FILIP]

Har

PART I

CHAPTER ONE

APRIL 2018

FILLIPO'S GAME

I jump over the wall and the scent of wild garlic hits me. Overhead the wind meddles in the trees, a lush reverb through their leaves. I stand inside the Woods, gazing at the nature of this quiet kingdom, and I'm held by its beauty just as I was in youth. 'The Woods', that's what we called this place in childhood, as if this small woodland, hushed away from the city, was not a destination, but an ideal.

The Woods, walled off from three districts of Edinburgh. Once owned by a family wealthy in the 19th century and once the host of a school and a watermill down by the river. The school and the mill have been derelict for over two hundred years, left as skeletal ruins now lying under carpets of ivy.

When I was little, I would watch the Woods through my bedroom window at night, wondering what kinds of ghosts, be it the schoolchildren or the millworkers, would wander through the darkness.

The paths that these long-gone peoples made are still here, running through the ivy and stone: little brown passages hewn in the soil, scattered across the Woods. This place is a living gamble of history. I still love its sense of lost stories, now as a woman of 25 years. The sad footballs, the broken bottles, the spent bonfire sites, the soda cans which have the old logos from the 1990s, the stolen bicycle carcasses.

I wonder who stole the bicycles, who they belonged to? I imagine who kicked the footballs and why they left them here. Who lit the bonfires and smashed the bottles? And I don't feel angry that people litter here, or that other generations of children claim to own this place. Because they don't. The Woods belong to *me*, and I am one of their original guardians. And I know more about the stories of this secretive, nigh-forgotten place than anyone else.

I bet that there are more secrets to be found within these walls. I come here after such a long absence, and already I can feel more tales.

My name is Dolina.

It's early morning, and there's a zippy presence in the clouds. April has been slow to bring spring, but now the Woods are beginning to bloom with growth. I look around, to see how much the land has changed. It's much different from when I last came here. The two largest ash trees by the valley lie cloven at their bases, one capsized onto the other, charged by a wind's storm long ago.

Other things are unchanged – like my cousin Filippo's Tarzan swing when I get to the river. It was the mightiest Tarzan we had in the Woods, because it dipped over the river's valley, and you got a proper rush when you sailed out in the air over the water.

I feel the old nylon rope and the wooden saddle. The rope's frayed now and the saddle mouldy, but Filippo's Tarzan is still intact. I can't believe somebody's not cut it down yet. I look around me, wondering. Maybe I could have a little go of the swing. Nobody's around to see me this early in the morning.

Of course, I feel like a kid, but it still feels good to whoosh out on the swing. I imagine the old neighbourhood kids here watching me. Not as my current self, but when I was little, when we used to play *Filippo's Game*. I suddenly remember it all now. *Filippo's Game*. The *Game*, wow, I must have been five years old the last time I played it.

It was a game my elder cousin invented. Filippo was a very clever boy who everybody in our neighbourhood loved. His *Game* acted as an initiation-course for his Gang, which he ran. Kids had to complete the *Game* in order to join up. It was nothing serious, not like a violent Gang or anything, only a bit of fun as kids. But it was super intelligent, what Filippo created.

So, throughout the Woods, Filippo constructed physical puzzles. They were made out of ropes, ladders, tunnels and secret dens. Quite like army assault courses, except you had to use your mind to complete them because they included tricky riddles and mazes you had to solve.

After you passed LEVEL 1, you'd move onto LEVEL 2, 3 and so forth in a different part of the Woods. And there would be hidden clues you'd need to look out for as you passed each LEVEL.

LEVEL 1 involved this very Tarzan I'm swinging on. It was a simple task – what made it nervous was that everybody in Filippo's Gang would be watching you whilst you did it. What you have to do in LEVEL 1, is: collect three stones from the riverbed, and, whilst you're swinging out on the Tarzan, throw them up into a basket perched high up in the tree. If you throw all three stones up into the basket you complete LEVEL 1.

I've already been swinging over the river for five minutes, this early in the morning, that I may as well play *Filippo's Game*, one more time, just to experience what it's like. Indeed, when I look up into the tree above the Tarzan, the old Safeway shopping basket is still there with rocks in it from previous players.

I collect three stones from the river and start playing. I get one into the basket on the first attempt and have got the other two in within minutes. I cheer to myself. I do it so well, I wish everybody from the old Gang were still here to see. (I did pass this LEVEL when I was a kid too, and all the boys who were watching didn't cheer because they didn't want me in their Gang).

As I've passed LEVEL 1 so spectacularly, I go to LEVEL 2 next. I remember where it is: down the river, so I go off in search. LEVEL 2 is a bit simple, and quite frankly (no offence intended) a bit boyish. What you do is start running from an oak tree one side of the river, run through this prickly group of trees, and then jump the full width of the river: you have to do it under five seconds. When I say it's boyish, I mean you need to be tough physically when you do it. But I did do it when I was a kid, and shut the teasers up.

And I do LEVEL 2 at the first attempt today. I even time myself to be assured I'm under five seconds. Then lie across the far bankside chuckling.

Filippo's Gang would laugh at me back then because I was their leader's little cousin, far younger than anyone else. I really wanted to be part of the Gang, but I could never get past LEVEL 3. And they were all, including Filippo, too cruel to help me out when I got stuck at LEVEL 3.

They told me I needed to find 'Filippo's House'. But I could never find it, and I still don't know where this 'house' is. Maybe I was just too young to figure it out. But I'm old now, and I'm sure Filippo's House is still hidden somewhere in the Woods.

For LEVEL 3, they gave you a clue. I remember them telling me it, the exact words:

LOOK IN THE HOLLY TREES

USE THE OLD TROLLEY TO FIND THE HOUSE

The holly trees are still there downriver, so I head down. The emerald leaves sparkle, and their boughs arch over a semi-circle of earth, shading me underfoot. When I remember the Gang's mockery there's a charge of envy and competition in me. There's still time to complete *Filippo's Game*.

There lies the trolley, by the back of the trees, stumped by one of the trunks, rusted and beaten.

Use the old trolley to find the house. It seemed so difficult a clue as a kid, as they kept jabbering the words to me. I thought then that you needed to take the trolley somewhere. The trees seemed too big and the leaves too jagged as a girl. I'd never guessed you were supposed to use the trolley to climb.

I step up onto the trolley. It's rickety, yet holds my weight, and I see a convenient branch nearby my head. I pull myself up into the branches. When I get up into the canopy, I see arrows pen-knifed into the branches below me. Arrows, carved by Filippo's knife, leading onto further branches. "Wow," I say aloud, "he even made a pathway through the trees!" All designed above the canopy and so neatly hidden that I never had any idea it was here.

I balance myself and crawl across the branches, following the arrow circuit. It's easy to go across, the branches are so well placed. I finally get to a bigger arrow pointing straight ahead into a thick bush of holly, joining onto an oak tree's branches. I go through the peppery leaves. I can barely see, the leaves are so thick, but then my hands bump into something hard. It's a wooden board.

The words 'Filippo's House' are painted in green paint against it. I realise, with astonishment, that this is Filippo's *treehouse*, perched between two boughs of the oak tree, and disguised completely by the foliage of the holly trees. I gape at this little building made in the air. It's a great treehouse as well. Properly constructed with make-shift timber, and a diagonal roof lined with tarmac. It has an open doorway which entices me in.

It's snug and warm inside. Moss and leaves smother the floor, but otherwise it's dry. It's big enough to fit my adult body. I feel blessed to be here, experiencing this. Not just to have finally got to LEVEL 3, but to be beholding something so amazing my cousin created.

The wind leans against the oak tree, a lunge of passion continuing through the timber and into my spine as I feel the treehouse sway. I want to share my discovery, so I bring out my phone. I'll take a photo of the treehouse and send it to Filippo.

As I'm about to take the photo, I notice something colourful jutting out of the leaves, the far end of the treehouse floor. I go across to see what it is. After turning the leaves away, I find an old cap. It's a football cap. I recognise the cap instantly, because I know who used to wear it. But I haven't seen it, or its owner, in 20 years.

The cap is regalia from the *France '98* World Cup football tournament. It has a picture of that little tournament mascot – the cartoon bird with the red hair and the yellow beak holding a football.

Under the cap I find another item. It's a digital watch, very old, from when teenagers still wore watches. I turn the green light on at the side of the watch and it comes alive! And it still has the correct time too.

I remember this watch just as clearly as I do the cap. I always envied the watch because it seemed like such a cool possession when I was five years old. I loved when the screen of the watch turned green.

This cap and watch belong to a boy named Henry Fowles. He used to live in our neighbourhood when I was little. Was the same age as my cousin. He was never part of Filippo's Gang. But he was just as well-known as Filippo was, and just as big a character. He was one of the most important members of the old neighbourhood guard.

I'm beginning to feel a dullness in my head. There's an illness creeping in my stomach. Maybe I shouldn't be here in this treehouse, because something's wrong about this. Henry Fowles constantly wore this *France '98* cap and his watch. He was never seen without them on. This disturbs me, because I've just found his precious items, 20 years after I last saw him.

Henry Fowles went missing from our neighbourhood in the summer of 1998. And he has never been found since.

Memory thunders down on me. I remember the police in our neighbourhood, the reporters. The crazed attention the city had for months after Henry vanished. I thought I had blocked those dark times away in the past. But it was all real. It all happened. The police never concluded Henry Fowles' case, nor gave any explanation as to where he went. Henry remains a mystery. The weight of these thoughts clamp around my throat.

I've found something important here. I put Henry's football cap and watch inside my coat pocket. Then I leave the treehouse, and quickly climb back down through the trees. I exit the Woods as fast as I can and see nobody as I walk home. I'd gone back into the Woods suspecting a new story, and now that I think I have one, I'm afraid of what it all means.

CHAPTER TWO

JUNE 10th 1998

HENRY

There's a big football game on today. Scotland are playing Brazil in the World Cup, and all the streets are quiet because everyone's inside watching the game. I was supposed to watch it at Tommy's house, but Tommy was being mean earlier, and his Dad was drinking too much beer. So I came down to the Woods, to play by myself.

It's a hot, sunny day. I go down to the river and I see my face in the water. Mum face-painted Scotland flags on me and Tommy's cheeks earlier. We were getting ready for the game by dressing up and painting our faces, and I liked all the buzz. But then Tommy spoiled it by being mean, and I don't want the paint on me now. I wash the flags off my cheeks in the river and watch the blue and white paint swirl away. Hah. I don't need stupid football or beer to enjoy things.

And now I have the Woods all to me. There's a pink-flowered plant which grows by the river. I always love the smell of the flowers and the bumblebees obsessed with their pollen. It has a minty smell, but with something special too, not like other plants. I start picking the flowers together and I make a little envelope around them with these big ivy leaves. It's like a bouquet without wrapping paper.

I'm there a long while, sitting under the pink flowers with the bees, making this bouquet. It's the kind of thing Mum likes, so I'll go back home when I'm done and give it to her as a present. I'm pretty chuffed with it.

I stand up to head back home. I feel my blood come to my head.

Smash.

I freeze. What was that?

Something violent. In my dizziness I'm not sure what the smash was or where it came from. Then the alarm on Mr Walker's house starts screaming. I crouch down under the flowers, scared. I can see Mr Walker's house over the wall of the Woods. The siren flashes and the screams hurt my ears even from here. Mr Walker's alarm has never gone off before.

I need to go home. Trouble is, the only way home is by going over the wall next to Mr Walker's. And it's too loud, so I stay crouched down, waiting. I can't see anything in his garden. Nothing moves.

A man leaps over the wall, into the Woods. He appears so fast I can't react as he begins running down the path right towards me. My first thought is to run away from the flowers. But the man is already charging closer to me. Hide! I have to hide. I push my face down against the earth, but I realise how useless my hiding place is because it's just next to the path. Running footsteps come nearer, fast and terrified. I quiver there as the man comes closer and closer and then something tells me to stand up, because he'll see me anyway:

"Argh!" he shouts when I shoot up.

"Henry!"

It's Henry Fowles.

"Dolina?" he says, "What are you doing here?"

"Just playing …"

Henry scares me. He's covering his nose with his hand and I can see dark purple blood spilling through his fingers. It makes my eyes water.

"Oh no," I say, "what happened?"

He gallops towards me and I feel my chest tighten up because I want to scream. But I can't because I can't let air out. Henry flies under the flowers next to me.

"Get down, Dolina," he whispers, "and be quiet."

He lies pressed down on the ground, gaping at Mr Walker's siren flashing. I watch his nose bleed. He's holding his cap with the football cartoon in one hand, cupping his nose with the other.

"Dolina," he says to me, "I'm in trouble – but I didn't do anything bad, okay?"

"Okay. But what happened to your nose?"

He doesn't answer, eyes darting around. Then he says:

"Is anybody else in the Woods?"

"No, I don't think so."

I'm crying silently. His body feels huge, vibrating next to mine. Henry always has his cheeky grin on his face when you see him. I've never seen him hurt before.

The alarm on Mr Walker's house stops. We're left with the peaceful sounds of the Woods. Henry pants into the quietness. He brings a pathetic tissue out his pocket and holds it to his nose, and says to me:

"Dolina. Don't tell anybody you saw me here, please?"

"I don't understand. What's wrong?"

"I have to go. Please, Dolina, don't tell anyone you saw me."

He jumps up and puts his cap in his pocket. Then he sprints off down the path and disappears further into the Woods.

I'm shivering and must get back home. It feels like *I've* done something bad, and I need to be near somebody grown-up. I head back down the path and I can only hear the birds singing. They sing happily like nothing's happened. I get to the wall where I can jump out the Woods and am just about to climb up when a face pokes out from behind the other side, and this time I scream properly.

It's my cousin, Filippo.

"Dolina, what's up?" he says, perched on the wall. "What's with you?"

His big frowning eyebrows hang down on me. It feels like Filippo's caught me, but I don't know what I was doing wrong.

"Why are you crying?" he says.

"I heard Mr Walker's alarm …"

Filippo stays still, scanning the trees behind me into the distance.

"It went off by accident, don't worry. But why are you here alone, Dolina?"

"I was just picking flowers by myself, that's all." I remember I left my bouquet back at the river, and it hurts that I forgot all about it.

He watches me curiously, blocking the way out.

"So you heard Mr Walker's alarm go off, and you've been here the whole time?"

I nod.

"Did you see anybody after that?"

I think about Henry and all I can picture of him is his nose bleeding. I know I'm about to lie to my cousin but it seems like the right thing to do. I shake my head quickly.

Filippo smiles. He springs up onto the top of the wall and holds his hands down to me. "Come on, Dolina: you should go back home." I go to his arms. He lifts me up easily and lets me out the Woods. His shoes thump as he jumps down after me. He's still smiling and I don't like it because I know he's only pretending to be friendly. "Go, Dolina. Head back home and watch the game. Scotland just scored, even, against Brazil!"

I'm wondering why he isn't inside watching the game himself. Why's he wanting to go into the Woods instead? I just want to get away from him. I head back up the road towards home. I get into our street where the sunlight pinches my eyes. When I look back down into the road behind me, Filippo is still standing there under the shade of the trees, watching me.

CHAPTER THREE

APRIL 2018

THE OLD NEIGHBOURHOOD

Filippo isn't my cousin's actual name. His real name is John, but the neighbourhood peers gave him the nickname 'Filippo' in the 1990s because he looked like the Italian football player Filippo Inzaghi. That's why it was a good nickname, because he had a normal name like John and was Scottish, but he had these exotic handsome looks like he was an Italian celebrity. And he was big and well-built. Which is probably part of the reason why he had such influence around our area, back when he reigned it.

Let me go into a partial history of the old neighbourhood, if we rewind time by 20 years. I turned six years old in 1998. Filippo and Henry Fowles were sixteen. If there was a title of 'king', of all the kids in those days, it definitely belonged to Filippo. Filippo was a magnetic, nonchalant character, and a leader above all. I felt charmed to be his little cousin, even though he wouldn't let me get close to his aura. I was his blood relation, but I didn't have any access to his kingdom. Mostly because I was so much younger. The only other kid my age was a boy called Tommy who lived next door to me. We were at least a decade younger than everyone else, so Tommy was my only real friend.

Filippo was incredibly intelligent. He was a prodigy with everything at school. Got the best marks in his classes, was a great guitar player, was the star striker of the local football team. All my memory says of him is a sense of perfection. He left the neighbourhood when I was still very young, going off to London to study business at a top university.

As soon as Filippo left the neighbourhood, the resonance in the streets seemed to wither. People stopped going into the Woods to drink and smoke and light bonfires. Nor did they hang out on the road kicking footballs about any more. It was as if the spirit of the neighbourhood rested within Filippo. He left to study nine months after Henry Fowles disappeared.

I saw him last Christmas visiting his parents down at the end of the road. He's working in London now as a manager of a marketing business. His wife is exquisitely beautiful and they have a young son. Filippo's excelling in the world, and he hasn't changed from my girlhood impression of him.

I'm thinking about the neighbourhood in 1998, compared to now, and how it's all changed. Drastically changed. I'm the only one of the old-guard left that still walks about this place. It's the night time, following the morning when I found Henry's cap and watch. I haven't told anybody yet about finding his stuff. I hid his things under my bed, and now I can't sleep because their presence bothers me.

We'd all been stunned by Henry's vanishing in '98. I remember the police coming to question my mother and I about him. They spoke to everybody in the neighbourhood. The nearby streets were thronged with reporters for weeks after he vanished. Images of Henry's face were plastered on tabloid front pages. Everybody at school heaped attention on me because they knew I came from Henry's neighbourhood. But then it all died, and everybody lost interest, because Henry Fowles never appeared again.

We were only left with gossip and theories as to what had happened. I think if Henry hadn't been living in a suburban area, they wouldn't have cared as much. The normal teenage boy gone missing from the suburbs was something that didn't usually happen in Edinburgh.

Yet when I was little, I didn't understand the media hype, because I thought they'd got it wrong. I didn't think of us as living in the 'clean suburbs'. Our community was very small and surrounded by rough and run-down districts.

Youths from these areas would often carouse down our quiet road at night. My Mother and I have a big house, and our windows were bricked through many times. And my friend Tommy often got beaten up, because he was shy, and weighed nothing, and the other, bigger boys could get away with it.

Therefore, I didn't see our neighbourhood in the way the newspapers saw it. They couldn't have known what happened to Henry unless they'd lived here. Nor was Henry the normal suburban teenager. So just who was Henry Fowles?

If I were to make the starkest of comparisons between Henry and another person, it would be with my cousin Filippo. They were so different in every way, and yet I remember them always being so close. Whereas Filippo was handsome, Henry was weird-looking. Not ugly, but had a thick, drooping nose and heavy eyelids. He was a lot smaller than Filippo. Filippo wore expensive designer gear and Henry wore baggy jeans and jumpers. Henry never looked sober, ever, whereas Filippo would never be seen drinking or smoking.

Everybody crowded around Filippo, but nobody liked Henry. And that was the main thing: Henry wasn't a popular kid. But he was still always hanging around. The kids tolerated rather than accept him. While Filippo excelled in his local fame, Henry remained as the local outsider. And I can't explain how odd it is, that they were together in the same place so often. When I remember Filippo today, I naturally think of Henry.

I listened to the gossip surrounding Henry in the years after he disappeared, and developed a perverse interest in it just as everyone else did. Henry lived with his mother down the street. It was well-known that his mother and step-father were drug addicts. Proper bad stuff. Heroin. Henry was often left alone by himself when he was little, and he often didn't attend school. It was a gritty way for Henry to grow up with the addict household, but I don't think it damaged him. I always thought Henry was an okay boy. He wasn't a bastard. Just mischievous. With that constant smile on his face he deflected his unpopularity with good nature.

Henry got in to dealing drugs of his own in early adolescence. He didn't have to go to school, so had the time, and he knew the provincial areas where people were looking to score. He only dealt marijuana, and nothing as obscene as heroin. But it was still foreboding, and he was far too young to be in that kind of field.

Many of the rumours linked Henry's disappearance to his dealing. He didn't have a tough edge, and anybody could take advantage of him. The police must have suspected that too.

That Henry sold to the wrong person, and the deal had turned violent, and Henry couldn't defend himself. Then they erased the evidence. But somehow I've never bought these rumours. I'm sure it was something else.

Why do I keep thinking about that day in 1998, when Scotland were playing Brazil at football? When I saw Henry Fowles with a gory nose. He was obviously petrified, and somebody was chasing him. And I know that my cousin Filippo was involved in it in some way.

What made that smash that I heard? What was it that set the alarm off in Mr Walker's house? Why did Henry run into the Woods? Did Filippo *hit* Henry? Why did Henry ask me not to tell anybody he'd been seen? These questions keep batting me about the mind. I know that day was significant. Because Henry vanished four weeks later. What happened within those four weeks after that day, so long ago?

CHAPTER FOUR

FILIPPO

I wake up next day to a glittering April morning. The sun glorious in the trees outside the window. The house is silent. Mum's already gone out to work. I have a pulsing mental energy this morning. A galvanised feeling, as if I know progressions will be made today. And it's all due to these memories of the old neighbourhood.

Knowing that I need to know more about it all, I message Tommy Hepburn, the old childhood chum I mentioned. We stopped seeing each other regularly after we embarked to study in different cities years ago. But we're still good friends whenever we message each other:

Hey Tommy, I just wondered if you could call me soon? I was playing 'Filippo's Game' yesterday. Remember that? The old game my cousin made in the woods? It made me think about the old times and I'd like to chat to you about them, but it'd just be good to catch up with you in general, if you like, so let me know.

He messages back within minutes:

Hi Dolina, I'm at work at the moment, but I'm actually coming back to visit home next week. I have a two week holiday and I'll be staying there for a few days so I'm sure we can hang out then!

I reply, sure, I'd love to see you. I get a thrill to know one of the old-guard members is coming back to the very neighbourhood. Somebody I can vent my growing intrigue for the Woods and

Henry Fowles with. I'm dying to tell Tommy about finding Henry's things in the treehouse and about that disturbing day in '98 with Henry's nosebleed. I realise I've never told anybody that story. I was too scared to talk about something I didn't understand when I was five. I just went home and shut myself in my room that day.

Tommy will be here in three days' time. It's Friday morning now, and I'm working all day Saturday and Sunday, but I have a free day today. I mooch about inside the house, until it gets to noon. The heat of the burgeoning season thrums outside. Nature in a vibrant resurgence. The maniac birdsong. The clangour of the river. The temperature of the day nags me until I have to do something about my mind.

I should just call cousin Filippo. Call him, pretending it's a random how-are-you? call to catch him out. My cousin is a good man. I know he is. And he's my own D.N.A. He will know things about Henry, these other things which I'm curious of. Maybe I only need clarification from his perspective of things. I should be able to speak to my cousin, like I would speak to my friend, right?

I figure that he's working today but he's probably on his lunch break, from 12:00. So, I wait until 12:30 (so he's had a chance to get something to eat) and then call him. I have a plan for how I'll ask him about Henry.

"Dolina!" Filippo says, picking up instantly. I can hear loud communal life in his background. "How are you doing?"

"I'm good, John – I just thought about calling you, since I figured you were on a lunch break."

"I am! Just out having food with the boys. How are you? Everything okay? You're back home in the old hood now I hear?"

"I'm back home with Mum, yeah. I feel a bit stupid calling you now, and I know you're working. But do you remember that *Game* you made in the woods? Your *Game*. We all used to play it when we were little. It started with the level on the Tarzan where you had to throw stones up into the tree-basket. You remember?"

"Oh! The *Game*. Of course I remember. Yeah, that takes me back a lot. My *Game*, I haven't thought about that in years. Why you ask about it?"

"Because I was just walking in the woods yesterday, and I saw your old Tarzan: I thought I would play the *Game* again, just for fun. You remember me playing it when I was wee, and you and all the Gang watched?"

"Yeah, I do! Fond memories, for sure!"

"And you remember how you and the gang used to tease me because I could never get beyond LEVEL 2?"

"Haha, yes, I know we picked on you a lot, Dolina, but we were just stupid kids. I'm sorry. Why you asking me about this anyway?"

"I finally got to LEVEL 3. Yesterday. I found your treehouse."

"Amazing! You finally got the clue with the trolley? That's cool – this is weird remembering that time. It's an ace treehouse, isn't it? I made it with Mr Walker, a long, long time ago."

Something glimmers in my imagination here, and I pause.

"Mr Walker? You made it with him?"

"Well, yeah. The treehouse was so good, it would be hard for a kid to build all that by himself."

"Hmm."

I continue my pause. The noise of the London café in Filippo's background rockets about my hearing as I'm trying to think.

"So what was it you wanted to tell me about the *Game*, Dolina? Just that you made us boys look like bastards?"

"No, well. When I was in the treehouse I *found* something."

"Okay?"

"Henry Fowles. I found his old *FIFA '98* cap, and his watch too. They were just lying there inside the treehouse."

I wait for his response. But it doesn't come, and the seconds pound by. Gabbling Londoner voices fly about down my earpiece. Clanks of cutlery. People giggling. Filippo's silenced.

"John? Are you there?"

"Yeah, yes! Sorry, it's just that that seems very strange. Henry? Henry. Are you sure those things were his?"

"His cap with that cartoon mascot he never took off. And I don't know if you remember his digital watch as well. He always showed it off to us?"

There's another long gap where I wait for him to say something. He then sighs.

"It was scary what happened with Henry, I agree. We all wonder where he is. He was a nice boy, though he had his flaws. I hope he's somewhere better than our neighbourhood. I hope we weren't too mean to him."

"So you think Henry's still alive?"

"Jesus, Dolina, this is all a bit much for a Friday lunch break!"

"I know, sorry John. I'm being rude."

"You're not being rude, it's just it's only a lot to take in. That's freaky as hell you found Henry's things. Nobody knows what happened with him, and now you remind me of him, I still feel creepy about it all. But can we talk about it another time? I should get back to my boys, and I have a meeting at one o'clock. That okay?"

He hangs up the phone quickly after this. He says farewell and wishes me well in his deep voice, which always has that rollicking delivery. You always recognise Filippo's voice instantaneously, whenever you hear it. It has a unique charisma.

CHAPTER FIVE

RETURN TO THE TREEHOUSE

It gets to 8 p.m. The afternoon's heat pries onward. The air's stuffy and I listen to the Woods throbbing through my open window. I bought a bottle of wine earlier and it's working on my thinking. Wine was supposed to be a way to hinder my compulsion with the stories of this neighbourhood, but it's only making them more enticing.

I try to call Tommy, but he doesn't pick up. Instead I send him a message:

Tommy: I got to LEVEL 3 in Filippo's Game. I found the treehouse John built. Please call me back because I'm needing somebody to talk to. Or if not: could you please tell me about LEVEL 4? I didn't think to progress to LEVEL 4 when I got into the treehouse. You got there, right? So could you give me a clue about it?

He texts back eventually:

Ah, Filippo's Game. Wow, I wish I was playing it again too. Yeah, I got to Level 4 back then. But, why should I tell you how to get there, Dolina? If you like the game, just go play it more. I will tell you, though, that there is a clue at the treehouse. Night night for now. I'll see you on Monday.

The sun has set and it leaves a long cyan gradient across the sky. The air meets my window as if there is nothing between myself and the Woods. I know I have to go inside there again this evening, back to the treehouse. I get my things together to head out.

The zest of the spring plants floods me as I go outside, my heartbeat tumbling. I go past Mr Walker's house on the side of the hilly road towards the Woods. All his lights are on in his big house. Walker's lights are never turned off, no matter what time of day it is.

Hopping over the wall, I stumble as I land. Maybe I've had a little too much of wine. I laugh at myself and go on. I pass Filippo's old Tarzan swaying over the river silently. Then follow the riverbank until I come to the Ribes plant which has the pungent pink flowers I adore. I stand inhaling the flowers' scent, wondering how many bees will be here by tomorrow.

I go under the holly trees and I find the *Safeway* trolley, and climb up it and into the branches. Using my phone's light as guidance, I go along the network of arrows. I reach the bridge and crawl up to the treehouse. It's amazingly cosy. I could just sleep here for the night if I liked.

But I have to figure out how to get to LEVEL 4. There's a clue here somewhere. I search. I scrape through the dry leaves with my hands. But find nothing. There's nothing on the walls as I shine the light around. I'm there for a fair while, getting more irritated in my tipsiness. It annoys me that I'm 25 and I'm still flummoxed by *Filippo's Game*.

Then I look out the window. Its positioned oblong to the side of the oak boughs, the boughs stretching underneath it. I peer from its ledge. Something unnatural then catches my eye. A bird's-nest-box! It's attached to one of the boughs, and I see that I can climb out the window across to it.

I listen beside the bird's box, in case there's a nest inside. But it seems defunct, so I reach inside its hole. I feel a slip of something hard and flat and bring it out. An envelope, already opened at the seal. I open it, pulling out one piece of paper. In bold colourful letters are the words:

GO TO JUNE'S WATERFALL

And I'm struck by the wonder of *Filippo's Game*. Carefully I put the paper back in the envelope, the envelope back in the bird's box. Then climb back inside the treehouse. I hear the bats and the owls shriek and hoot in tandem, forever in holler and response to music we'll never understand. I'm lucky to have grown up near the Woods. I feel that I belong here.

I sit down listening outside. I'm beginning to feel drowsy and am starting to nod off, when suddenly my eyes are attacked. Harsh light cuts through the treehouse window. I crouch down in the leaves.

There's a white beam darting about the walls of the treehouse. I duck under the beam as it flings overhead. Somebody is standing underneath the treehouse with a powerful torchlight, and they know that I'm up here. The torch hovers on the window.

"Who's up there?" A voice comes. "Who's up there in the treehouse? I know somebody's there."

I stand up and head to the window, recognising the voice. I go into the blare of the torchlight by the window and blindly look down.

"Who is there?" I say, aggressively as I can.

The light holds my face. My toenails tingle with panic.

"Please, tell me who you are?" I say.

"*Dolina*? Dolina – John's little cousin, is that you?"

The man brings the torch up into his face. It's my neighbour, Mr Walker. The torchlight sends two disks of silver over his glasses. I chuckle nervously.

"Alec? Alec Walker. Dear lord, you gave me a fright. What's happening?"

"What's happening with me? Nothing, I just heard some noise up in the trees, and was scared myself. Why don't you come on down here and we can talk?"

Alec Walker is my oldest neighbour, and I like him. But I don't understand why he's inside the Woods with me. I crawl back down through the trees, calling out to him in clumsy gibberish, "Oh, I'm sorry Alec. I was just wandering about. And I found John's old treehouse. And I'm a bit drunk and stupid, so sorry. But how is everything with you?"

I come down to the ground where Mr Walker stands. He holds the torch down by his waist and the light sends a schism upside his yellow jacket.

"So what you up to?" I say.

"I was just taking my usual evening stroll. And I saw some light above me, so thought I'd see who it was. But, it's all okay now. How you doing anyway? How's your Mum?"

"She's good, yeah, she's thinking of retiring soon, so that should let her chill out a bit finally."

This is absurd standing here with Mr Walker. We're in humming darkness, and he's just making conversation.

"So are you heading back home? I'm going that way too." I say.

Why is Mr Walker in the Woods? He obviously knew I was in Filippo's treehouse, that means that he must have seen me go into the Woods. Why is he standing in my way as if it's normal for him to be here too? His eyes blink in accurate dots of intelligence underneath his glasses.

"I'll just keep going with my stroll. But I'll see you soon, Dolina."

Mr Walker casually walks off down the path away from me. I don't waste time in getting away from him. I reach the far wall and exit the Woods. I run up the hilly road. When I get back into my house, the first thing I do is to lock my front door.

CHAPTER SIX

JUNE 16TH 1998

SCOTLAND V NORWAY

I come out of *Spar*, sucking on an ice pole, when I see somebody I know inside the phone booth. A tall lad, leaning against the window, holding the phone under his cheek. When he turns around and I see the blue *France '98* cap, I realise it's Henry. His head bobs about as he talks. He looks happy.

It's another shiny summer afternoon and the sun zaps the black phonebooth. Henry hangs the phone up. He sees me standing here stupidly when he comes out and grins his gigantic grin.

"Oh! It's little Dolina! How are you, chum?" he holds his palm out for me to high-five it. Which I do, and I'm happy to see him too. I smile up into his weird face.

"What's up, Dolina: why you no speak?"

Because the last time I saw you was in the Woods when you had a bloody nose. And now you just look like normal Henry again.

"Not much, Henry. What you up to?"

"Just mooching about. What kind of ice pole is that? *Cola* flavour! I loved cola the best when I was a kid too."

I offer him a chunk of my ice pole. He laughs in a friendly way, and says no thanks.

"You heading back to our hood, Dolina?"

"Yeah, let's go."

I've never walked home with Henry before. Home is ten minutes away and I'm shy of his company, though I don't mind it. First thing he does as we set out is take out a chubby cigarette from his pocket and light up. It's weed. He's always smoking weed – Filippo's friends always do too. The tangy smell of it constantly floats about our street. Henry lets a gust of smoke out his big nose.

"So, you watching the Scotland game v Norway tonight, Dolina?"

"Yeah, I'm going to Tommy's to watch it."

"Do you *like* football, Dolina?"

"Hmm … I like the flags and songs and all that. But, I don't know. I don't understand why people get so angry when they're watching it. Like Tommy's Dad, when he drinks."

"Ha ha. Oh, I agree. They take it so personally and go raging. But it's all just a bit of fun, and I'll watch the game too. It's nice to see Scottish people care about something other than drinking, I suppose."

My ice pole melts in my hand. It seems mean to eat it when Henry doesn't have one, so I'll just leave it until after I get home. I watch him carefully. He's wearing his green hoody and baggy jeans, even though it's 20°C. He has the usual twitchy head when he talks, and just seems relaxed, not bothered about our last meeting at all. That was … six days ago – and I haven't seen Henry around, anywhere, since it happened. I really want to ask him about it. Just to see if he's okay. But I don't know how to ask him.

We cut into our neighbourhood's street, where the trees of the Woods block the sunlight. Henry checks his watch, with the green glowing screen. (I want his watch – wish I had it).

"You have a hot date?" I say.

"I do, I do. A date with your very own kin, little Dolina."

"What do you mean?"

"I'm meeting your cousin down the road."

"Filippo?"

"Yes."

More questions burst in me, but I don't have the courage to ask them. I thought Filippo was the one who was chasing Henry last week? And now they're friends again? Seconds later we spot Filippo standing at the end of the shadowy road. He's doing keepy-uppies with his feet skilfully. Keeping the ball in the air like his feet have spiderwebs.

"Filippo!" Henry calls in a sing-song voice. "Pass the ball."

Filippo kicks the ball down to Henry, who runs up and thumps it off down the street. Filippo watches it sail past him. Henry laughs. Filippo rolls his eyes.

"How are you, Mr Inzaghi?" Henry shakes his hand.

"Hey, Dolina." Filippo says to me. He yawns, runs his hands through his curtains-haircut, then turns and walks away from us towards his ball.

We follow him. And pass the white Hospital which looms at the back of our neighbourhood. It's a strange building, and it creeps me out a little. Because you never see anybody go inside the building or hear any ambulance sirens. Filippo gets his ball and then does more keepy-uppies as he walks.

"You heading to Tommy's to watch the game, Dolina?" he says to me.

"Yeah – you coming too?"

"I already got plans. Next game, though."

"Hey, Filippo," Henry jumps in, "you should invite Dolina to *our* game tomorrow night."

"Yeah, she can come watch, of course."

"What do you mean, what game?" I say.

"Filippo's organising a football game with all the cats from the hood, little Dolina! On the field next to the Hospital. It's tomorrow night. I'll even be playing."

"You'll be a substitute, Henry," Filippo says. He stops by the wall of the Woods where there's a lamppost next to it and picks his ball up.

"Well, just you wait. I'll be a star," Henry stops by Filippo. "But you can come."

"Tomorrow evening?"

"Yeah just come up to the Hospital. We'll all be there."

Henry finally finishes his joint. He stubs it out whilst Filippo throws the football over the wall, then climbs up to the top using the lamppost as a frame. He sits on the top with his back to me, looking into the Woods beyond him. Henry climbs the lamppost too.

Where are you going?" I say, a dumb question.

"Just off to do some things, little Dolina," Henry says. His smile is kind – he knows I want to go with them too. "We'll see you tomorrow, okay?"

Filippo disappears over the wall. Henry waves at me then goes after him. Leaving me standing alone, sad. I wish I could go inside with them. Why can't I? I hear them scuttle off through the trees, talking until their voices fade. It's obvious they don't want me with them – but why?

It's not too late to give up. There's another way I can go into the Woods to see what they're doing. Walking faster down the road, I put my ice pole in a bin. I head down to the next part in the wall where it's easy for me to climb up, next to the bushy holly trees. I dip down quietly into the Woods, duck down on the path and crawl over to a little hilly bit. From here I can see through the trees and onto the path in the distance.

And *there they are*! Filippo and Henry. It's amazing to spy on them. They walk down the path and come to the river which they hop over to the other side. Then they stop in the broad part of land above the valley, where the two gigantic ash trees dwarf everything else. They hover around, Henry checking his watch and Filippo looking about for something.

A shape darts out behind one of the ash trunks. It's a person. Henry and Filippo jump and spin around when they see her. It's June Walker, the deputy of Filippo's Gang. I don't like June. She makes me nervous. She's wearing a white sweater over her curvy breasts and her dark hair bats about her shoulders. The three of them talk but I can't hear any of the words. Henry's grinning – I can see his teeth from here – and Filippo shuffles on his feet. June is just straight and serious, and then she says something which makes Henry stop grinning.

Henry then goes towards her, bringing a parcel out his pocket. The parcel is the size of a brick. June nods and takes it from him. Henry then offers June a handshake. June melts away from him, ignoring his hand, and walks away down the far side of the valley.

Filippo claps Henry on the back and then follows after June, disappearing, leaving Henry looking after them. He stands there for a while, then shakes his head and turns back. After jumping over the river, I realise he's taking the path which leads directly up to my hiding place. I panic, and climb back over the wall fast as I can. When in the street, Tommy's house is luckily near the wall. I nip over the road and go behind the gate of Tommy's garden.

I should really just go up and ring the doorbell, but there's something about spying which thrills me. I wait behind the fence, watching through a gap in the planks for Henry to appear over the wall. And he does, climbing into the street calmly, whistling a tune. I try to find something in his expression that might explain what's happening with him. But he gives nothing away, and I watch him walk back up the road towards the Hospital.

CHAPTER SEVEN

APRIL 2018

TOMMY

I used to tease Tommy Hepburn a lot when we were kids. He was always easy to pick on, and smaller than me even though he was a boy. Everybody picked on him, because he was such a sweet, innocent chap. I'd annoy him because I wasn't shy like he was (super shy), because he didn't have the same skills I did; painting, music, artsy stuff.

But whenever we played games as children, Tommy would *always* win. We played endless games of badminton and ping-pong, and I'd love the combat, but he'd beat me every time. Even with games like Monopoly too – where the game rests in chance – Tommy would be the victor. He'd never get smug about it either. Puzzles were just what he was good at.

Things are not that much different in the spring of 2018. I graduated from Art School in December last year and now live with my Mum and have a crappy part-time hotel job. My paintings have never received much acclaim aside from through friends and I have a developing feeling that I will never be a popular artist. Tommy lives in Glasgow with some well-paid finance-research job. His life situation is more stable than mine is. Serves me right for having bullied him when we were little.

What we do have in common is a deep love for the Woods. I love Tommy, too, and I'm excited about seeing him this Monday lunchtime. When I spot him walk up to the garden my chest lifts up and I rush to the front door. He's bemused by how tight I hug him, but he hugs me back. "Come in, Tommy, to the kitchen. Let's get some coffee!"

He's just the same quiet, humble guy as we sit with coffee at the table. When you ask him questions he never really expands beyond two lines of dialogue. But he's always powerful in his shortness when he does speak.

When he asks about me, I can't really say anything more than that I have a Fine Art Degree – whatever that means – and I don't know what to do next with it, or know what to do in life in general. But he doesn't judge, only listens and says encouraging things. As I speak, he notices how distracted I am. How I keep tapping my feet. And he guesses what I'm agitated about.

"What is it you really want to talk about, Dolina? It's *Filippo's Game*, isn't it?"

This ignites me. I go on a feverish rant about what's been obsessing me the last week. It comes out so spluttery and loud that Tommy's intimidated, but he listens methodically.

First, I tell him I passed LEVEL 3 and found the clue to go to *June's Waterfall*. Then I tell him how creeped-out I was when Mr Walker found me in the treehouse with his torch. And that I spoke to Filippo. But I leave the most important part out until last: that I found the *'98* cap and the watch which belong to Henry.

I'd had Henry's things ready under the table, and I bring them out and place them between our coffees. Tommy stares at them for a very long time, not saying anything. There's a mix of fear and confusion in his eyes. Which isn't the reaction I was hoping for. The cap and the watch sit there, decades old, the cartoon-bird smiling at us with a thumbs-up. The digits on the watch keep turning.

"So, you called Filippo?" Tommy finally says. "And told him you found these?"

"I did."

"Well what did he say?"

"Nothing much, he was just surprised. Dazed, almost. Then he ended the call soon after."

"And Mr Walker came out to you, the *same day* you spoke to Filippo?"

"Right. And, get this: Filippo said he made the treehouse *with* Mr Walker."

I can tell I've gotten Tommy hooked on this. It's a new puzzle for him. He doesn't show it in his face, but I know the hook's in him now. He sits back in his chair, thinking. And I wait for him to say something.

"You've got a free day today, right Dolina?"

"Uh hu."

"Let's go back – to *Filippo's Game*. We'll go complete LEVEL 4 – *June's Waterfall*."

CHAPTER EIGHT

JUNE'S WATERFALL

It's a lot colder today than it was last week, with shaky rain and wind. Tommy and I head out to the Woods for the first time together in over ten years. It feels just as special to be doing this with him as it was in youth.

June's Waterfall lies down in the lower parts of the Woods, where the river gets wider. The 'waterfall' is not a real waterfall. It's part of the old mill ruins, where they built a long, slanting part under the river for the water to channel down. It looks like a long rock-climbing frame, held underwater. I'm not sure why they built it this way, though I'm guessing it was to control the current at the fall's bottom, as the collected water there is very deep. The falls were named after June Walker, who was Filippo's closest ally in the old neighbourhood. It is said she had a key part in making this LEVEL.

As we go down the hilly road, we pass June's father's house, and both of us go quiet. Mr Walker's place is by far the wealthiest house in the street, made in Edwardian times, with that old-fashioned black-beams and white-walls style. There's a sign on Mr Walker's front gate which says: 'CCTV Cameras in Operation'. When we're far enough down the hill from the house, we begin talking about LEVEL 4 again.

Like me, Tommy never completed *Filippo's Game*. He always got stuck on LEVEL 4. From the fourth LEVEL, it was said the puzzles got harder. But now that we're adults, we want to investigate it again. We get to the farthest part of the Woods' wall, where you climb up and under an arching horse chestnut tree. We enter our land of beauty. The buds are held in half-explosions of green. Spring provokes the weeds and shrubs into glossy inks, aside a constant soundtrack of birdsong. We head down to the riverbank, and just as we get to the part before the waterfall, a band of birds rush away above us. We watch them fly off, leaving trembling hoops in the water's surface.

We arrive. When I found the note: 'GO TO JUNE'S WATERFALL' back in the treehouse I knew instantly where it referred to. I'd often been in this part of the Woods when Filippo's Gang were around. They always talked about *June's Waterfall* admiringly. I'd was envious because I really wanted to know what lay in LEVEL 4. I was still uselessly marooned on LEVEL 2. I couldn't imagine anything you could do with a man-made waterfall.

Now, Tommy is with me. And he says he got *inside* the LEVEL. As we hover there by the bankside, I still can't guess how a puzzle can be made out of this scenery. It's been raining and the water's brown and flowing fast.

"You do know you have to swim, right?" Tommy says. "To do LEVEL 4?"

This is typical of Tommy. How he fails to mention something incredibly important unless he knows it himself.

"Swim?" I say. "I.e. you have to go into the water?"

"Well, of course: what'd you think June's Waterfall involved?"

He's already taking his shirt off, then taking his wallet and phone out his pockets. I stand there staring at him.

"Clothes off, Dolina," he says, cheerfully.

"I have to get into my underwear?"

"We have to swim underwater into LEVEL 4. Nobody's around to see you in your undies – come on, let's go."

We undress. I keep my jeans on but I don't want my top getting wet. My trainers can get wet though, so I keep them on. It all feels surreal, being next to Tommy (both of us 25) half naked. Tommy jumps into the river without hesitation. I follow feebly.

"Come on, then, Dolina."

"You haven't explained anything Tommy. What is it we do?"

"We swim *under* the mill ruins. There's a secret tunnel there."

"A tunnel? So the tunnel's underwater?"

"Yes, and you swim through it."

"You know I'm not a good swimmer," I say.

"You don't have to be ... God, Dolina – I thought you were the one who wanted to do this? Now, let's go."

We swim over to the mill walls the far side of the water. Tommy points down into the depths below us.

"Do you see the tunnel opening?" he says.

"No."

"You have to dive down, and below the water is the tunnel. You swim through that and you come out into air the other side."

"But how far is the route?"

"Not long. Just follow me."

This is typical Tommy as well. He just dives under the water and begins swimming into this abyss and expects me to follow as if I have the same talents. I take a long heave of oxygen in and put my head under.

I always found it hard to keep my eyes open against water. I remember practising in the bathtub when I was little, but couldn't really do it. So, now I'm swimming down into the river following the blob of Tommy's body, my eyes wincing. My lungs are already tearing at me to give up. I hadn't thought the water at the bottom of the falls was this deep. But eventually I bump into Tommy. His calm image reassures me, floating before a circular hole – the opening to the tunnel.

He motions for me to come with him. I swim and swim, and his blob grows darker, losing shape. My feet kick against the tunnel walls, and claustrophobia begins to attack me. Then the wall above me loses force, and I swim upward instinctively. I

37

launch out the water and reap in huge pales of air. Tommy's in front of me, chuckling. He treads water a few paces from me.

"Where are we?" I ask him.

I behold a canal-like passage, with a domed roof above us. We're in a long tunnel, half-filled with the water, the walls made with leaky old boulders. By the far end of the tunnel there's a metal gate with criss-cross bars, leading onto further tunnels and water.

"This is where they'd work with the water," Tommy says.

"It's amazing. I didn't know all this history was here. I've walked by it so many times and had no clue."

"Me neither before I was a kid. Follow me to the end, Dolina. Let's see if it's still there." He swims towards the gate and then finds something in a hole in the wall. It's a tube of paper, bound with string. "Here it is, the Map for LEVEL 4."

It's a hand-drawn map, detailing the circuit of these underground tunnels.

"Did Filippo draw this?" I ask.

"Of course he did. Who else?"

It's further evidence of Filippo's genius, drawn over two decades ago. Brilliant pictures in felt ink. Didn't know he could draw too, but of course he can.

"Right," Tommy says, "I'll swim under the gate, and you pass me the map through the gaps overhead?"

"We go through there? But it's too dark. Are you sure this is all safe?"

"There are lights around the other side – I'll show you."

I'm stunned all over again how Filippo had the daring to make all these LEVELS. I go under the gate (after I pass Tommy the map) and out into a rectangular tunnel where the water is shallow. I call out Tommy's name nervously, because I can't see anything. Then there's a scratchy ripping sound, and a plume of fire erupts to the side of me. Tommy's holding a live match.

"Wow," he says, standing on a ledge by the water, "the matches are still dry enough to work."

He sidles along the ledge until he stops at something else dug inside the wall, and holds the matchstick into it. A glorious bulb of light blooms, and I realise it's a glass lantern! I watch the room burgeon in light.

I hop out the water and join Tommy on the ledge to witness the room from a proper angle. It's filled with ropes, wooden beams and ladders, which jut and hang from the walls like some fantastical assault course. I shiver with adrenaline.

"This is the bit I could never get past," Tommy's saying, bringing the map out. "Let's take a look."

On the map the pictures mark the steps in the course. There's a rope-swing first, and a host of beams you have to climb up. Then a ladder we can see by the very end of the room. Although there is no plotted route to it, '*June's Room*' is where you need to get to, marked with a star.

"I always got to the ladder part," Tommy says, "but never figured out where *June's Room* was."

He believes he can still remember the swing and climbing-frame part, and asks me to bring the lantern along so he can see better. The lantern is an antique, maybe a century old, with a glob of wax. It's as if we've stepped back to a concealed part of history.

Tommy begins the game. He uses the swing to glide across to the beams. There is no seat, so you have to hold on by your hands. But the drop to the water below isn't far enough to hurt if you fall. I leave the lantern on the ledge and it takes me a few times to get across, but I reach the beam and Tommy catches me. We're standing on the beam, looking around at the other parts.

"You see the ladder from here?" he asks. I do. It's about 20 yards away. "So you have to climb up and over between the beams in order to reach it."

The beams hang between the two walls in tandem. I marvel at their size, great hunks of timber as you'd find stranded on beaches.

"Why'd you think the mill people built these beams like this then, Tommy?" I say. My voice is quiet and trembly. I just want to chat a little, to hear his voice. He only says he doesn't know, and I can hear he's a bit nervous as well. I'm glad he's with me. The chamber echoes with the hollow sounds of dripping. I wonder how far we are underground.

Tommy takes the lead, climbing, and I follow. The beams are easy enough to climb over, and we reach the last one which overlooks the ladder leaning by the far wall.

"Okay, so you see how the ladder leads up to the roof?" Tommy's saying, "and there's a little hatch there, where what looks like a drain cylinder is? Like you'd find on the street to go into the sewers?"

I spot the metal circle. It looks solid with rust and age.

"So I always used the ladder to climb up there. But I could never get it open. Plus –"

"Plus it's too small for us to fit through. Even for a child it couldn't be done. Let's see the map again."

I study the map in the dim light. The star symbol for *June's Room* is drawn beyond the boundary outline of this chamber. It's placed just to the right, beyond the wall.

"So I thought maybe there'd be another clue if I opened that hatch. But I could never budge it. Maybe if I tried now, that I'm stronger?"

But the hatch doesn't seem to be the way forward. I study the ladder. It isn't fixed to the wall, but hanging against it. You can clearly move it. What if the hatch on the roof is meant to be a distraction? I look around the walls. Suddenly I see a patch in the lower wall to the right, where the stones turn black.

"Tommy!" I cry. "Down there! There's another hole in the wall! You have to move the ladder down to it."

I lean one shoe out and find one of the ladder-steps, then scale down it. Tommy comes after me. Then when we're at the bottom, we lift the ladder sideways so that it acts as a bridge to this little hole in the wall. I climb over and peer inside it.

"What can you see?" Tommy calls.

"There's another arrow here!" it's in fluorescent paint pointing into a passageway. "And big enough for me to crawl through! This is it, Tommy."

Tommy cheers. I peer into the dark passageway. There's no light by the end of it, and there could be anything inside. But we've gotten this far, and I have to go in.

"I think I'm going to go in," I call.

"Are you sure? You don't want me to go first?"

"I'll be fine. Other people have done it before, right?"

"Okay, I'll be right here for you."

I crawl through into the passageway. It's big enough for an adult to move through; the ground is dusty dry under my hands. I feel my way through the dark. Then gradually a faint glow by the end becomes brighter; the passageway rises and then broadens. I come out to an oval room with a strand of light shining from above. 'JUNE'S ROOM' is painted on the wall. I stand up and go forward.

"We've done it, Tommy, we've found it!" I yell out behind me.

Just as I step forward, something snags my foot. I hear a swirly sound, followed by a lumpy thud behind me. I turn. A beam of timber has fallen down in front of the passageway. The beam blocks the entrance. I tell myself to breathe for a few moments. That's what you should do before you panic. I go to the beam and try to lift it free. But it's far too heavy, too thick, entirely covering the passage. I'm locked inside the room.

"Tommy – *Tommy*! Are you there? I think the door's shut on me ..." I try to budge it, using my full body weight. My heart's yammering in my chest. The room's filled with my racy breathing. I stand up, sweat rolling down my temples.

I look up towards the light. A thin white blade coming from a slat high above me. I'm at the bottom of a long chimney-like structure. The walls narrow until getting to the light at the top, about 25 yards above. There is no way to get out.

Something catches my eyes at my feet. A thick coil of rope. The rope is ripped off at one end. Then I find the other end of the ripped rope. It's tied to a hook, attached to the top of the block of timber. Now I start to panic properly. I've broken the seal on the door.

"Tommy!" I yell through the wall. "Tommy, I think I shut the door after me by accident. The rope on the door is snapped, and I can't get it open. Are you there? Tommy, please."

I go on pleading like this against the door. But my voice flails uselessly around the room, and I can't hear anything from Tommy. I think I might start crying, I'm so scared. I can't call for an ambulance. My phone's back in the Woods. Even if I could, what on earth would I tell them? I barely know where I am.

Then I try to rationalise things.

"It's just a game, Dolina. Just a game. There must be something I can do."

How do I get up to the top of the chimney? I search the room. There is the sign JUNE'S ROOM on the wall. I go over to check it. I notice one of the rocks there isn't attached to the wall. It looks loose, incongruous. I feel it and find that it moves. I pull it out. Inside is a little piece of paper. I unfold it and place it in the blade of light to read the message. On it are written the words:

IF YOU BEAT PANIC – YOU'LL SEE MORE IN THE ROPE

Right. So, the 'panic' must mean that you're supposed to be scared at first, when the door shuts. Therefore, the door is *meant* to shut you in. It's a trap. I snagged the rope underfoot when I came in – so the rope acted as a trip-wire to release the block of timber.

I go to the rope, and uncoil it. It's very long, and when I get to the other end of it, there's a loop tied in with firm knots. Again I look up into the chimney. "You have to climb up to the top. That's daylight out there, for sure." Then I just see a metal pole jutting out from the wall near the top, beyond the blade of light.

"'You'll see more in the rope'. So you use the other end of the rope, and throw it up to the pole at the top. Then when you catch it with the loop, you climb up using the rope."

My mind pelts through a range of possibilities and fears. What if I never get out of here? What if Tommy can't find me, or tell the police where I am? What if I'm wrong, and the wooden door is the only way out? All these things attack me as I continue to throw the rope up, again and again, and fail. Yet my entire body becomes focused towards an essential zone. The zone you need to be in to complete *Filippo's Game*.

I catch the pole with the loop. I gasp, and joy sweeps over me. It's easy to climb up the chimney walls because you mostly use your feet to propel yourself up. I clamber up onto the pole and then reach out for the light at the top. There's a wooden hatch there which I push open.

Then I leap out into the colour and pang of the Woods again! I lie on a floor of ivy, staring up into surrounding trees of bright green. I whimper a little. "Christ," I say, "that was a scare."

When I stand up, I spot a sign near me. The words are painted with that same merry multicolour paint, on a pane of wood stuck into the earth:

Okay, so I've accomplished what I came here for, and now I know where LEVEL 5 is. But right now I just need to get back to Tommy.

I recognise where I've come out in the Woods. I'm on the far side of the river where there are no paths. It's overgrown with fallen trees and curtains of ivy. My clothes are sodden and my trainers squelch as I work down through the growth. I find the mill's masonry which overhangs the waterfall where Tommy and I came in. Just then I spot Tommy far below me swimming across the river to the bank. He's thrashing his arms in a front-crawl, aiming for our clothes.

"Tommy!" I call across to him and my voice rings out below the water. I feel powerful from where I am, overlooking the Woods. Tommy whirls around to me.

"Oh, God, Dolina. Are you all right? I was just about to call for help."

"I'm fine. I got past the LEVEL. I did it."

"But when you didn't come back, I got so frightened."

"Yeah. So did I."

"What happened inside the *Room*? What did you find in there?"

"Tommy. Let's go home and get dry. Then I will tell you all about it."

I sidle down the bank towards the river. There is a zeal in me, a guilty pride, that I've progressed farther into the *Game*.

CHAPTER NINE

JUNE 17TH 1998

FILIPPO'S GANG

Tommy said he didn't want to come, because he doesn't like Filippo's Gang. I didn't know what he meant by that, and I want to go see the football game Filippo's hosting. So I go up to the Hospital by myself. I go past Henry's house, which is the last house on the street. Then the Woods is one side of me over the wall, with the Hospital's odd shape at the end of the road. It's like these are the only two places in the world. Like we're not inside a city or a country at all.

The Gang have lit a fire. I smell the woodsmoke as I walk up the street. They've just lit it on the field under the Hospital. I don't think they're allowed to do that, light bonfires there. But I like the scent and atmosphere of fires, and it draws me closer.

They're all loud and partying, and there are more people than I expected. I go up the little mound and onto the field. The field lies away from the road. At the end of the road is the Fence of the Hospital. Beyond the Fence is an enormous Liquid Nitrogen tank. Thick tubes run from it and the tank constantly makes this buzzing noise as if it's about to burst.

I reach the field and scan the crowd. They're smoking and drinking, batting footballs about. There are a lot of strangers around, strangers to our neighbourhood. I spot Filippo. He's doing more keepy-uppies in front of a group of people sitting on the grass. He has his hair swept back over his forehead, hanging down to his shoulders. He makes the ball look effortless, of course. Just showing off.

I'm standing there alone, so I try to catch Filippo's attention. I wave at him and he spots me for a moment. But he just drops his eyes back to the football again. It's embarrassing that my cousin ignores me whenever he's around his Gang. I look around for somebody else I know, and I find June Walker sitting not far from me. June's with a group of girls her age. I don't know them. They're sitting in a circle, very serious. They've all put heavy make-up on and styled their hair, but they're not talking to any of the boys. They intimidate me. June suddenly sees me, and she calls out.

"Hey, Dolina. You okay?"

"Yeah, I'm good." All the girls are looking at me.

"Come sit with us."

I really don't want to sit with them, but then, I do at the same time. I go over to June. It's like approaching an Army General, or the Prime Minister or something. June's in her usual white sweater, which makes her boobs look huge. I sit behind her, just out of the circle.

"Girls," she says, "this is Dolina, Filippo's little cousin."

"Aww, she is?" the group suddenly stir. "She's just as pretty as Filippo is handsome!"

I blush under their eyes.

"So you came to see the game?" June says.

"Yeah."

June's eyes are darker than anyone's. Like there's no lines between her pupils and irises. And they're always dry and robotic.

"You enjoying the World Cup?" she says.

"Uh hu, it's fun."

I don't know why June's asking me questions. She spoke to me before in a nice way ever. She barely says hello on the street, even though she's my cousin's Deputy.

Shriek. We all hear a whistle. And everybody goes silent. There's a boy standing in the middle of the field. That's Robin. He has a fantastic afro haircut which bobs about as he runs. He's holding a whistle in his mouth. Robin's the referee for the game tonight. He's always the referee.

"Okay, people. Let's get started with the game!" he calls to the crowds. "Both teams come up to me, please."

Whilst a group of older boys go towards Robin, including Filippo, all the other people sit down in a rectangle around the field. Lots of Gang members and the others sit near me. I feel little and stupid compared to them, but I'm also excited about the match.

Robin's talking to the boys in a circle. Filippo's holding the football. Then they do the coin-toss thing, and Filippo's side wins it. I recognise the boys on Filippo's team from our territory. The opposition are all strangers. Immediately I want Filippo's team to win, because they're from here, our neighbourhood. And when Robin blows his whistle to start the game, I clap and cheer as loudly as everyone around me. I want June and all the others to notice me as one of them.

People were chirpy before the game started. Now that it's on, most people have hushed up, even June and her girlfriends. It's weird how a football game does that, makes people dark.

Then our team scores, and I go wild with everyone else. Nobody's even looking at me, though. Filippo then adds a second goal. He's much better than the other players. He dribbles through two defenders and zooms the ball under the goalie. I wish I could be hugging him with his teammates too.

As they're celebrating, something interrupts the scene from the trees by the side of the pitch. A sound makes all the players turn and look. I can't believe I forgot all about him. Henry. He comes dancing through the trees, grinning, holding a bottle of wine. Immediately there's a flutter in the crowd. People groan. June rolls her eyes and tuts.

"Oh, no," she says. "Here he comes again."

The play in the game is still paused since Filippo just scored. Henry's dancing between the players, offering high-fives which nobody accepts. He's drunk. Filippo shoos Henry towards another group of lads sitting by the field-side: the Gang members. When Henry goes and sits with them, he offers the wine to the others. They all look at him like he's crazy.

The game continues. The opposition pull one goal back. Then threaten to score again. The spectators are getting nervous and angry. Henry, in his gangly green hoody, is up shouting encouragement to Filippo's team. I like it. I'd rather be sitting with him than with June.

Suddenly one of the opposition players crashes into one of our boys. He slides in with his boots and the other goes flying in the air. Everyone goes, 'Oh!" and Filippo's team swarm towards the tackler like wasps. I wince because it looks like they're going to fight. But Robin goes in between them and manages to stop them shouting. Robin shows a yellow card to the tackler. But the hurt boy is still holding his legs in pain.

"Looks like he can't play anymore," a voice says. "We need a substitute."

Filippo's looking around helplessly, muttering to his teammates. I realise what's about to happen, and for some reason I know it's a bad idea. Filippo turns around, to Henry on the touchline, and waves him to come on and play.

More groans in the crowd.

"Oh, God," June says, "not *Henry*."

Henry takes his jumper off. He's still wearing his baggy jeans, when all the other boys have shorts. He puts his *FIFA '98* cap on when he runs on.

"Who is that, June?" one of the girls asks.

"Henry Fowles. Just some slime-ball from our street. He only wants to play because he wants to be in our Gang."

"How does he get to be in the Gang?"

"He must play *Filippo's Game*. Filippo made a bet with Henry that if he scores tonight, he'll give him a chance to play the real *Game*."

"Oh, *Filippo's Game*. I've heard about that. It sounds mysterious."

"Hmm, well, we'll see if Henry can even manage a goal. Look at him. He's a drunk."

The game kicks off. Now I'm afraid, about a whole load of things. Henry? They'll let Henry play *Filippo's Game*? Why? I don't get it. I'm always afraid for him when he's around the Gang, especially when they're drinking like this. Even with the way June talks about him. She hates him and I don't understand why.

I'm surprised they're even letting him play in their football team. And he's so bad at football, too. He just looks stupid, running about in his heavy clothes with all the other lads, and they're all bigger than he is. He's blundering about, sweating. One time the ball comes over to his feet. He aims to kick it, and misses completely. Everybody on the field laughs except me. It's embarrassing: I wish the game would end. Filippo's side are still winning 2 – 1. Just let it end and then Henry can go home.

But why on earth would Filippo make a bet like that with Henry? Why would he give Henry a chance to get into the Gang, or let him near the *Game*? Everybody in the neighbourhood is jealous of the *Game*. They want to be part of it. Including me. Why let Henry of all people play it?

Another girl arrives by June's group. It's one of June's friends and she's carrying a bag of alcohol. June greets her and they open the bottles happily. I watch June drink some of the wine. Her eyes flash down to me as she has her mouth on the bottleneck, like I've caught her being cruel.

Roars come from the other end of the field. The opposition have made it 2 – 2. I look at the watch. The game has nearly finished.

Filippo barks at his teammates. He never really gets angry except when he's playing football. The game becomes clumsy and frantic. The boys keep kicking the ball up high. They're all scared to lose the game, and I'm scared to watch. I don't even know why I came. It all got worse when Henry arrived.

I back away from June's group. I try to slip away and leave. But the game holds me back just as I stand up. Filippo has the ball and looks up to our goal down the field. The only player we have there is Henry. Filippo hesitates. All the eyes are waiting to see what he'll do. Then he puts his face down and whacks the ball to Henry. It lands pinpoint at Henry's feet. Henry ducks away from the defender and thumps the ball under the goalie and into the net.

3 – 2. Henry's won the game for us. He begins whooping up and down, then runs the length of the field where the opposition fans are. They throw things at him and one of them spits as he passes. But Henry only grins and celebrates to himself. And nobody else makes a sound. Filippo claps, then stops.

I want to yell and shout for Henry, but the others trap me shut. I'm stunned by his goal, it was so good. When I look at June she's just concentrating on her wine bottle. I happen to look over at Filippo, and I *think* I see him, but I'm not sure, looking to see how June has reacted. Because Henry won the bet. He's scored. That means he's allowed to play *Filippo's Game*, right? If so, June must be mighty angry, and Filippo must realise he's made a big mistake.

The game starts again. It's nearing the end. I've sat back down again and suddenly I'm enjoying myself. Henry has shut everybody up, for once.

Filippo is running with the ball. He races past June and the girls, who hoot after him. He gets nearer the goal, then makes a pass and it comes to Henry again. I can see a huge defender running to him from behind. The defender doesn't even make it look like a mistake. Just as Henry's about to kick the ball, the defender trips him up from behind. Then, as Henry's falling down, thumps him in the back of the head with both his kneecaps.

Henry drops flat on the grass. Then he stops moving. I cover my mouth.

The opposition teammates snicker to themselves. None of our fans or teammates do anything. They don't laugh, don't protest. Robin blows his whistle for a free-kick. But he doesn't show any card to the big defender. The defender only walks away, leaving Henry's body on the floor. It should have been a red card.

Filippo goes over to Henry and kneels by him with a blank expression. Henry very slowly sits up, holding the back of his head. He looks totally dazed. Without saying anything, he walks off the field. Instead of calling after him, Filippo only takes the free-kick, and the game continues.

I watch Henry collect his wine bottle by the touchline. He hobbles away back to the trees at the edge of the field and disappears behind them. His head is bowed, and he sways about, not only because he's drunk. I'm the only person watching him. Everybody else has just returned to the game, and they watch our side go on and win.

CHAPTER TEN

APRIL 2018

WHAT NEXT?

Tommy's already asked me several times whether I'm okay. It's obvious *he* isn't okay, and he wasn't the one trapped in an underground tunnel a few hours ago.

We're back at my house, late afternoon. I showered and put clean clothes on after we got home from *June's Waterfall*. I made Tommy shower too, to get the river water off. Now we're sitting at the kitchen table, with wine rather than coffee. And, I am okay. At least, not frightened anymore. In fact, I'm grinding with stimulation, becoming more obsessed with *Filippo's Game*. It's neither a good or bad obsession, yet. I need to learn more about who the people were in our neighbourhood.

"Stop asking me if I'm okay, Tommy!" I finally snap at him. He looks a bit hurt when he shuts up. But I go on. "I just want to discuss what happened earlier at *June's Waterfall*."

The wine's making me ruthless, but I'm also thinking about the *Game* in a new way. I didn't expect that the *Game* itself would get disturbing. I hadn't thought the LEVELS could be dangerous. Maybe it's the danger that makes the *Game* become something beyond entertainment.

"You were seven years old when you played Level 4?" I say to Tommy.

"I was."

"Filippo let a seven year old play LEVEL 4? I mean, what if you'd got into *June's Room* and couldn't get out? How would a little boy be able to climb up that chimney bit even?"

Tommy just shakes his head.

"You said June was the one who invented LEVEL 4?"

"No – Filippo did. He made most of it. But June came up with the idea for the *Room* at the end."

"Why, though?"

"I don't know. I just remember the others talking about what June added to it. They'd say things like, 'June makes the *Game* scary at LEVEL 4, so watch out'."

"So you weren't alone when you played it back then?"

"No, I remember Robin was there."

"Robin Lainson?"

"Yeah."

We're quiet for a while, drinking. There's an anger in me and I don't know why it keeps building.

"June Walker ..." I muse. "Did you ever like her?"

"Hmm, June was a bit strange – don't you think?"

"Yes. I never liked her. I always thought there was something ugly with her."

"Why?"

"You don't remember her? What she was like?"

"She never really spoke to us."

"Yeah, and she was my cousin's best friend. Don't you think there's something up with the Walkers in all this?"

Tommy shuffles about, drinking his wine slowly. He seems reluctant to go further. I'm annoyed with him, because I want him to help me with this. Tommy was always great at games and puzzles, right? Now we have this real-life puzzle. He could never get past LEVEL 4, and I beat him to it earlier today. He needs to make up for that. I want to know why June made the *Room* part of it.

"What do we do next, Tommy? What next?"

"I think you should calm down a bit, Dolina. You're obviously vexed."

I glare at him for several moments, until he drops his eyes.

"Tommy: there are things I haven't told you yet about Henry. Things which happened in 1998."

I begin telling him about my memories as a child. I describe the incidents in June '98, of the alarm on Mr Walker's house and Henry's bloodied nose. Then how I saw Henry gave June a package the week after that. Then the bizarre night when Filippo allowed Henry a chance to play the *Game* if he scored in the football match.

Tommy takes a sip of his wine. I notice a spark in his thinking, and I realise he really is with me on this.

"Filippo and June must have owed Henry something," he says.

"How'd you mean?"

"They gave him a chance to play the Game that would induct them into their Gang. That's huge. They must have been allowing Henry to make propositions."

"But why would Henry want to be in the Gang, if he knew everybody hated him?"

"Maybe it was convenient for him. Perhaps he needed protection. The package Henry gave to June in the Woods: maybe that was formal acceptance into the Gang, and he needed to be publicly accepted into it, by playing *Filippo's Game*."

"What was in the package, I wonder? I'm guessing both Henry and June Walker needed something from each other." We sit around, our brains rolling. It's frustrating. At least somebody else is as frustrated as I am. "So what about the essential part? Henry's bloody nose?"

"Yes, I remember something about that." Tommy takes another drink of his wine, prolonging my expectance, in his usual absent-minded way. "Not about the bloody nose. But about Mr Walker's alarm, and the smash sound. I heard that Henry broke Mr Walker's window."

"Henry broke Alec's window! Why?"

"It wasn't on purpose, apparently. Him and the others were playing football in Mr Walker's garden. And Henry kicked the ball through the window by accident. That sent the alarm off. I remember the lads laughing about how shit he was at football."

"But Henry didn't even play football, *because* he was shit. And plus – the World Cup game was on that day. Everybody was inside watching it."

"I'm just telling you what I overheard."

"How do you explain the gory nose then? Somebody thumped him in the nose just because he made a mistake with a football?"

Tommy doesn't say anything. It almost feels like I'm the only person who cares about Henry Fowles.

"Well who was it who told you Henry broke the window with the football?"

"Robin Lainson."

"He was there that day?"

"I think that's what he told me, yes."

"Do you know for sure if Henry ever played *Filippo's Game*?"

"No, I don't know if he did or not. I don't remember anyone talking about him playing. I've never thought about it that way."

"I'm going to go and talk to Robin next then."

"Okay?"

"Because we need to know whether Henry played the *Game*."

I'm already looking Robin up online.

"I think he did play the *Game*. That's why I found his cap and watch in the treehouse. But we don't know how far he got – which LEVEL he got to. So I'll go talk to Robin about it next."

As I scurry away at the keyboard, Tommy looks at me searchingly.

I imagine Henry standing inside the chimney in LEVEL 4. I wonder if he was as scared as I was. I wonder if he got to the chimney at all. But somehow, I believe he did. I believe he played my cousin's famous *Game* further-in than I have.

CHAPTER ELEVEN

ROBIN

Robin Lainson was probably Filippo's best male friend, back in the 1990s. He was a key figure in our neighbourhood. Robin was seen as a top member of the Gang, behind June the Deputy and Filippo the King. He's bound to have essential information on Henry.

I haven't seen Robin in a long time. But he's still close with Filippo. I liked him when I was a kid. He was friendly and didn't mock me as much as the other Gang members did. Maybe I was jealous of his closeness to Filippo, but the jealousy made me respect him too.

Robin was the only kid in our neighbourhood who wasn't white. When he was young he had this terrific afro haircut, a huge, bulbous thing. Everybody loved his hair and it was a rich source of banter, in a jovial way.

I messaged him earlier and suggested we could meet to catch up. He messages me back this afternoon, and says yes, he'd love to see me. I can come around to his place tonight to catch up.

Tommy didn't want to come and see Robin, so I go into Edinburgh on my own. It's a long bus ride, but a pleasant one, with hazy sun playing shadows on the streets. It's weird to come out of the leafy lull of our neighbourhood and into urbanity. It's strange to think of Robin as now belonging to this urbanity. He lives in an affluent flat with his wife and two young children.

I'm still a bit drunk from the wine earlier, and maybe my detective skills aren't at their ripest. And when Robin and his wife answer the door and welcome me in, I'm blushing constantly. I don't feel like an adult compared to them. They seem, not old, but settled. Robin has no afro these days.

He invites me in to his sitting room, where his boy and girl are. I realise how awkward I am with children. I just don't know how to act with them and feel like a freak. Which I generally am when it comes to socialising.

Robin offers me wine and I instantly accept. His wife tells us she's just putting the children to bed, so us chaps can catch up properly. The kids go and hug their Dad at the sofas, and I give them each a clumsy hug in turn. Everyone's embarrassed at my clumsiness, but all are too kind to register it, even the children. Ha – I'm such a social failure – it's laughable.

So, by the time Robin and I are sat on his sofas together, I'm a bit deflated mentally. No longer the shrewd investigator keen on mystery-solving.

"It's strange to see you all grown-up, with a big flat, and a nice family," I say to him. "I still feel like a child compared to you."

"Haha, thanks Dolina. You'll do good in life. Don't worry."

Robin has a way of laughing after everything you say something to him, and after everything he says something to you. Not in a fake way, he just laughs a lot. We talk about my plans for life, what I intend to do. All that conversational scaffolding where nobody remembers your answers next time you speak.

Despite my impression of his superior maturity, I realise he's still the same person who grew up with my cousin and I. As I talk to him, I see the same boy who used to play with Filippo. It's as if this large flat and his nice family aren't real, that there is a misconnection between the past and the present, which makes the present flawed at its roots. He's a 36-year-old man and he must have secrets. He cannot dodge the history he shared with Filippo, Henry and I, just because he's older.

The conversation lags, until I see he's getting bored with me. So, I decide to introduce the topic of *Filippo's Game*. (I have my tactics. I'm not going to tell him I found Henry's things in the treehouse.)

"This might sound strange," I begin, "but I've been playing *Filippo's Game* again. Just by myself, in the Woods. You remember the *Game*, right?"

"Hahaha ha ha! Yes, of course I do! *Filippo's Game*. That was great fun. Your cousin was a genius, I'll admit. A smart guy to have built all that in the Woods. So you were playing it recently?"

"Today in fact! I was playing *June's Waterfall*."

I go on to tell him about the *Game*, and my experience in LEVEL 4. Robin only listens with a fond expression.

"I'll admit, when I got stuck in the *June's Room* part, I was terrified."

"Oh, ho ho. Yeah, I know it was a scary bit. But it was made to test the players, to see how far they could keep their heads. The other LEVELS are a lot scarier than that, believe me. Have you gone to the *School Ruins* yet?"

"The next LEVEL? No, but I will, soon."

"*School Ruins* is amazing. You'll love it. All the parts will still be working."

Robin suddenly springs up and puts his wine glass down.

"Actually – Dolina – come with me!" he walks out the room abruptly. I follow him into his flat's corridor. He opens his hallway-cupboard, cranes into it and begins lifting stuff out behind him. He produces bedsheets, books, a whole bunch of things, and I wonder what he's doing … Until he finds a big red box. "This, Dolina, is where I keep all my stuff from back then. From the 1990s."

We take the box back into the sitting room and open it. It's magical, what's inside. A miniature museum of boyhood. Catapults, green and white Hibernian Football Club scarves, *Star Wars* action figures, Top-Trump cards. There's an old *Nintendo '64* games console, and all the *Mario* and *Zelda* game cartridges.

"This is amazing," I say, "you kept all this? Does the *Nintendo* still work?"

Suddenly I'm flooded with memories of playing this very *Nintendo* with Henry, Filippo and Robin when I was a girl. Videogames were ways to compete with each other peacefully back then.

"I'm sure it does," Robin says, "it must be an antique by now, but yeah."

I'm getting emotional seeing all this. I long to be a child again.

"But here's what I wanted to show you," lifting something out from the bottom of the box, "it's one of the original maps, for *Filippo's Game*. Your cousin drew it and made all the pictures."

He hands me a scroll of hard, yellowed paper, A3 size. It offers a bird's eye view of our neighbourhood, the Hospital and the Woods. Drawn with oil pastel, pencil and ink, there's an elaborate outline of all the paths throughout the Woods, with little pictures representing each LEVEL.

"There are only three of these maps. John, June and me all had one. It plots all the points in the Game. Pretty cool, huh?"

"It is, it is. Ah, I really want to head back and play the next LEVEL."

The map is more than impressive. It's as if it reinvents the Woods as something fictitious. A fantasy world, or videogame, or graphic novel. Yet the geography of the drawings, the way he's depicted the river and the mill/school ruins, is all as perfectly scaled as a real map.

"You can keep it, if you like?"

"Thanks, Robin I will, thanks a lot. But, wait, just one question. Why are you giving me this map? If it tells me where to go? Doesn't this spoil the *Game* for me?"

"Ah, ha. But look a little closer? The map doesn't tell you anything about how to do each LEVEL – it only plots their location. All the clues are held physically within each LEVEL. And, if you look again. What do you notice? What's missing?"

I look over at it. It takes me about two minutes to realise what's not included, even though it's so obvious:

"Oh! Right, the last LEVEL? LEVEL 8, it's not there!"

"Exactly, Dolina. John left LEVEL 8 off the map. You'll have to find it, my friend. But you'll do it, if you use your head." Robin stands up. "You want some more wine?"

I accept. I'm enjoying this visit, and my curiosity's being fed so well, I've forgotten why I came. And yet, I don't know how to bring up Henry without the mood turning dark.

"Well, again, this is an odd question, and random …" I begin. "But, do you remember the *World Cup* in 1998?"

"Yeah, of course. It was the last time Scotland managed to get into any tournament. Why?"

"You remember that day Scotland played Brazil?"

"Uh hu. I watched it."

"Well, I remember it too, even though I was little. But I wasn't watching it with anyone. I was in the Woods. And I heard Mr Walker's alarm go off."

He's looking at me and I can't read his expression. He waits for me to continue speaking.

"And, well that was pretty scary … Do you remember that day? I heard a smashing sound, then the alarm. Filippo was there at Mr Walker's."

"Yes, I do remember that actually. I was there at Alec's too. Because we were all watching the game, and the alarm interrupted it."

"Do you remember what caused it?"

"Hmm. It was so long ago, it's hard. But I think it was something silly, and it ended quickly."

"I heard that somebody might've kicked the football at the kitchen window, by accident? It was Henry Fowles."

"That's it! Yes. The ball broke the window. But, it wasn't Henry: it was June."

"June? Are you sure?"

"Yeah. Just a clumsy mistake. I think Alec even made her pay for the window repair, though, just so she wouldn't try play football again. Ha ha ha ha."

"But, somebody told me it was Henry who broke the window."

"Umm, no. Henry was watching the game with us. June was with her girlfriends in the garden. The alarm went off, and it was so loud. But then it was not that big a deal. We just watched the rest of the football."

"So Filippo, Henry and you watched the game after that?"

"Um." Robin sighs. I've noticed he's not looking at me anymore. "I don't *think* Henry was interested in the game that much, so he left early."

"And Filippo?"

"I really can't remember, Dolina. Why you so interested anyway?"

I blush.

"I don't know, Robin, I'm just curious. So, it was you three and June and her friends there that day?"

"I think Chelsea was there too."

"Chelsea? Filippo's old girlfriend?"

"Yeah, she was there."

Robin checks his watch, drinks more of his wine. He seems more jaded, rather than surprised or evasive, as if he literally can't remember that day. But I wonder whether he's pretending about it. Maybe he's not telling me something. Regardless, I can tell my visit is nearing the end of its tenure, so I jump in with my final important question.

"Just one more thing, Robin, then I'll leave you alone. Do you know if Henry ever played *Filippo's Game*?"

"Henry? I don't know if he did or not. Maybe."

"You don't remember being in the Woods watching Henry play the Tarzan LEVEL?"

Robin shakes his head vacantly, thinking. Then suddenly he jumps up:

"But, but, but: there is a clue which will tell you whether Henry completed the *School Ruins* part or not."

"There is? Tell me, please!"

"Ha ha ha. That would be telling you too much. I thought you wanted to play the *Game* anyway? If you complete *School Ruins*, there's a part at the very end of the LEVEL which will tell you if Henry got that far too. You'll see what I mean when you reach it."

He finishes his wine.

"Right, Dolina. It was great to see you. Sadly I must head to sleep. I've got work in the morning. Not that I mean to chuck you out. Please keep that map though. It's a gift. And let me know when you complete the *Game*."

I thank him and we trade hugs and goodbyes. When I'm back outside, my head's plying down different routes all at once. It's too much to handle, this excessive thinking. The map coaxes me inside my jacket pocket. I just want to stare at it, study it dry. But I need to rest too. I'll just head home and sleep for now. There's more work to be done tomorrow.

CHAPTER TWELVE

A DREAM

I had a dream last night and I think it's important. Here it is.

I'm heading home on the bus. It's a heavy summer day in full sunshine. The bus goes up an arching road, and at its pivot I can gaze out to a landscape stretch of Edinburgh. I see my neighbourhood far in the distance.

The housing districts, dazed dominoes in the sun, lace upside the final hillside of the city. The houses are carved out by a bulging green slab of trees. These are the trees of the Woods.

The Woods lean across the horizon, distanced only by countryside fields many miles away. I wish I could jump into the greenness. Across from the Woods stands the Hospital, a silent white cube clinging to the edge of vegetation, It doesn't seem urban, only lost and just as mysterious as the Woods. It speaks nothing of a Hospital's trauma. Its frame places no shadow across the trees. Before this far-off painting, my mind races with stories, the flesh and wonder of the characters moving through its world.

Suddenly the vision collapses. The window frame darkens as my eyelids drop. I'm quickly going blind. My lungs begin to slow, then stop working, and I can't breathe. My body hits the floor.

The only thing left is sound. The volume in my ears intensifies as everything else plummets. Then I realise I'm not on the bus anymore. I've been transported. I'm in the Woods, rushing with birdsong, the river, insects.

I wrench for air but my throat's stuck.

"Dolina?" A voice I know well. "What are you doing?"

When I try to speak my voice comes out in a gurgle.

"Are you hurt? What's the matter?" Henry says. "Maybe we should get you an ambulance. But, don't worry."

Henry pulls me up whilst I suffocate and my body charges down. I lean into his arms. He's holding me hard, as if pressing life into me.

"We'll get you to some doctors, don't you fret," and he begins pulling me somewhere. I feel his chest dip and surge like the hull of a boat. Though I'm dying, I know he'll try and help me.

But then his body leaves me, and I hear him scream. "No! Don't do it to me!" he hollers, so loud it bangs my eardrums and I feel my body descend further into oblivion. I rebel at myself.

Stand up Dolina, stand up Dolina – Henry needs help! I try to call his name and force myself to stand up.

His body and his presence have already gone. Something's ripped him away. His voice comes no more. And I lie there degenerating on the ground whilst only the audio of the Woods trills onwards. Until I wake up.

CHAPTER THIRTEEN

SCHOOL RUINS

I go up and under the valley, where the white blossom trees shed warm meandering snow through the air. The blossom flakes dangle against the background of wild garlic. Lilac flowers have declared a meadow underside an amber-leaved plant glowing with sun. These are the Woods in their visual pinnacle, this time of year. I'm off to find the *School Ruins* today, where LEVEL 5 comes.

Tommy has gone back to Glasgow even though he said he'd stay a few days. He didn't speak to me much after *June's Waterfall*. I think he was a bit freaked after all that. I'm angry with his sober attitude. Feels like he's already bailed on me, when I thought he was as enthusiastic as I was. But I'm anticipating he'll come back.

I've been thinking about what my meeting with Robin Lainson meant, going over what he told me. My main conclusion is fairly simple. Robin must have been lying about what happened on that Scotland v Brazil day in 1998. He told Tommy back then that Henry had broken Alec Walker's window. Now he tells me that June broke it. One of the versions must be a lie. Moreover, there is no mention from him of why Henry had a bloody nose.

So, I'm heading to speak to Chelsea – Filippo's old girlfriend – tomorrow. She was there that day, and she'll have a different account, I hope. I haven't seen Chelsea in a long, long time, but I found her on Facebook, and she agreed to meet me for coffee in town tomorrow.

Although I know Robin's lying to me about something, I believe him about the clue at the end of *School Ruins*. Also, I was surprised how indifferent he was about Henry in general. He didn't really register any emotion when I brought him up. And, he gave me the map of the *Game*, when he didn't need to. What does that mean? I don't know yet.

I brought Robin's map with me today. The drawing of *School Ruins* is one of the best on the map. It's just beautifully drawn. The ancient urban structure within the Woods, subdued now by nature.

The *Ruins* lie in the very north-east of the Woods, far away from the neighbourhood. To look at the Woods from outside the walls, you wouldn't expect a school to ever have been there, and yet, the paths in the Woods are formed by the schoolchildren who walked here 200 years ago.

When I arrive, I find the mossy slabs of stone set around in a perimeter. The ruins are so old that the trees grow within the perimeter walls. Beyond these walls are some of the oldest trees in the Woods, which were planted that long ago when the school was built. The oaks and elms there surge magnificently over the Woods, the tallest vessels here by far.

I begin looking around the masonry, for a first signal on what to do. This is the first LEVEL when I've had no hint of any kind on what to do at the start. But, I remember one part in the ruins from childhood. It's this abrupt hole in one of the walls – a hole at the bottom. I used to crawl through it out to the other side when I was a girl, playing with Tommy. I go there now.

Of course, I'm too big now to fit through the hole. I crouch down to it, and search around the rocks inside, suspecting maybe another paper clue hidden behind a removeable one? But none move. Something about the hole seems important though. I can't fit through the hole, but I can climb the wall at this part. Maybe there's a clue on the other side of the wall.

When I climb up, I instantly find a fluorescent arrow, pointing diagonally down the length of the wall. I've never scaled this wall before as a child. Now I'm an adult I'm finding the clues straight away. I head along the wall.

I'm four meters off the ground, edging down this thin wall-top. The ivy is so thick that I have to traipse through it, and I have nothing to hold my balance onto. When my foot's snagged by something under the ivy, I trip over and just manage to catch myself on the ivy strands before falling off. I'm lying in front of a long plank of timber, disguised under the ivy growth. Alongside it, painted in graffiti-like style, are the words:

USE ME ONTO THE NEAREST TREE

THEN PROGRESS WITHIN THE AIR

Okay. What does this mean? I search around my area. It's as if I'm being judged as I figure out what to do, my performance in *Filippo's Game* being scrutinised, surrounded by the ivy leaves, little gloating faces watching me.

"I don't understand the clue … 'use me'?" It's just a heavy plank of wood. It runs to the end of the wall, which breaks off onto nothing. 'Nearest tree'. I look across to an oak tree hanging near the wall.

I take Robin's map out and study it. When I look at the picture of *School Ruins*, I notice the spaces between the walls of the school. The tree I'm standing in front of is plotted prominently, prompted by a series of other trees marked with distinctive dots. The other trees are left out of the picture. 'Use me onto the nearest tree'. "So the LEVEL is played within the *trees*, and within the air."

I lift the plank of wood up, and crane it across to the bough of the oak tree across from me. Sure enough, if fits perfectly onto a branch leaning out from the trunk. I climb across the plank and onto the oak tree. Hugging the bough to keep my balance, I feel something jutting out from the bark. It's another long plank of timber, nailed at the bottom to the trunk and tied with rope at its top. The map depicts the next tree, a fir tree this time. I climb up to the plank and undo the rope at the top.

Filippo's even built-in a lever at the bottom of the plank, so that the wood eases over to the branches of the fir tree smoothly. I nip up the plank and dip into the fir. This fir is huge and fat with lush needles. I snuggle into the branches, which splay wide to save you falling. I spot the next sign on the main tree trunk:

CLIMB TO THE VERY TOP

I ascend, with the leaking sap from the trunk browning my fingers, enriching my scent. It's a real easy climb because the branches are everywhere. And Robin was right about another thing. *School Ruins* is a fun LEVEL. And when I get to the top, I can see out for bounds across the Woods. I pause for a while, admiring the scenes.

Then there is a rope, just below me. It's secured by a metal bolt to the trunk, and it arches across to a birch tree across from me. Then there are two more ropes attached to two more birches. A triangle of birches, the ropes connecting them.

I'm sweating as I ponder how to get across. I'm not the best with heights, and I can't tell how far I am off the ground, but it's not a short distance. Plus, there is no swing or saddle or anything to journey along the rope. You just climb by with your hands? Well, I assume so. So I go for it.

Action films and the actors in them are so unrealistic, how easy they portray physical feats. I hoist onto the rope with both hands and begin to scale across, holding my full body weight, realising I'm dangling now from a proper dangerous height. If I drop from here I could break my legs. The *Game* has instantly turned nasty again.

My muscles zap and burst and when I finally get to the birch trunk, it's straggly and bare of branches. I stand here above the drop, sweat whipping off my face, with only one foothold. And the only handholds are the two ropes. The Woods give no cessation as I tackle these ropes. The Woods care not for my presence. The animals in it chirp and thrive, indifferent to my self-induced tussle.

I make the end of the final rope after much swearing. The ropes have arched over the last *Ruin* wall, and I'm sitting under the first heaving bough of an elm tree. I hold there for a long while, panting. Why didn't I bring a bottle of water? I'm resting before the next challenge.

I happen to look up and notice something unusual in the trunk above me. It's a square of wood from the trunk, cut free of the main body and placed back in, acting as a little door. I take the door out and inside the hole there's a piece of paper:

AT THE TOP YOU'LL FIND THE BOX: ADD YOUR NAME
TO LEVEL 5

BEWARE THE BLACK-SHEEP STUMP

I study the gaping trunk above me. On it are nailed stumps of wood, trailing high up beyond my sight. That's the task: I have to climb to the highest point in the Woods.

I can feel the members of the old Gang again. They're smirking, nagging at my confidence, goading me to give up with *Filippo's Game*. It's difficult to describe how enormous this tree is unless you're sitting on it. I'm supposed to climb it, with no safety ropes? How do I know that there weren't ropes back in the 1990s? Plus, the 'beware the black-sheep stump' – that sounds bad … But perhaps it's through the fear of it – the challenge – that pelts me on. I know that I'm supposed to be doing all this. I start climbing.

The climbing blocks are positioned so well that it's easy to climb. I take it very slow, because I'm scared, but the blocks are kind to the grasp. My limbs tremble and time saturates, but when I finally brave a look down I'm already a long way up and near the top. Plus, there's a not-so-vertical part in the tree now. The trunk leans diagonally, and I can see something promising at the top, shining. That must be 'the box'.

The blocks diverge, and I see that they split into two climbing routes heading up to the top. Two routes leading to the same place. I pick the one that seems the simplest. I put my hand onto the first block and launch myself up; go up to the second block, resting my feet on the first. Then there are two more above me. (The box at the top is just there metres above – I'm so close). I put my foot onto the first block above. The block under my shoe shudders … I have nothing else to cling to. The block gives way. I plummet. I scream.

I fall fast and heavy. The tree catches me back as I'm caught in the crevice of a bough. My leg crunches between the trunk and my body weight. I howl. My leg's trapped underneath me as I'm sitting on it, but it's so painful it's hard to unlock it.

When I do, I dangle it down into the air. Stinging muscle. I can barely move it. It's seized up so badly I fear it's broken. I'm nearly sobbing with pain and fright. But thank God I didn't fall right to the bottom.

I realise what I did. I missed the warning clue from earlier. Beware the black-sheep stump. One of the stumps is a dummy and designed to give way under you.

"Filippo, you bastard! You sadistic bastard! You made the *Game* this dangerous?" Ranting aloud to myself in my anger. "So that's what the catch is? There are two routes and one of them is a dummy, the one that looks like the easier route. Jesus, though, Filippo? What's with you?"

I look down to the forest floor. The dummy block lies there placidly. I caress my leg, trying to soothe it. It's not broken, just severely strained at the calf. It will be fucked for a good while. Obviously, it's hurting me mentally too, that I forgot about the warning clue. I climbed onto the trap. And I notice that the trunk I'm perched on is directly below the dummy-block position. Anyone who got there would fall right where I am now.

I'm angry, but I'm still alive. So I head back up the tree-trunk, my leg scathing all the way, taking the other block-route up. I make it to the top. What I find there is a little blue safe. It's sitting calmly in a central space between the boughs. It has a key lodged in its lock. I turn the key and open it. Inside, are an old-fashioned camera, a black felt-pen, and a bunch of little photos. I'm breathing fast and I feel the relish pulsing in my head. Underside the lid of the safe are scrawled the words:

ADD YOUR PHOTO AND NAME TO THE LIST

LEVEL 6 IS WHERE THE FOXES RUN

I study the camera first. It's a polaroid camera, looking brand new. It's not battered or worn or anything, and there is still unused film under it. It's been kept dry, held in this safe after all this time. Next, I study the photos. They're selfie pictures of people sitting exactly where I am now. I sift through them.

The first photo is of Filippo. He's staring confidently at me with his pretty face. Next is June Walker, then Robin Lainson with his afro superb and dominating the frame. Underneath each photo is a date, written by each of them with the black felt pen.

"So when you complete *School Ruins*, you have to take a polaroid photo of yourself, record the date at the bottom, and leave it in this safe."

Across the pictures I recognise all the other old Gang members. Every single member who got this far in the *Game*. A catalogue of history; portraits of youth, their faces bright in the light of the '90s. I get to the last photo, the last of a thick line of the Gang held in chronological order. Its date is June 18th 1998.

Henry Fowles grins at me. With the green hoody and the big nose, indifferent as to how weird-looking he is, happy that he's completed LEVEL 5.

Henry sat where I am sitting, nearly 20 years ago. He has the final photo date, the last person to ever get this far in *Filippo's Game*. This means something very important.

The polaroid camera still works. Of course it does. I put some fresh film inside it.

I take a photo of myself, and watch my image seep into life. Write today's date at the bottom, and place the photo in the safe, under Henry's card. I'm getting closer to Fillipo's Gang and closer to Henry.

I'm light headed and spent physically. I don't really know how to feel mentally, which emotion to pick. Am I elated to be progressing in the *Game*? Why am I still sitting atop this tree, suspended loftily above the Woods? Why I haven't I climbed down to the bottom just yet? Is it because I'm closer to Henry than I have been before?

What does it mean that he got this far? Why does he look so happy in his photo?

CHAPTER FOURTEEN

CHELSEA

I really busted my leg good yesterday. I'm walking with a jagged limp and it hurts with every step. Bloody scrapes all over the shin, the muscles jolted in. I won't be fit to play LEVEL 6 for a few days yet. But I make it into town to meet Chelsea, this afternoon. My leg will heal.

Chelsea was the glamorous queen of our neighbourhood, for a very short while, back in 1998. Solely because she was Filippo's girlfriend. She lived in one of the districts outside of our area so she technically wasn't of the neighbourhood's ilk. But she was inducted into the Gang. Filippo and she then broke up after the summer of '98, and she just stopped hanging out with the group.

I was surprised she even responded to my Facebook message, or remembered who I am. But I remember her as being chirpy and harmless as a character. She'd stop and talk to me when I saw her around the streets because she knew I was Filippo's relation.

When she walks into the coffeeshop this afternoon she greets me quirkily and kisses me on the cheek. She looks mature, professional, like she's succeeding in life. We get some coffees and sit down by a table.

When I'd messaged her I'd been blunt with my intentions and why I wanted to talk. I'm investigating Henry Fowles. Chelsea readily agreed to come meet. She messaged me back saying that she's still spooked about Henry's disappearance. And she wants to help. The first thing she says to me is:

"Are you a journalist, Dolina?"

"I'm not, no. I'm just trying to find out what happened with Henry. I remember you being around the neighbourhood a lot that summer he disappeared. So I wanted to ask your version of things."

"Sure, okay. You've got me for an hour before I'm heading back to work. Ask away – I'm all yours."

I've prepared a list of questions for her.

"So, the Gang, Filippo's Gang. You got in, right? That must mean you completed *Filippo's Game*?"

"Yes! Yes I did. Those were great little games!"

"I just completed the *School Ruins* part yesterday."

"The one with the ropes around the trees? It's all still there in the forest? That's amazing."

"It is. But just one thing I wanted to know: did you ever find out if Henry got into the Gang? Did he complete the whole *Game* too?"

"Hmm … I think he did, but am not sure. I remember other people saying that Henry was *playing* the *Game* but not whether he got to the end of it. But I was never there to see it when he was playing."

"So do you mean people would usually watch a contestant play the *Game*, all the way through?"

"Yeah, John was always there with me when I played through it. I enjoyed the puzzles he made. He was there as I did the LEVELS, and I think he helped me out a bit when I got stuck. Because the *Game does* get quite … alarming, at points."

I want to tell her about my leg injury, and how terrified I was in *June's Room*. But with everyone I've spoken to about the *Game* they're more impressed with it than they are sceptical. And so am I.

"John was an okay man," she continues, "I mean, I disliked him for a while after we broke up. But we were only, what, sixteen years old? Just a teenage relationship which petered-out. He was relentlessly smart and he made me feel stupid maybe. But was largely a decent lad. I don't have any dislike nowadays.

"But actually," she's frowning, "now I think about it. The *Game*, and his Gang, it all got a bit weird sometimes."

"How do you mean?"

"Well, take the *Game*, for example. I liked it, and it was fun, but I only saw it as play. The other Gang members saw it as a hardcore initiation thing, which I didn't understand. It became serious after that, like being a Gang member was something almost religious. And with John as well, how they all respected him so much. He was talented, but I didn't think of him as an icon or anything. That's what made it creepy."

"So, you thought John was weird as well?"

"A little. But more so with the others."

"Who? You remember June Walker?"

"*June*, oh, yes! She was a right cold little ..." she stops herself and drinks more coffee. "Sorry, it's mean to say it, but I never thought she was right. There was something off about her, like she had a dark influence on the Gang. June is an example of what I mean."

I don't like coffee in general. I'm forcing myself to drink it to seem like I'm liking it, because I'm trembling so visibly. I try to control my shaking hands.

"I'm glad you came in to talk to me, Chelsea. Thanks for the time."

"No problem, Dolina."

"There's another thing I wanted to ask about. And I might be wrong. But, do you remember the day back in 1998, when the World Cup was on? Scotland v Brazil. You were with John, Robin and June – at June's house. Henry was there too?"

"When Alec Walker hit Henry. Of course I remember."

"Alec Walker *hit* Henry?"

Chelsea eyes are wide.

"Yes, Mr Walker punched Henry in the face. I saw the whole thing. Henry flew back from the punch and smashed into the window."

I gape at her.

"I thought everybody knew that?" she says. "It was a plain assault."

"Okay … Chelsea, could you just explain the whole thing to me, please? What happened that day?"

"I was there, with John, Robin and the others, like you say. We were all watching the football game on the TV in Alec's living room … Umm … Scotland had just got a goal back against Brazil and we were all cheering and hugging each other. Then John and June asked Henry to go into the kitchen to speak to Alec.

"I remember seeing them through the kitchen door talking to each other. I didn't know what about. Robin and I were sitting on the couches watching the game. Then out of nowhere Mr Walker just thumped Henry in the nose. Henry flew back and he landed into the window. Then the alarms went off. It was crazy."

"Jesus Christ," I say, "are you sure? Alec Walker? Why on earth would he hit Henry?"

"I don't know. It was disgusting. Alec was in his forties and Henry was just a teenager."

"But can you guess why? Were they arguing or shouting or anything?"

"No. I really can't explain."

"What happened after that?"

"Henry's nose was bleeding. He ran out the kitchen and out the house. I wanted to go after him but John stopped me. The alarm was blaring in my ears so I didn't understand what was happening. I just wanted to get out of there, away from that thug Alec. So I did, I got my coat and bag and left. And I never went back to the Walkers' house again."

"Did John run after you?"

"Yes. Except, he ran to the end of the driveway with me. I said I was going home. He said he was going off to see if Henry was okay."

"So *he* just ran away from you?"

She laughs ironically, darkly.

"Yes, I guess he did. In fact, we broke up pretty soon after that. I was being a coward, how I didn't go to check on Henry. How I didn't even call the police or anything. I hate violence, and I feel ashamed I didn't do anything about it. I asked John about it later, why it had happened."

"What did he say?"

"I think he said Henry and Alec had made up for it. He made it seem like just a stupid fight between two boys. You know, the classic way where boys hit each other and then they make up straight after."

"Well, did you believe him?"

"No. I saw Henry around the neighbourhood after that. He was just his usual self and didn't seem bothered by anything. But no, I didn't believe John, that it was *nothing* what happened that day. A man doesn't punch a boy in the face and get away with it.

"And this is like what I was saying earlier, how it was odd in that neighbourhood. And especially with the Walkers. There was something dodgy about it all, and that's why I left it." She finishes her coffee. "Hmm. I'm feeling all jittery talking about that now. That's the only time I've seen somebody be attacked violently like that."

I'm quiet for a while. Chelsea seems very serious now, when she came in earlier buzzy.

"Henry was a goofy kid," she says, "but only because he was different from the others in the Gang. I mean, I distanced myself from him when I was younger, just because of popularity and all that shit. I probably would've liked him if I was older. He was a lot older than the others. *We* were the immature ones."

It's gotten to the end of her hour. It went so quick. Chelsea tells me she has to head back to work and gets her things. She becomes flowery again.

"Sorry our talk wasn't so cheery! I hope it was helpful."

I tell her that it really, really was. I want her to stay and tell me more. What she's said has sent revelations through me. But I can't stop her leaving. Maybe I don't want her returning to her own life, her own proper job, looking and being functional.

Watching her disappear through the window into the sunny street, I'm bothered by how easily she moves on from what she's just told me. Violence and crime have left her head already. Because she's abandoned all that in her past.

But what happened to Henry is not abandoned in history. The past is not gone. With Henry Fowles, it's not even discovered. Within me personally it is pulsing with life. And I'm not going to desert my old friend.

A sixteen-year-old boy got physically attacked by one of my neighbours, a man, 20 years ago? And Alec Walker never got charged for it? This is crucial news. Robin Lainson witnessed this same attack and he lied to me about it, very casually. Why?

I look at the shiny frames of cars passing outside the window. Hear other people chatting in this coffeeshop. Suddenly, I have to leave, be free of this scene. It's just all too scandalous, and I can't be near people whilst I'm this upset. I leave and head home.

PART II

CHAPTER FIFTEEN

JUNE 19TH 1998

THE FOX

School was so bad today. It was so hot out, but we had to stay in. Loads of wasps flying about the classroom. I can't wait until school holidays. Only one week away! It's evening now, and still a hot evening, and the Woods look very pretty.

Tommy's out with his Dad tonight, so it's just me to play with. But that's okay. I go into the Woods by myself.

It's *loud* inside. The bugs clog the air and the midges chase me as I go across the river. The atmosphere in the sun is amazing. I want to explore. So I walk a different way from where I normally go, beyond the holly trees and cut off from the main paths. I want to find the fox again. Haven't seen him in a while.

In the sunshine I see gold spiderwebs in the tangle of plants and trees. Long, single lines of web hanging meters across branches. It's a miracle how they can do that, build webs that far apart. (But I also hate spiders, and the webs keep getting in my hair).

The fox lives around this part of the Woods, where it gets overgrown. I'm just curious to see where he lives. I only see him ever in the distance and he's always running away. But his den is somewhere inside this big block of purple bushes. The bushes are made of sharp sticks underneath and it's too hard to climb into them. But the fox has a way.

I creep closer to the bushes. I'll try and snoop on him. I go around the back of the bushes instead of the front. Then I notice something I haven't seen before. It's a little tunnel through the sticks ... Is this the fox's tunnel? I go into the opening and begin to crawl through. I see that the sticks have been cut away above me, and this tunnel stretches deep into the bushes. I'm confused. A fox couldn't make a tunnel like this.

I hear a whooshing sound behind me – I turn – there's the fox! He's running away from the bushes. I dive back out the tunnel and run after him. He's heading for the river. This is the closest I've ever been to him. I run along the riverside whilst his dark red body flashes into the weeds.

But the thorns here are too thick, and I can't keep up. I hear the fox rustle ahead of me through the thorns and then there's no sound. I can't get past these bushes: they're bigger than I am. I look beyond the river. Then I spot the *Fence*.

The *Fence* is the end of the Woods. Beyond that the land belongs to the Hospital. The *Fence* has barbed wire. It's tall and looks terrifying. My Mum told me to never ever go over it. "Never go further than the *Fence*, Dolina," she says. But I don't understand. Because the Woods don't stop there. There are more trees behind the *Fence*.

Plus – from here I can just see the Liquid Nitrogen tank. That spooky tank that always makes that sound, like a massive fridge about to stand up and come alive. I can only see the roof of it and it's small from this distance. But yeah! That's it. I've never seen it from this place before.

I realise, that, chasing this fox, this is the farthest I've ever come into this part of the Woods. And I really want to go over *The Fence*. The Woods can't belong to a Hospital! The trees glitter over the top of the barbed wire, and I want to go over and discover what's there. Why does Mum not want me going that far?

But I'm just too scared to go closer. I turn back. Oh well. At least I got to see the fox up close. And there's still more time to explore. I go back along the river, climbing over the weeds. I've never seen these parts of the river either, and I keep finding new things. Like this tree which has fallen over the water, making a bridge. It's so perfect a bridge that I have to try it.

I walk across the trunk and sit down on it half-way, watching the water flow under me. Feels like I'm a queen, perched above the river, safe and hidden in the wild. The midges swarm in clouds above the water. They're bound to find my skin soon enough. But then I see something shiny in the water, under the midge cloud. It's made of glass, whatever it is. I can't see any closer from here on the bridge.

I need to find something, today. So I go for it. I take my shoes and socks off. And dip down into the river. The coolness rushes up my legs as I go closer to the shiny glass thing. The riverbed's sharp, and the midges instantly clamber over me when I get there. But when I crouch down, I find a glass bottle.

The bottle's lodged in between two boulders. It has a cork on the top, and there's something stuck inside it. I can just about shift one of the boulders free, then I lift the bottle out. The midges are flinging into my eyes and nose, so I take the bottle to the riverbank and climb up onto the weeds.

It's clear glass with a long neck. Inside is a silver key. I take the cork out and study the key. This is the best thing I've ever found. I'm sure it means something. I look around me to see if anybody's seen me finding it. But there's only the hazy Woods. This is mine, and I want it all to me.

I put the key into my pocket. I don't know what it's for, or what it's doing in the river. I just know I have to have it. I put the cork back on the bottle, and the bottle back in between the two boulders underwater. It doesn't seem right to take the bottle as well as the key. After putting my socks and shoes back on, I leave the river, and go past the fox's den. I need to go home and hide this key.

I keep checking to see if it's still hidden in my pocket. Hide it. Hide it. Hide it. I exit the Woods and go up the street. I go around the back of our house and into the back garden. Mum is in the house upstairs … She won't see me. The first thing I spot is the shed – that seems somewhere good to go, if I can find the right place. I open the shed door as quietly as I can.

All Mum's garden things are stacked here. Her tools and her pots cake the floor, so I can't hide the key anywhere on the ground. The roof? I look up and study the ceiling. I notice there is a gap in the corner of the walls between two roofing planks. I find my Mum's bag of compost and lug it over to the wall, then use that to climb up to the roof.

I slide the key up and behind one of the planks. Climb back down and put the compost bag back. Mum won't find it there will she? I close the shed door again and go into the house. I must leave the key there. I'm already too afraid to go and bring it out again. Just like I'm too afraid to go beyond the *Fence*. The key belongs hidden. It's all too weird for me. I go into my bedroom and shut the door.

CHAPTER SIXTEEN

APRIL 2018

DEPRESSION

Walking around at work the last few days, with this bad leg, in this awful little hotel: God, it's been a strain. I've just been heavily depressed of late, having to be here. Carrying food to rude people, serving drinks to drunk people, washing stubborn dishes, doing errands for the hairline-aggressive chefs.

I have a degree from a top art school, and this is all it has qualified me for? I'm good at making paintings. That's it. How does being a good painter make you money?

I miss the campus where I studied in the other city. I miss the notion of youthfulness, that something great was sure to happen with me. I miss the scent of oil-paint, the charcoal stains on my fingers. I miss the old easel in the art class where I'd stand creating for hours.

Now I'm standing in a hotel doing nothing meaningful, on minimum wage, with these other colleagues being mean to me because they're doing the same thing. The chefs especially. They've chosen me as a target. I choose to placate them, but they just keep attacking.

I haven't been fit to do anything else for days, it's too painful to walk. But there's a reason why my leg's nailed. Because I was playing a kid's game in a woodland somewhere I'm 25, have nothing prospective in life, and I'm playing little games, like I'm mentally ill.

What if that's all *Filippo's Game* is? A forgettable adventure. A cult, belonging in childhood. Why go back to it now?

But this is only a simple resolution to distract me from the real problem. What I'm most angry about is the mystery of Henry Fowles. And why the history of it keeps bothering me. Am I angry because I want *Filippo's Game* to be something more? Or do I want to prove it to be what it actually is? Am I on the cusp of discovering something great?

The Walkers are the characters I keep thinking about most of all. Alec and June Walker. Compared to me, the Walkers are far more successful. They've always been super wealthy. Does that mean they have something I don't?

June Walker lives down in London these days, working with the same business branch as John. I can't even think how much they're earning. I know money doesn't grant happiness, and so on, but they also don't have to work shoddy hotel jobs.

Alec Walker hit Henry Fowles in the face, a very long time ago. Alec is more than double the age of Henry. And he lives happily in a wealthy house, now, in the suburbs of Edinburgh. Who are the real villains in our society?

Why are men allowed to be violent? Is a punch ever excusable? Punches happen so often in films, on TV, with that ridiculous *Poosh* sound, to make it more cinematic. Films have to augment violence in order to justify it. Real life violence is much different.

I've just completed the Sunday shift at the hotel job. I managed to control my temper with the chefs earlier on when it was hectic busy. I could have exploded at them, stormed out and quit my job. But didn't.

I ride the bus home. Need to recuperate, but I need to smash this mystery as well.

CHAPTER SEVENTEEN

THE WALKERS

When we were little, Tommy and I used to play basketball down at the bottom of the hilly road beside the Woods. We made this hoop out of bendy sticks we got from the Woods. It was great fun for about three days, playing basketball. Tommy always beat me, but still. We stuck the ring up at the top of a wall which leaned away from the main road and put rocks on it to keep it in place. That wall belonged to the back of Mr Walker's garden.

I remember I was the first one to lob the basketball up past the ring, into Alec's garden. We couldn't reach it from the wall, or climb into his property, so we nervously went up to Alec's door and confessed we had lost the ball there. He was charming and jokey about it the first time. He said it was no problem and let us go around the back to get it.

His garden is huge, by the way. He has an outhouse which looks like something out of a 1980s action film, with CCTV cameras all around it. And a long lawn, mown perfectly: everything suggesting the plush idleness that wealth allows. We got the ball back that day, and we liked going somewhere we hadn't seen before.

So when we threw the ball over the wall a second time, we didn't feel hesitant in going back to ring at Alec's door.

"Ho ho ho," Alec said, smiling "go on and get it back then, little-uns. Be careful with your aim from now on." And he shut his door quickly.

It was a classic miserable overcast Sunday when I threw the ball into the garden a third time.

We rang Alec's doorbell and when he answered this time, he *exploded* at us. He ranted that we shouldn't come around to the door on Sundays. "Sundays are for family time!" he kept saying. "Come around another time!" Tommy and I were genuinely scared of him. So much that we never asked to get the ball back again. We took our hoop down from the wall, and didn't return.

I realise that we annoyed him. But we were also only kids. Plus, the 'family time' comment was a lie. We saw June walking ahead of us on the street when we went home that same day. It was maybe 20 minutes after Alec's row, and June wasn't home, being part of the family time.

Who are the Walkers, then?

As I said a while ago, the Walkers are the oldest neighbours we have. My mother moved here a long time ago and this is where I always lived from birth. As long as I can remember, Alec and June have been around. Alec would always greet you boisterously when he saw you. He walked his dog a lot in his distinctive bright yellow jacket. June was very different. She'd keep her face down and walk by you silently, so eventually I knew not to say Hi when I saw her.

The Walkers are also by far the richest neighbours beyond anyone else in our area. Alec is the C.E.O. of a marketing company based in London. John Filippo works for Alec's company. Filippo is the manager of one of the company's branches and June is a director in one of the others.

I assume that this is a key link between my cousin and the Walkers, both for what happened in 1998, and what resonates now? As to why there might be something to hush up about Henry Fowles?

When Filippo was sixteen, Alec had recognised his talent, and had given him an internship opportunity in his marketing work. Filippo had performed so well that Alec had offered him the London job after he finished school. I assume it was much the same process with June, although she was the C.E.O.'s daughter.

My mother had always been proud that Filippo had done well, and she praised Alec for giving him opportunities. Mum liked Alec a lot. *I* liked Alec too; he seemed like a decent man, yet there was a distance within his joviality. Something false about his greetings.

Why would I be afraid to go up to Alec's house when I was little and ask for my basketball back, when Filippo was at Alec's all the time? A few days after that occasion when Alec shouted at Tommy and I, I saw him again with his dog. Alec just waved and gave a friendly hello, as if he didn't remember being angry with us. And if he did remember, he'd surely just give a ball back to a kid after he'd calmed down, especially if she lived right across from him?

I'm making connections between what happened then and now, after what Chelsea told me. Comparisons between my vague unease about him when I was a girl and what I know now.

I believed Chelsea's account completely. She wasn't lying when she told me Alec hit Henry. With such force that it propelled him back into the kitchen window … That was a crime that needed to be hidden. And I know that Robin hid it and is still hiding it. I know that Filippo disguised what happened from Chelsea.

June was there too. I see a triangle between Filippo, June and Alec. Henry is the mark outside of that shape. Why was Henry Fowles there with them that day? The biggest 'freak' of the neighbourhood. Why was he allowed into Mr Walker's house when I felt dubious about going there?

Soon after that day Henry got hit, I saw Henry and Filippo together. I spied on them, and I saw them meet June Walker in the Woods. Henry gave June a package. I need to discover what was inside that package.

Let's fast-forward to 2018.

The other week I called Filippo in London in the daytime. He went silent when I told him that I'd found Henry's possessions in the treehouse. Later that night, I went back to the treehouse, and Mr Walker comes out on me with a flashlight. He knew I was there, and he came into the Woods to confront me. Filippo must have told Alec I'd found Henry's things. And Alec Walker doesn't want me going into the Woods to complete *Filippo's Game*. Why?

There is one fact that I'm hooking this on. Before I told Filippo on the phone that I'd found Henry's things, he mentioned that he'd built the treehouse with Alec. Alec Walker therefore knows about *Filippo's Game* intimately. It reveals new information about my cousin's making of the *Game*?

Alec, June, Filippo and Robin are not the routes forward with this mystery. They're the people I need to *investigate*, not the people I need to get information from. Henry is correct route. I need to ask myself, who else was properly close to Henry Fowles?

CHAPTER EIGHTEEN

JUNE 23ʳᵈ 1998

SCOTLAND V MOROCCO

The World Cup game is on at nine o'clock tonight. Normally, Mum wouldn't let me stay up to watch anything this late. But it's the last week of school, and we're only watching videos in class anyway. So she's let me go over to Robin's to see it.

Filippo picks me up from home to take me over to Robin's. He looks so tall in the door, and he has a nice smell of aftershave. Mum stands behind me and she speaks to him. She giggles after everything he says. I watch how they talk and I want to join in, but I know I can't. Filippo says bye to Mum and takes me down the street. The roads are pink and quiet and I'm thrilled to be alone with the king of the neighbourhood.

"Think Scotland will win tonight, Filippo?"

"Hmm, we'll see … Will need a bit of luck."

"Can Scotland *win* the World Cup?"

He chuckles.

"I don't think so, Dolina. Scotland don't usually win trophies."

"Do you think *you'll* ever play for Scotland?"

He laughs his manly laugh.

"No," he says. "I couldn't be a real footballer."

"But you're really good at it."

"Not good enough. What would you like to be when you're older, Dolina?"

"Hmm. I think I'd like to draw and paint. Be an artist."

"Yeah? That's cool. Your Mum showed me some of your drawings at the house at Christmas. You're brilliant at art. I'm sure you could be an artist."

I blush. I try to hide it but he notices it. He doesn't point it out though.

"Just keep painting, Dolina."

We come to Robin's driveway. Robin's sitting smoking outside his front door. Filippo suddenly turns to me:

"Okay, so you're going back to your Mum's before ten o'clock – right? That's the deal? You can watch the first half of the game, but then you've got to go home." I nod. He turns back and walks away towards Robin. I really wanted him to stay and speak to me more. Robin jumps up and tosses his cigarette away and gives Filippo a bearhug.

"Hey! It's King Filippo. *And* Dolina! Come inside, my friends."

I can hear thumping music and voices clambering upstairs. Makes me nervous and excited at the same time. Soon as we go into Robin's house a waft of dog food hits me. It's very hot. Robin offers us a can of Pepsi and I say no thank you even though I want one. Filippo leads the way upstairs and I'm trembling as I follow Robin. When we go into the room I discover Chelsea, June and Henry sitting around the room. The air's smoky and there are bottles about the floor. Rap music's pounding – I can feel the floor bump with the beat.

Filippo goes over to Chelsea and kisses him. Chelsea waves to me as I stand in the door. June's watching the TV screen. Henry's on the floor beside me as I stand in the door wondering where to sit. He offers me a fist-bump, which I do.

"Sit next to me, little Dolina! If you want."

I sit by him. He's holding a bottle of wine in one hand, knocking it back and forth into his mouth. His lips are already caked purple like he's wearing lipstick.

"Think we'll win today, Henry?" I whisper to him.

"I think the Scots will *annihilate* the Moroccans, little Doli!" he whispers back. "Is little Dolina allowed to drink, Filippo?" he calls over to him on the bed. Everybody glares at Henry, who's grinning. "Gee – it was just a joke. But I'm going to open the window for her. Not good for her to be in this smoky room."

He nearly falls over as he goes across to the window. When he's coming back, he pauses in front of the TV. Blocking the screen, he pretends to yawn. Then he stretches and stands there, blinking.

"Out the way, Henry," Robin says.

"What? I was just stretching my legs."

"Just get out the way! The game's about to kick off."

He sits back next to me. When he notices me smiling he winks at me.

Robin turns the music off and turns the volume up on the TV. The others begin to cheer when the Scotland players come out in blue and white. I cheer and clap with them and it's fun to join in. I like the bit before the game when the players line up and the national anthem is played in the stadium. We all sing it together in the room – 'Flower of Scotland' – and our voices mix together at different pitches.

Then the Moroccan anthem is played: the camera goes along the faces of the Moroccan players. Henry keeps commenting on how they look. "Oh! This one's looking *devilishly* handsome ... Oh – he looks like the baddie of *Lawrence of Arabia*! ... Wow look at his hair! Robin: his afro is even better than yours!"

Nobody else in the room talks. Robin and Filippo nervously watch the TV. Chelsea fondles Filippo's hand but he's not noticing it. The game starts. I don't understand the rules of football. Or why Robin and Filippo shout when something wrong happens to Scotland. It's just men running around in shorts, chasing a ball.

Robin lights a cigarette and the sick smell of it finds its way over to me. *That's* something I really don't get, how people can put that stuff into their lungs. Henry keeps drinking and playing with his new digital watch. He's taken it off and keeps checking the time. I gaze at the green disk; it keeps distracting me from the game, I want it so badly.

Morocco score against Scotland. The boys all flap about. The girls roll their eyes.

"Oh, of course," Robin says, "typical Scotland. That's us done. We're out. I know it."

"Nah," Henry announces, "5 – 1 to Scotland: you just wait."

The game starts again and Scotland keep losing the ball. Even though it's sad I'm still enjoying being here. Being this close to the Gang. I wonder if I'll be in the Gang one day …

Morocco score again 20 minutes later. Filippo goes out the room silently and walks downstairs.

"Oh, no!" Henry's smiling. "Don't be sad, Filippo!"

It gets to half time. Henry starts chatting to me about what I'm going to do in the summer holidays.

"Only three days away until the holidays, aye?" he says.

"Yeah. Mr McGhee's just showing us films tomorrow."

"Ach! If you're not learning anything, just stay at home! Don't go in to school."

"Henry," Robin interrupts, "*you never* went to school at all."

Chelsea and June laugh.

"I need no schooling my friend!" Henry says. "I am the walrus."

Filippo comes back into the room with a big bag of crisps. He walks past me, goes over to the girls and gives it to them. Them and Robin talk to each other. Henry talks to me. He's so drunk that he barely understands what I'm saying. He asks me what films we're going to watch in school, then when I say *Toy Story* he starts talking about it. Then talks about *Toy Story* as the game goes on. As it drags on it's obvious Scotland are going to lose.

Henry keeps urging Scotland on sarcastically. He claps and gives the Scotland players directions as if he's their manager. He keeps pulling his blue cap down over his eyes; half the time he's not even watching the game. This annoys the others. Everyone's annoyed with Henry (except me), and Robin and Filippo are so depressed that Scotland are getting beat. Eventually Filippo snaps.

"Henry!" And everybody gets a fright and stares at Filippo. "If you're not enjoying the game why don't you leave?"

Henry drops his eyes and his smile.

"Also," Filippo lowers his voice, "don't you need to see *Jim* this evening?"

"Jim. Oh, yeah," Henry, "I should go …"

He stands up clumsily and puts his bottle down. I don't want him to go and leave me here with them. The others aren't fun at all.

"Yeah. I forgot I have to go meet Jim. Okay folks. Will see you cats soon!" he holds out his hand to me for another fist-bump. I watch him go.

Suddenly I feel alone, sitting in one corner of the room as the others are on the bed. The game goes on but they've lost interest in the football. Except June – she just sits staring at the screen and sipping a can of cider. Filippo and Chelsea play fight and kiss and it's a bit disgusting to watch. I really wish Tommy was here.

Then Robin lights another cigarette and I get a proper guff of it in my face. I think I'm going to be sick. I need to leave. I'm trying to think up an excuse to go home. I look around me for a clock to check the time –

There! –

Henry's digital watch. It's next to his wine bottle. He left it behind. I grab it. Turn its green light on. I've always wanted to do this! I can't believe Henry forgot to take it with him.

"Hey, guys?" Everybody looks at me. "Henry forgot his watch."

"Not surprised," Robin says, "did you see how drunk he was?"

"Well, what should I do?" I look at the time on the screen: it's 21:02. "I can go give it back to him?"

"Yeah, Dolina," Filippo says, "Henry went round to his house. It's not so much fun watching Scotland get beat anyway."

"So I can just pop along to his?"

"Yeah, sure. Head back home after that though – before ten, remember."

"Okay, I will do," I stand up to leave, "Thanks for having me around Robin."

"No worries, Doli. See you soon."

They all say bye as I exit the room with Henry's watch. I realise it's the first time they've spoken to me tonight. I step out Robin's house into the milky night. I go fast down the street, past my house and head up to Henry's.

It's weird, I've wanted his watch all this time. Now that I have it, I could keep it for me. But I only want to get it back to him soon as I can.

The streetlamps have just turned on, glowing orange. They make orange mirrors on the ivy walls of the Woods next to me. I go past all the houses until I see Henry's, and the Hospital's shape beyond that. I've never been to Henry's house before, but I'm not afraid of ringing his bell. So when I get to his driveway I walk straight up through the gate and head to the door.

But then I hear shouting from inside.

Men, shouting. Angry. I stay still, meters from his front door. There's a light on inside the glazed window. The voices are muffled and jumbled up. I can't hear the words. But there's some huge tantrum going on. I begin to back away from the front door.

Then a *woman* shouts. That must be Linda, Henry's Mum. After she shouts everybody else goes silent. I pause, listening. A shape appears behind the glazed window, coming towards the door. I shriek and run back down the path and out the gate.

I just make it out of their garden before the front door opens. I press my body tight to the dark wall in the street. The front door slams shut and I jump. Slapping sounds come down the garden and then a body appears in the street.

It's a man. He turns the other end of the road and goes striding towards the Hospital. He didn't see me hiding at the wall. I know him. That's Jim. Jim the Janny who works at the Hospital. His shoulders twitch and he's speed-walking. He moves into the darkness down the road.

Jim didn't see me. But I shouldn't be here near Henry's house. I need to head home.

Then I hear Henry's front door open and shut again. And I start running down the street. I run and run and feel the cement bang under my feet until it's sore. But I'm too frightened to stop, until I get to my house. I can feel somebody coming behind me down the road. I jump behind my gate and duck in the bushes, and wait.

I try to control my breath. The soil is squishy under my hands. I want to pee myself.

Silently, a man in a bright yellow jacket appears. Mr Walker. He's very calm, looking straight ahead through his glasses. Just like he normally does when he's walking his dog. Except his dog isn't with him tonight. He just came from Henry's house.

I watch him go up his garden. I see his shape move against the bright lights of his house and then he disappears inside.

CHAPTER NINETEEN

JUNE 24TH 1998

SUPER MARIO 64

I pretended I was ill this morning, and Mum let me take the day off school. I think Mum knew I was pretending, and she was just being kind. She's already taking her summer holiday so probably didn't have the heart to send me to school.

I'm up in my bedroom, though, and I'm kind of trapped in here, pretending that I need to rest. What I need to do is go give Henry his watch back. He must be looking everywhere for it. I know he likes it as much as I do. But how can I go out if I'm staying off school? Mum will know for sure I was fibbing.

What makes it worse is it's a boiling day. My room's already steaming in the morning, and it gets worse when it gets to the afternoon. There must be some way I can sneak out.

I go to the bathroom. From there I peek out the window into the back garden. Mum is doing some gardening. I go back to my room and get Henry's watch. Then tiptoe downstairs and duck under the landing window so Mum can't see me from outside. I can just pop up to Henry's quickly and come back again. Will only take a few minutes. Mum won't notice me gone. I head out and run up the street.

I ring Henry's doorbell. Seconds go by. The door opens. It's Linda. She's wearing pyjama bottoms and a vest without a bra on.

"Hi, there, Dolina," she says quietly. "what's up?"

"Hi Linda. I just came to give Henry his watch back. He left it at Robin's last night when we were watching the football. And I was going to give it to him last night, but it was too –"

"Sure, sure, Dolina. No problem. He's in his room, just head up."

She looks tired and peaceful and she's already leaving the door open for me. She walks away down the corridor.

"Just go up to his room?".

"Yeah, go on, lass. He stays in the first room on the right," and she disappears behind a stained door and shuts it.

I close the front door and move down the corridor. The house is huge, and very *new*, as if they've only just moved in. There are no decorations or carpets and all the wood sparkles. When I go past one of the rooms and look inside, I see it's stacked full of all sorts of things; toys, televisions, dumbbells. All in a scattered pile like it's been forgotten about.

Quietly, I go up the stairs. On the right door I knock. I knock three times and there's no answer. Then the door whooshes open and Henry's standing there. He's not surprised to see me in his house.

"Little Dolina! How are you this fine day?"

"Henry … I found your watch last night! You left it at Robin's." I hold the watch out to him. His face jumps into a grin.

"Oh! Dolina! You found my watch!" he crouches down and hugs me. "Brilliant! I thought I'd lost this when I was stupid drunk last night. Thank you so much!"

I'm proud.

"You want to come play *Mario*?" he says, pointing behind him at a TV and a *Nintendo 64*. The screen dazzles blue. I've seen the others play *Super Mario 64* so many times and nobody has ever given me a shot. But, I have to get back home before Mum finds out I'm not there.

"I do want to but I should get back home."

"Oh, you didn't go to school, did you? You took my advice last night! So you're trying to pretend to your Mum you're ill, am I right?"

I laugh.

"Just come and play for five minutes – it's a present for finding my watch." He leaves the door open and goes into his room just like his Mum just did. I go inside. I've always wanted to play the *Nintendo*, and *Mario* especially. Henry hands me the controller. It's like stepping into a spaceship or something.

"Right, well this is where you fight Bowser, the baddie boss," Henry explains, "so it's quite hard. Press start, the middle circle button first."

Bowser runs towards Mario on the screen. Henry tries to instruct me on how to beat him.

"So you catch him and twirl him around on the joystick!"

But I can't do it. And Bowser keeps throwing Mario off the ledge.

"Ach! Here, Dolina. I'll beat Bowser for you, and then you can play in the world afterwards. Deal?"

He takes the controller back and beats Bowser easily and then he takes Mario onto green fields with castles in the background. He hands me the controller.

"Go explore, my friend."

Henry goes over to his bed and lies down. He's still dressed in the clothes he had on last night. He puts his hood up over his strange face and closes his eyes.

I learn how to control Mario, and it's amazing. All of the game is. The jangly music, Mario's Italian exclamations. I know Mum might be worrying where I am, but the game is too tantalising.

Henry's room is just as empty as the rest of the house. He has a TV, the *Nintendo*, and a bed. That's all there is. His bed is not even a bed. It's just a mattress on the floor with a sleeping bag over it.

But he doesn't seem to mind. After five minutes I hear him snoring. He's fallen asleep, forgetting I'm here.

I keep on playing.

CHAPTER TWENTY

MAY 2018

A SURPRISE

My leg isn't healing. It's getting worse. The bruising's gone from purple, to blue, to black in two days. The calf muscle's gone hard and heavy. It's too sore to move, too sore to sleep. There's something seriously wrong: probably internal bleeding, but nobody's around to help me.

The Woods have overtaken the neighbourhood. The tree foliage presses against my bedroom window, so that I'm constantly under the canopy's pulse.

I begin to fear my leg might be infected, because I can feel fever setting in. I call out for my Mother, for Tommy, but nobody's around. Nobody's around in the world, it's just me lying in creeping poison on my bed.

I have to do something. Have to get out this room.

I hoist myself up on the windowsill above my bed and rest my weight on my good leg. Open the window from the bottom. There's a thick branch splayed under the window, leading into the canopy. I crawl onto it, then go across it on my backside. Below me, the road is overgrown with soil and moss. Yet the streetlamp still glows orange in the shade. I go through the brush as the wood pigeons taunt *do-doo doo doo* to me and the squirrels scarper away by my intrusion.

I break through at the top into light. There's a violet morning sky and I can see the rooftops of the houses in our neighbourhood. The Woods ring up until the Hospital in the distance, smothering up everything save the neighbourhood rooftops.

Then I spot something on the final rooftop. A person. A boy, sitting there watching the Hospital with his back turned to me. It's Henry with his hood up.

"Henry!" I cry out to him and my voice sails over the land. But he doesn't hear me. "Henry!"

I crash over the branches towards him. The hell with the bad leg. I *need* somebody. I hop up onto Tommy's house's rooftop and roar his name again. He turns. And stands up and sees me. "Henry, I need help."

I can't see his face, he's too far away. He calls back to me but I can't hear him. Then he starts signalling to me with his arms. He's pointing at something beyond the Woods, and I look over. The treelines stretch into the horizon onto those far fields outside of Edinburgh. "But what's he pointing at?"

I lean to see, and lose my balance. My bad leg buckles and I drop to the floor. The roof tiles slide out their parts and drop off the edge. My lungs seize up. And my vision darkens, the sky falling with it. My last sight is Henry jumping over the rooftops to me. As I haul for oxygen like I've just been punched in the stomach.

I wake up with another pull of air, brought back into life. Well, that was a good dream. I lie there on my bed. The daylight's bright through my window.

It's Tuesday, and I have a full free day. But, God, I feel awful. Hungover. Dehydrated, feel like mud. Ugly thoughts and memories begin to attack me. That same stagnant question of what to do in life seems unanswerable.

I trudge downstairs to the kitchen and drink two pints of water. But it doesn't help, the dehydration is so bad. I sit at the table and put my head in my hands. I've been drinking so much lately. The hotel job fuels over-drinking. Maybe I could just go get some wine. Would waste another day, but at least it'd make me temporarily happy.

Bring! The front door bell whacks me. It gives me such a fright that I'm furious as I go to the door. I open it wildly.

I find sweet little Tommy Hepburn on the steps.

"Dolina," he says, "hello."

"Tommy? You're back again?"

"Yeah. I'm still on holiday for another week. And I wanted to come back and help you with your quest."

My anger evaporates and I invite him in and hug him in the doorway.

CHAPTER TWENTY-ONE

FOX DENS – PART I

Tommy's arrival has brightened me immensely. I speak to him about how I've been feeling at the dinner table. Typically, he's nice about it and has some wisdom. He remembers experiencing the exact same thing after graduating. But he also guesses that it's this mystery which is making me crazy.

There's another thing bothering me. Since I completed *School Ruins*, I haven't returned to the Woods. I've been *wanting* to head back there, but I've had an aversion for the place. As if it's scared me, and not just because of the physical wound. I'm still scared, but Tommy's presence makes me bold.

I inform him of what I've learned since we last spoke. About what Robin said and how he gave me the map, about LEVEL 5 and how I know Henry got that far, and Chelsea's revelation about Alec Walker.

"Hmm." Tommy says, after I get to the Alec part."

"Aren't you shocked?"

"Of course I am. Something that bad was never made public. Robin and the others must have been ordered to lie about it. So they could protect the Walkers. Henry must have threatened Alec that day. Or, maybe he antagonised them. You remember what he was like – he always took things too far."

"Yes, he did, but in a jokey way. For a man to actually smack somebody like that."

"I agree. That's sick stuff. And I think there's something else we haven't learned yet. And just by the by, I'm sorry for leaving you last week, Dolina. But I admire you've done all this work by yourself."

"It's cool, Tommy. I like that you came back."

"We should stick to *Filippo's Game*. I'm reckoning there are more clues in the *Game*. Let's look at the map. Find out where to go next."

*Fox Den*s is the name of LEVEL 6. Filippo hasn't drawn it as brashly as he has the other LEVEL drawings. It's drawn as an oval purple shape, surrounded by tree shapes. The purple oval represents a great stretch of bushes. I remember where they are in the Woods. Beyond them, following the river, is the *Fence*, which marks the territory between the Woods and the Hospital.

"Well, I feel bad that you did LEVEL 5 and 6 on your own," Tommy says, "but why don't we go do *Fox Dens* today? I can help?"

"Okay, but, Tommy: aren't you a bit scared?"

"Of what?"

"Of going back into the Woods."

"Why?"

"You know why. Because of Mr Walker."

"Well, yeah, I am. But, look at the map. *Fox Dens* is the other side of the Woods away from his house. We won't pass his house on the way. He won't see us go in to the Woods."

"You're right. Let's bounce out."

This is the first time I've enjoyed going outside for what seems an age. Tommy and I quickly embark up the street, filled with the aura of summer. We pass Tommy's Mum's house and the others, then come to the end of the road, where Henry's house used to be.

Except it still is Henry's house. Nobody has lived there since 1998 after Henry vanished and when Linda moved away. This big house has been derelict since then. There are weeds growing out of the rain pipes, grass smothers the driveway, the windows are boarded up.

Apparently, a band of robbers broke in back in '99 and looted all the valuable building materials inside. Then they turned the taps on downstairs and flooded the place, like the baddies do in the film *Home Alone*. I didn't think robbers actually did that in real life – it's such a sadistic thing to do.

The house just seems like a classic haunted mansion now, reinforced by the silent Hospital in its background. Seems like only Henry can ever live there.

"How'd you think Linda ever had the house? If she had problems with drugs and all that?" I ask Tommy.

"Well, it sounds mean. But I heard other people saying they were squatting there. I really don't know, though, how they could've bought the place if she was an addict. Not many people could buy that place when it was brand new."

Linda moved out in the Autumn of '98. I don't think she could stomach the reporters bombarding her. I detested the media as well. I don't blame her.

I remember the Gang members mocking Linda for being a drug addict. Often when Henry was present. But to me, Linda was always a nice woman. I don't judge her. I wonder what's become of her these days and I hope that she's still alive.

We get to the farther parts of the wall, where the final entrance to the Woods is. When we climb over, it's all overgrown. Nobody's used this entrance in a very long time. And when we land inside, we find this part *super* overgrown. The trees and woodland floor are choked with ivy, flies and weeds. We journey down to the river through heavy thorns and nettles.

I don't recognise this part. It's changed so much since when I was last here. And when we get to the river, we find it's morphed in new shapes, making new circuits through the land. I remember net fishing for minnows with Tommy when we were little this side of the river. Now this side is just mud and stalks of hogweed. I like all of this though. It's like the jungle area of the Woods.

We jump over the river routes until we get to the far side, then head up through the trees towards the purple bushes. Now that it's further into summer, the *Ribes* plants have wilted, the pungent pink flowers have turned wispy and the bees have gone. The wild garlic sheets, too, have flopped down. But summer has churned out those white cone flowers on the horse chestnut trees. And the hawthorn flowers are bloomed, with their sonorous scent.

We reach the purple bushes of the *Fox Dens*. They have grown much bigger since I was a child.

"You think the foxes still live here?" Tommy says.

"Hope so. I remember this is the way I used to come see the fox. But you can't get through these parts, it's too thick. Why don't we try the other side?"

We search around the perimeter. Tommy notices something immediately:

"Dolina! You see that?"

It's a hole under the thorns, and it extends in a tunnel under the bushes. It's body-sized. Tommy stoops down to the hole.

"It's definitely man-made."

He silently crawls into the hole and begins going down the tunnel. I follow him. The thorns scrape me and it's a struggle to get through, but Tommy broadens the space. The tunnel descends into the land and I can feel the force of the bushes overhead. Until we get to this circle where the thorns are cut out above us in a dome.

"This is pretty cool," Tommy says.

We're sitting inside a dome of wan light cut under the bushes. The tunnel stops here. There are no more openings.

"It is. But what do we find here?"

Tommy scouts around the dome.

"Maybe it was something to do with the foxes," I say, "but the '90s foxes can't help us now."

"Or maybe the thorns have grown over what you could see back then, and the clue has changed with time."

He studies the main branches of the roots, as far as he can before the sticks override him at the top. He feels the roots alongside the dome's perimeter. I'm getting despondent. Maybe the *Game* is too old now.

"Here," Tommy says.

Hidden inside a little hole in one of the branches is a 50p coin. Its metal's still bright and looks newly made. Underside that is a carved arrow, pointing to the floor.

"The clue is hidden inside the soil," Tommy announces, "and the root has grown farther off the ground after 20 years, so it's less obvious now."

I watch him marvellously duck to the floor. He digs into the soil, scooping the earth out with his hands. Just as mathematically as he does everything else. Until he uncovers a glass jar. He brings it out. It's all slathered with earth, but the top still comes apart when he opens it. Inside is a silver key. And a piece of paper, with the words:

FOLLOW THE RIVER TO THE HOSPITAL

LOOK FOR TWO MORE SHINY THINGS

"Wow," Tommy says, "this *Game* is amazing."

Instantly I'm struck with memories! Altogether I realise the links between girlhood and now. I remember finding a silver key in a bottle in the river. I found it when I was very young. I put the bottle back in the river, kept the key and then hid it in my garden shed.

"Tommy, I remember it all now."

He looks at me confusedly.

"I hid a key inside my shed. My garden shed at home. I found another key."

CHAPTER TWENTY-TWO

FOX DENS – PART II

It took me a while to explain to Tommy what I meant about the other key. I persuaded him to come back to my back garden. I'd totally forgotten about that key I found until now. I'd never connected the key with *Filippo's Game* when I was little. Tommy was suspicious of my revelation all the way home.

And he still is now as I open the shed's door. I go inside and look up to the ceiling – in that little gap in the corner of the roof. I'm about to reach up … But I notice a massive spiderweb gaping across the corner.

"Oh, shit. Tommy, are you afraid of spiders?"

"Huh?" he's standing outside the door irritably.

"There's a huge spider web there. And probably a huge spider."

"Dolina, why are we going back to your garden shed rather than being in the Woods, completing *Filippo's Game*?"

"Tommy! I'm telling you, the key's in there. I'm just terrified of spiders. So could you reach up and get it for me?"

He comes into the shed. My arachnophobia battles with my intrigue for the *Game* as Tommy reaches up, behind the spiderweb and feels into the corner.

"But where is it, Dolina?"

"To the left, sitting on the ledge."

"Ahh …"

He brings the key out.

"You were right," Tommy says, "I'm sorry."

We go back into the house and make coffee.

"It's weird how I forgot about it so easily."

"So, the clue means there are three keys altogether. We have to find the last key."

"Near something shiny, yeah."

I'm feeling healthy again. Blood's thumping and my wits are zipping around. I need to get back into the Woods already. I don't know why I thought coffee was a good idea, we're both so hot. But I pile the vat, pour the water and wait for it to sit. Then stand by the sink, looking out the window.

"There's Mr Walker," I say, quietly.

Tommy looks at me.

Alec's just come out of his house with his lemon jacket. I can see him easily from here and though he can't see me I shrink from the window. Tommy comes over and we watch him turn down onto the hilly road. He's not walking his dog.

"You think he saw us?" I say. "Saw us going into the Woods earlier I mean."

"Oh, Dolina, stop making him a super villain."

But I can tell Tommy's nervous too.

"Maybe he's just heading down to the shops," I say, "but he'll be back soon. So why don't we head back into the Woods now, before he comes back up the hill."

"Yes, okay. Pause the coffee for now."

We race back up the road silently. And dive back into the Woods. We agree to follow the river, as the clue told us to. We traverse until we see the *Fence* in the background. The *Fence* is still barbed-wired, yet it's smaller to an adult eye, and the ivy has conquered its long frame. I'm filled with a longing to see the other side of it. The trees over the other side of the Hospital territory call to me.

"But how are we supposed to find something shiny amongst all this?" Tommy says.

"The river goes beyond the *Fence*. Maybe it's closer to that."

We trek on across the sharp jungle of riverbed life, advancing towards the *Fence*. We reach the old wall with the *Fence's* metal above it. I look around. The wall is part of the classic masonry of the Woods and I follow the masonry pattern onto the other side of the river. Where it joins onto the perimeter wall of the Woods.

"There wouldn't be anything shiny on the *Fence*," I say, "but what about the wall?"

I scour this side of the river's wall but can't see anything. I dip down to the edge of the river and jump in before Tommy can say anything. I think I'm being heroic – but I've misjudged how deep the water is. It comes up to my waist and my lungs seize up with the cold. "Are you all right?" Tommy calls.

"Yeah." I go across the pool, the water fluming under the concrete wall against me, until I get to the far side. Then scramble up the bank, thorns pricking my hands.

"What are you doing, Dolina?" Tommy calls.

I don't answer him. And go along the *Fence* until it stops, and the Woods' wall takes over. Then discover a pathway through the thorns, go along it, until I come to the very end of the masonry. Something glints in my eye and I know I've found it. It's the third and last jar, placed inside a hole in the wall, where one of the boulders has been taken out.

"I've got it Tommy," I call.

He's still standing the other side of the bank looking confused. I open the jar. Inside is a long, old-fashioned key. And there's another piece of paper:

FIND THE FOX ON THE FENCE

I take the items back across to Tommy. I'm all sodden and shivering, but I just want to snatch this LEVEL up. I hand the paper to Tommy.

"Find the fox on the *Fence* …"

"So we need to search along it."

I jump into the thorns. My jeans are wet and they deflect the jags, and I've been stung by nettle so many times I don't care anymore. I scan along the *Fence*. There seems nothing except metal sheets blocking us from the other side.

"The fox. What would that mean?"

Then something nicks by eyes underneath the ivy on the metal. It's red spray-paint. Tommy spots it too, and we begin tearing the ivy strands away. Until we behold a spray-painted picture – a cartoon of a red fox. Underneath the fox is an arrow, pointing into the earth.

"There, the arrow. Like the purple bushes there must be something hidden underground." Tommy says.

We don't have anything to dig with, and the ground is so blocked with weeds, that I'm tempted to go back to the house to get a shovel or something. But Tommy feverishly plucks away at the earth until he discovers a sheet of blue plastic, inches under the ground.

The sheet drapes over a square block of wood. When he lifts the plastic up, we find a trapdoor. It has two keyholes in it.

"Pass me the keys, Dolina."

The two little silver keys work the locks, and when he opens the trapdoor, we find a hole dug into the earth. It leads under the *Fence* and to the other side. Except the hole is pitch black and there's no light the other side.

"There's still one key left …" Tommy says. He takes his phone out his pocket and switches the light on, peering inside the hole before him. "I can see another door the other side."

Tommy disappears into the dark. I then hear the clanking sounds of the key. Then the hole illuminates with light from the other side. "I've got through, Dolina!" he calls. "Come on up with me. It's safe."

I duck down into the hole, into the moist funky soil and aim for the light. I come to an open trapdoor with Tommy standing in its frame. I jump out into the light. We've suddenly come out the other side of the forbidden *Fence*.

"Look there, Dolina."

He's pointing to the trapdoor. On the underside of it are written the words:

SIGN THE LIQUID NITROGEN TANK TO COMPLETE
LEVEL 6

We look around us. The trees are less dense here, and there are no thorns. Plus, there's an open pathway just next to us. Looks like somebody maintains this side of the Woods.

"We *are* kind of in the Hospital's territory now," Tommy says, timidly.

Indeed, I feel naked. We've definitely come out of the proper Woods. The bulky cube of the Hospital can be seen through the trees in the distance. The soil and leaves above the trapdoor under us lie scattered across the path, clearly violated. It seems illegal, that we're not under the covert splendour of the Woods anymore.

"But we've still got to get to the Nitrogen tank." I say.

We can see it in the distance. Can hear it too with its unnerving throbbing. But beyond that is a road leading up to the Hospital. And trucks and ambulances parked dormant near the boughs of the building. Urbanity has shocked both of us, and we've both turned cowardly.

"Come on, Tommy. We're nearly there."

We move. The road to the Hospital's quiet. Everything's quiet save Tommy's creeping behind me. We reach the white tubes of the tank.

"What do we do, then, Dolina?"

I look around the cylinder of its bulk, until I get to its rear. There, I notice another spray-painted sign. "Here! Tommy!" The sign reads:

HEAD TO THE ELECTRICITY BOX: LEVEL 7

And underneath the sign is a list of names written onto the paint, scribbled in fat black ink. Filippo is the first, then June, Robin and so on. They are all there. And there's an arrow pointing under the tank's bottom. I grope down under the tank and I uncover another glass jar. When I open it I find a black felt pen inside. So you write your name onto the list to complete LEVEL 6.

The final name on the list is Henry Fowles. I get that same icy feeling, knowing that he was here so long ago. Knowing that I'm doing a profound thing by investigating him.

I sign my name under the list. The pen works as if it was freshly bought. I pass the pen to Tommy.

"No, Dolina. I don't deserve to sign my name. I didn't complete 5 or 6."

"Oh, Tommy, just sign your name. Come on."

I'm holding the pen out poised to him and he keeps refusing to sign. I can see the ink of my name glistening against the paint of the tank whilst all the other names are dried and faded. The tank throbs above us. Tommy's being stubborn.

"It wouldn't be fair …" he says.

I take his hand and wrap his fingers onto the pen. He accepts and squats by me. We're both watching him scrawl his letters. A voice barks at us from behind and Tommy's pen skids down.

"Hello?" We both jump. Then turn.

There's a man standing there behind us.

"Hello?" He says, again.

He has thick white hair and jagged black eyebrows. That's Jim, the Hospital Janitor. Jim the Janny.

"Jim?" I say. "Is that you?"

I stand up with Tommy.

Jim's holding a radio in one hand and it's snarling quietly.

"You shouldn't be here," he says.

"Jim – it's *us*. It's me and Tommy."

"This is Hospital property. No public access allowed. You should not be here." His brows simmer at us. His irises are small and blink ferociously. The rest of his face is static.

"I'm Dolina. Don't you remember us? When we were kids we used to play –"

"I know exactly who you are. Both of you. So what? I can call through this radio, get my colleagues to call the police?"

I start to speak but he cuts me off.

"Why are you just standing there? You're on NHS land when you shouldn't be. I can either call the police, or you can get away from here and don't come back."

Tommy puts the pen back on the ground. I feel so stupid.

Jim's standing in front of the path leading down to the trapdoor. He brings a caustic reality to the Woods. Slowly we walk to him. He stares at us.

"We were just playing the old –"

"*Filippo's Game*, yes." Jim cuts in. "Why, though? Why now? If I didn't know who you were and saw you here, what else could I do but get you arrested? Now, shoo, both of you."

He turns and he puts his radio back in his pocket and begins pacing towards the Hospital. He's a small man – always has been – but has such an aggressive walk. We're desperate to get farther away from him.

We dart back to the trapdoor through the trees.

"You still got the key, Tommy?" I whisper. Tommy lets me go back under the *Fence* first. I scurry through the passage and out into the other side. I hear him lock the trapdoor behind me. He comes out and frantically locks the final trapdoor down with the other keys. Tommy's embarrassed that he's so afraid. I'm embarrassed I'm more afraid than he is. We stand there, panting in the Woods.

They are supposed to be a place that conceal us, the Woods. But we've just broken territory by going under the *Fence*. We crossed the boundary into the Hospital yards. Even though it was part of *Filippo's Game*, to go there, it doesn't seem right that we did.

"Jim the janitor …" I say. "I didn't even know he was still *alive*."

Tommy doesn't respond.

"Can't remember the last time I saw him. He's still working at the Hospital – I didn't know," I'm just filling the silence between us. Tommy's silent for minutes until he breaks out:

"We shouldn't be doing this, Dolina. Whatever *Filippo's Game* is. It just keeps freaking me out."

"I feel the exact opposite, Tommy. I think it's very important, what we're doing."

"I mean, we could have been arrested, for God's sake."

"But we weren't. And we're not doing so bad. We still completed LEVEL 6. Only two more to go."

Tommy pants and pants.

CHAPTER TWENTY-THREE

PROGRESSIONS

When we get back to my place after *Fox Dens*, Tommy doesn't accept any coffee or wine or anything. He sits morosely at the table. I start drinking wine myself. I go up to my room, and I collect Henry's *France '98* cap and his watch from under my bed. Go back downstairs. Tommy's expression remains the same when he spots these things in my hands. I sit at the table.

"Tommy. Are you truly with me on this? On this quest, as you called it? Because I was really glad you came back to me today."

"I am. But I'm just afraid something bad is going to happen."

"Even if something bad does happen, don't you think it's important to discover it?"

"Don't you also think," he says, "that there's a better way to do all this? Why don't we just give Henry's cap and watch to the police?"

"I've been thinking that too. But, I don't know … It seems … To be back in the Woods, after all this time. It feels right. I need to find out something which has been ignored for so long. To me, it seems –"

"*Personal*? You want to find out where Henry went, and it's something to do with you personally?"

"Well, yes! Don't you feel the same way?"

"I liked Henry, and I want to know what happened to him. But we're not exactly professional detectives."

"Not everyone is. Besides, the police were already involved two decades ago. And what did they achieve? We're finding out more than they did just by ourselves. So why can't we just keep going with it? I could really do with a friend to help me. And who knows this area like me and you do?"

"Okay. Yes, but, Dolina: is it okay if we don't go back into the Woods for a while? I think it's important to lay quiet for a time. Alec Walker knows we've been investigating *Filippo's Game*. Now Jim knows as well."

"Jim definitely needs looked at."

"I agree. But we should stay away from the Woods for now. I'm going to go back to Glasgow tonight. And I'm back at work next week. But I'm on your team. I want you to call me whenever you need to – and I'll help – okay?"

"Thanks, Tommy."

I finish my wine. Tommy stands up to leave.

"Tommy. There's one more thing I want to ask you. Especially since you live in Glasgow." He's avoiding looking at me, because he knows what I'm going to ask. "Could you keep Henry's things with you? I know it was stupid to tell Filippo I found them. But Filippo and Mr Walker won't know that you have them." I'm holding Henry's things out to him. "I just think, if you take them, it'll be an important move. They'll be safe with you."

He takes the cap, touching it carefully, studying the cartoon mascot.

"I always wanted Henry's cap ..." he says, quietly. "That was such a good *World Cup* as well, in '98. And this little cap's an antique, now. Sure. I'll take his things and hide them in Glasgow. Give me the watch."

He gets his coat and puts them into the inside pocket. Tommy's turned dark, now, I see, when he normally doesn't do that. He doesn't even turn to me for a goodbye embrace at the door when he goes home. But he still says see you soon, and I trust him.

We've had a progressive day. The wine's bringing me down peacefully, and I plan to just chill for tonight. So I drink until I sleep. When I wake up in the morning I dispel the hangover with water and will-power. I have a shift tonight at the hotel, but it's not making me glum. My personal mystery is what's important. And I feel resurrected from my depression. This mystery has supplied me with purpose in life – and it's wrong to shield myself from it. I'm going to get to the end of it; my head's springing with ideas on what to do next.

When I head out to the hotel tonight, I'm sparky and in a good mood. When I get there, and after several hours into the shift, the colleagues are just as aggressive and angry as always. The head chef is the main culprit. It's not just me he's mean to. He switches at all of the colleagues. Just so happens I'm younger, and a woman, or that I look a certain way – doesn't matter what his problem with me is.

Whilst I'm waiting tables, I'm thinking about Henry Fowles. And how to bend two decades together, how to carve a solution out of 1998 and 2018, the Walkers and Filippo, Henry, Linda, Jim. How I can somehow use my memories from '98 to figure it all out.

And in my reverie, I put the wrong order through to the chefs after greeting a table. I put through the wrong type of steak – and after the customer complains 30 minutes later, the chef calls me into the kitchen and begins shouting at me. An unlucky, sad man, pulverised from years of working a job that he hates.

I remember teachers at school shouting at me this way, expelling their rage on young teenagers. And I would be terrified then. But now as the chef shouts at me, and the other chefs watch for my reaction, I find that I don't care. I just blink at him until he stops. Then return to waiting tables and resume thinking about Henry.

Whenever I go back the kitchen, the head chef's still shouting at people. The hours lag on and I'm finishing an hour before the kitchen stops serving. It's ten minutes until I'm done.

In the corridor next to the kitchen where we take food out, I notice a pile of bread crumbs on the floor. One of the chefs has dropped them, and I just step over it each time I'm going past.

Then it gets to the hour and finally I'm done and can head home. As I go back down the corridor, with my coat and bag on, the head chef spots me:

"Dolina? See before you go, is it okay if you sweep up those bread crumbs?"

I look at the bread crumbs. Then at my phone and check the time. It's one minute past the hour.

"No," I say.

The head chef goes silent. They all do.

"No – that's me done. See you soon."

I leave the hotel and go home.

CHAPTER TWENTY-FOUR

LINDA AND JIM

Tommy and I used to sing that song when we were kids to Henry, the kissing one. "*Jimmy and Linda sitting in a tree; K – I, S – S, I – N – G!*" It was known across the neighbourhood that Jim from the Hospital and Henry's Mum were dating. Jim was often around at Henry's house. To me, as a kid, I was just teasing Henry about it. There didn't seem anything wrong with two adults dating.

The older kids were scornful about it. 'Jim the Janny' was just a wordplay nickname, nothing insulting about it. But sometimes they called him 'Jim the Jake'. 'Jake' meaning that he was addicted to drugs as Linda was.

Jim was like a stern high school teacher, who, unlike my current head chef colleague or the school teachers from the past, wouldn't unleash their anger on you. He was fair in his discipline. He was a bit scary, with the white hair and the arrowhead eyebrows. But there was logic in the discipline.

For instance, when Filippo used to gather football games on the field next to the Hospital, Jim would sometimes appear out from behind the *Fence*. He'd come through the security door behind the tank. If things got too noisy, he'd ask us to quieten it down, because there were patients needing peace. Or if the Gang were drinking beer, he'd ask them to take their bottles with them and not leave them lying around.

And Filippo would always obey Jim. The Gang respected Jim, in a way, and hadn't the guts to call him a Jake to his face. I didn't think Jim was a Jake. But I didn't think Linda was a Jake either. To me, everyone in the Gang drank and smoked all the time anyway – there was little difference between whichever substance was involved.

Besides, Jim could be playful too. I remember one time, when there was a football game up by the Hospital, Filippo was playing with the others and I was watching the game with Tommy. One of the players kicked the ball over the *Fence* into the Hospital yards. And nobody was courageous enough to climb over and get the ball back. So it looked like the game was over and we'd all have to go home.

But then Jim called over from the other side of the *Fence*. We didn't know he was there, and could only hear his gruff voice.

"Okay," he shouted, "that's it: I've got your ball. I'm calling the police!"

Filippo went up to the *Fence*, to speak to him.

"Is that you, Jim?"

"Yes. I'm calling the police, this time. You've taken it way too far. Lighting bonfires, drinking too much."

"No, no, Jim. We'll just go. No need to call the cops."

Then Jim turned his radio on and we could hear him call through the static fuzz. And we were all properly afraid, speechless and ready to run away. We were all stunned for 30 seconds. Then Jim just threw the ball back over the Fence.

"I'm just playing with you, young ones," Jim called, and he turned his radio off. And we all laughed with relief.

"Oh – thanks, Jim," Filippo called.

"Okay. But be more careful with your ball. And it's getting late, so wrap the game up soon."

Everyone liked Jim the Janny. I certainly did.

But what did he have to do with Henry Fowles? When Tommy and I would tease Henry with the kissing song, he never cared. Henry also never got offended when the Gang called his mother an addict or junkie or anything, even though it was offensive. He barely talked about his mother at all.

But he was close to her. I remember seeing Henry walk around the streets with Linda. And sometimes I'd see him with Jim as well. Henry was always his typical self with anyone – grinning and telling stories – and they'd chat back to him.

When I saw Jim two days back, he hadn't changed much physically from my memory of him. He always had, and still did the other day, the physique of Martin Sheen: short in height, but tough. And he'd returned to disciplinary mode. Tommy and I were given a real row. Jim was right. What were two 25-year-olds doing in a No-Trespass-NHS zone? We shouldn't have been there and he was right to order us away.

There are still several things I learned from that incident. Jim knew who Tommy and I were, after all this time. He hasn't seen us since we were children. I would have thought Jim would've retired by now. He always seemed old back in the '90s and '00s. He drifted away after that, and I can't recall the last time I saw him, but it was a very long time ago.

He knew who we were, and he knew what *Filippo's Game* was. He knew we were playing the *Game* and was shocked that we were. Therefore, he knew about the trapdoor which led into the Hospital's territory. Jim was such a disciplined man, but he knew about children digging secret holes under the *Fence*? And allowed them to do it?

And he could easily have called the police on us, but he let us go. He told us not to come back. Is it the same with Filippo and Alec? That he's hiding something to do with the *Game*?

I remember that day in '98 when Scotland were knocked out the World Cup by Morocco. I found Henry's watch and I went back to his house to give it to him. I heard a big argument and I hid. Then Jim the Janny left the house, angrily. Then *Alec* left. Alec Walker? Why would he, of all people, be over at Linda Fowles' house? Debasing his upper-class status by going over to a junkie's household?

It's odd, and it's unnerving, how these little glimmerings of memory from 1998 keep returning to me. Like the dreams I keep having of Henry, which I don't understand. But the memories and the dreams are both helpful.

Before, I'd seen a plot triangle between Filippo, Alec and June. Henry was just outside of that shape. Is there another shape to be found between Linda and Jim? I still don't think Henry belongs to *any* shape, just yet.

I need to approach Jim again somehow. Without climbing through a hole in the ground. I also need to find out what happened to Linda Fowles. I realise she struggled with drugs, but there's a real chance she's still alive. Does she still stay in Edinburgh? There will be a way to discover.

These are the next steps.

CHAPTER TWENTY-FIVE

26TH JUNE 1998

HOLIDAYS

Just finished school! Summer holidays, now. Six weeks and no school!

I got a row the other day, because I played *Mario* for too long at Henry's house. Mum was scared she didn't know where I was, and when I got home she went pretty crazy. She knew I was lying about being ill on Wednesday – so sent me to school for the next two days. But anyway, it's all done now. Weeks and weeks of freedom. I get off the bus and go into the puffy air. Can't wait to get my uniform off and forget about it.

As I'm crossing the main road I spot two people waving to me. They're big and both wearing sunglasses. It's Mr Walker and Filippo. I'm shy but curious of them at the same time.

"Ho, there, young one!" Alec holds his hand out and at first I don't know what he means. It's weird, I don't think I've ever shaken a man's hand before. (His hand is clammy and powerful). Filippo's smiling behind him. Has his hair slicked back with gel and in his sunglasses he looks like a model in a shaving advert.

"So that's you off for school holidays now, Dolina?" he says.

"It is, yeah."

"A free bird!" Alec says. "Good for you. We're just heading back home – come with us."

We walk away from the rush of traffic into the rush of birds over the wall of the Woods. We're all silent for moments, and it's tense. And when I finally speak their heads snap across to me:

"So what you doing for the holidays, guys?"

129

"Ah, my dear," Alec sings, "the family and I are heading over to *Milan* for a few weeks. Yourself? You have any plans?"

I'm embarrassed that I've never been anywhere like Milan. I've never even left Britain.

"Crail," I say.

"Sorry?"

"Umm, Crail ..."

Alec looks confused.

"Crail is a little village in Fife, Alec," Filippo says, "Your Mum has a caravan near there, right Dolina?"

"Yeah, Mum's taking me up on Monday for a week there."

"Ah, sounds great," Alec says. Then there's more silence between us and the birds in the Woods take over again. We pass Filippo's house. Maybe Filippo's going to Alec's? I'm about to ask them what they're doing today. But then there's a *pop* sound from behind us.

Pop – it comes again. We've stopped and are looking back. It's coming from over the Woods' wall. A hand appears out of the wall. Just a hand, no body. The hand gives us a thumbs-up. Even though I can only see the hand, I know who it is instantly.

There's this hole in the middle of the wall. When I walk home from school with Tommy we always peek inside it. It's big enough to fit through. But inside, we see this metal box built among the trees. It has a steel fence around it and a sign saying 'High Voltage Electricity. Danger of Death.' So we're always too afraid to climb through.

The hand disappears and then Henry sticks his face out of the hole. He makes the popping sound with his lips.

"Henry," Alec says, "what are you up to?"

"Pop."

"Henry," I say, "you shouldn't be near that electricity box. It's dangerous."

"I'm fine, little Dolina. I was just sneaking up on you cats, trying to scare ya. And I got you, didn't I!"

He hangs there in the hole. It's as if Henry's gotten crazy in the last few weeks, more than he normally is. I'm just scared for him being so close to that electricity.

"Come on, Henry," Filippo says, "Let's get up the road."

"I already let Jim know earlier, Mr Inzaghi!" Henry pushes out an envelope, holding it in the air.

Alec and Filippo freeze, then look at me, and back at the envelope. I don't know why their expressions are so serious.

"And I have it here for you already, gentlemen. Take it!"

Alec goes to the hole and leans to take the envelope. Henry pulls it away from his grasp.

"Woops! Alec, you missed!"

Alec smiles and reaches for it; Henry holds it out and then pulls it away again. Alec's face twists in annoyance.

"Oh, Alec, chill out," Henry says. He finally gives it to Alec. "That makes it 2 – 1 to me, right? A bit of revenge."

Alec blushes. Only time I've ever seen him blush, and it's clear he's trying to disguise it.

"Got to go, folks. Catch you later, lady and gentlemen!" Henry says. "Dolina, come back to play *Mario* whenever you like!" He disappears behind the hole.

Alec storms up the road. Filippo tells me to come along. Filippo's smiling but it's one of his false smiles, and I can tell something's wrong with them. I think I should say something to Filippo.

"Was Henry mean to Alec?"

"No, no, Dolina."

"What was in that envelope he gave him?"

"Nothing. Nothing to worry about."

We walk fast until we get to my house.

"Okay, Dolina, will see you soon," Filippo says.

"Enjoy your Crail trip," Alec says.

They walk on. I stand watching in my driveway. But I notice they go *past* Alec's house. And keep walking up the street towards the Hospital.

I'm sweating under my school clothes. I should really just go inside and get changed and start my holiday. But then Filippo and Alec disappear round the road turn. Why did they say they were going home if they're not? And I have to follow them. I put my schoolbag just inside our garden, wait ten seconds, and creep up the road after them.

They've gone past Henry's house. Their shapes flicker in the heatwave above the road. I don't think they've seen me so I keep going. They go up the little hill onto the field by the Hospital. Crouching behind a bin back on the street, I watch them go over to the *Fence*. They reach the door which leads through it and Filippo knocks on it.

The door opens, but I don't see who opens it from the other side. Filippo and Alec go inside and the door shuts behind them.

CHAPTER TWENTY-SIX

29th JUNE 1998

CRAIL

Going to Crail today!

I made a load of sandwiches for the trip early morning before Mum woke up. I snuck down to the kitchen and surprised her with them set out on the table. She went wild and kissed me on the cheeks. I was chuffed. I had to make up for scaring her the last week when I didn't come home.

We jam the boot full of our things after breakfast and drive off out to Crail. When we're on the main road, Mum puts an R.E.M. tape in the player and zooms the volume up. It's the song 'Losing my Religion'. We both love this song and we sing the words together as we fly along.

Losing my Religion finishes just after the car passes the 'Welcome to Edinburgh' sign. We've left the city. Mum makes really good compilation tapes and her R.E.M. one is one of her best. I take the tape out and put it in back the other way. I'm just about to press play when something grabs my eyes by the side of the road.

"That's Henry!" I say.

"What, Dolina?"

"I just saw Henry."

I look back down out the back window. The car's still going, but I'm right. Henry's sitting in a bus stop at the side of the road.

"He's waiting for a bus. You see him?"

Mum looks back too and she spots him. She's slowed the car and the motorway isn't busy because it's an early Monday morning.

"Yes," she says, "but is he all right?"

Henry *doesn't* look all right. He's sitting in the corner of the seat, slouched, like he's mega tired.

"What's he doing outside of the city?" Mum goes. "Well – hang on – let's just see if he's okay."

Mum turns the car around and heads back to the bus stop. Henry looks totally different from normal. He's not in the green hoody or the jeans. He has a grey raincoat on, and a big hiking bag lies by a pair of walking boots. He's tired, but his face is white and serious, not red and grinning like normal.

He doesn't even realise a car has pulled up to the bus stop, until my Mum yells:

"Henry!"

Henry jumps up from the seat. His eyes are wide and terrified.

We sit staring at him. I'm closest to the open window and when he realises who we are, he walks towards us and leans into the window.

"Hi chaps," he says. "You off on some holidays?"

"We are, yes, we're heading out to our caravan." Mum says, "Are you alright, Henry?"

"I'm perfect, Louise! Just as perfect as always. Where about is your caravan, ladies?"

As Mum tells him about Crail, I watch Henry. He's become stiff, touching the roof of the car and hovering there. He's not typical twitchy Henry. He doesn't smell of alcohol or weed, for once. He's smiling, but his eyes are suspicious. What *is* he doing in a bus stop, miles outside of Edinburgh, this early in the morning?

"Well, I hope you have a great little trip, ladies." He heads back to the bus stop.

"Thanks Henry. But, just …" Mum hesitates, "Is it all right if I ask where *you're* going? You on a trip yourself?"

"I am, Louise. I'm heading to see some friends out west. Good to head out to the west, sometimes."

"Okay. We thought you looked a bit sad, is all."

"I'm just a tried boy. Not usually up this early. Thanks though. Enjoy your caravan times. I'll see you soon!"

Henry waves to us as we drive off. I wave out the window and then watch his shape in the side-mirror until it disappears. Mum doesn't speak. And I can tell she's thinking about him as I am.

To break the quiet, I remember the R.E.M. tape: it's there in the player waiting for me to press start. I press it, and Mum's picked the song 'Shiny Happy People' for the first one on side two. We had the volume way up for the last song earlier when we were in a good mood. As soon as the jangly bit comes on at the start, Mum winces and she snaps the volume down. So we can still hear this merry song, and we'd both be singing along to it too. But the atmosphere has changed, and it's too quiet. And I don't know what to say to bring it back.

CHAPTER TWENTY-SEVEN

MAY 2018

BONFIRE SITE

I'm in the Woods and I hear Henry singing through the trees. His voice lumbers through the air over the river. I want to catch him out because he thinks he's on his own. So I jump the river and follow his sound. Henry has a pretty good voice, and he's putting proper effort into it, as if he were performing to people. The sound comes from the bonfire site where the Gang party.

Henry's not usually by himself in the Woods. I thought it was only me who did that. When I creep out the bushes I spot him dancing around the fireplace. There are charred embers and bottles strewn around. Henry's drinking by himself, making his own party. His eyes are closed as he sings and I'm trying not to laugh. Then he opens them and sees me.

"Hey! Little Dolina," he's not embarrassed to be caught-out singing. He just keeps going and he beckons me over. "Finally! I thought nobody was going to turn up to my party. Come, dance with me, Dolina."

I take his hands, gladly. It's weird to touch his hands intimately. But he's not awkward with it – and that makes me easy with it – and he begins dancing me around. He doesn't know how to dance, and he's really bad at it. But that's why he's so good at it, too, with his jolty arms and jerky head. I sing with him. He has such a resonant voice that it's easy to join in with.

I twirl under his hand and we whirl around the bonfire. The cyclical green-blue-white of the Woods flushes by as we turn. I don't get dizzy. He picks me up and whooshes me in the air. His big face has a spark to it. The lazy, floppy Henry, unphased that only one person turned up to his party.

I pace away from him several yards. Then do the step-tap thing we do in Scottish dancing at school – the 'Gay Gordon'. So you step and tap with your feet in time with the ceilidh music and then the man and lady walk towards each other, embrace with their arms and continue in a line.

Henry grins because he knows what I'm initiating. So he does the step-tap thing with me, out of sync, which makes me laugh. Then he holds his arms out for me to come to him.

I leap out to get them, and I catch nothing. There are no hands. There is no singing.

Henry's vanished. I'm in the Woods, completely isolated.

The presence of the Woods spills onwards around me obliviously. I've just imagined Henry the whole time, and he's not really here. I look around to see if anybody's seen me. I'm humiliated. But it's something beyond normal embarrassment. I'm *demented*, to be here in the Woods, dancing with an imagined puppet.

The trees crawl down on me and darken and I feel them crushing my eyes. But then I realise it's not the trees. It's me, and it's happening again. I'm going paralysed. I hit the earth first, this time, then I'm gazing up at the air through the leaves as my breathing shuts off. I keep thinking Henry will reappear and lift me up, and as blindness takes me I try to yell for him.

But my lungs retract, taking jumps from my ribcage, and my tonsils suck back at nothing.

When I wake up I cough for minutes. My heartbeat's haywire in this dark room. I know I'm at home, but there's no relief at having woken up.

This was the scariest one yet, within this series of paralysis dreams. Maybe the dreams aren't so helpful, or revelatory. They worry me because the breathing breakdowns happen to me for real as I sleep, and I just manage to wake up before I run out of air. Why does this keep happening?

What is to be learned from dreams?

CHAPTER TWENTY-EIGHT

JIM THE JANNY

I've been thinking how to approach Jim again since I saw him last week. I'm thinking that if he'd have caught any other two people being weird in the Hospital's grounds he would've acted much differently.

I'm up in the early morning hours, pondering it all. How Jim and Linda are the next targets. I have no clue how to get in contact with Linda Fowles. I looked in the phone directories, sought her name on social media: nothing. She would be a little older than my Mum now – if she's still alive. And my Mum's 64 ... If Linda's dead, she might hold knowledge I'll never be able to access.

But I keep hoping. I've tried the same type of research with Jim the Janny. Looking literally for hours across the internet trying to find some shred of information about him. All I know about him is that he still works as the janitor up at the Hospital. At one point I considered calling the Hospital to ask if I could speak to him. But that wouldn't work. I don't even know his surname. Don't know if he's even the right man to talk to about all of this.

Lately, my sleeping has been composed of three or four hour blocks. I'll sleep in the afternoon in such a way, then around midnight, and wake within infant mornings. So I've got nothing to do this day apart from dread going back to the hotel on Friday. But I have 30 plus hours to work on the mystery.

The best thing about being a weird sleeper is the tenure it grants you over normal-sleeping people. Young mornings are fresh pages enticing you to paint, when everyone else is sleeping. They're always broken by the sound of traffic and the trail-routes of working people eventually. But in these hushed mornings (and especially in Summer, when the dawn bulges in the sky by 4 a.m.) you feel righteous to be a weird sleeper. Creativity seems best at these times.

I decide to go out along the road to the Hospital this morning. Grassroots fieldwork. May as well give it a try. I sneak out the garden door of the house so as to not wake Mum up, and I'm up next to Filippo's old football field within minutes.

The Hospital's cube saturates under the pink orange dawn light. As I go up the field the grass hasn't been cut for a long, long time. It used to be tended to regularly when I was a girl. It's thick and clumpy now and my shoes are sodded with dew before long. I can't imagine boys playing football here nowadays.

I look across to the old door by the *Fence*, which Jim used to use. Maybe I have gone a little mad myself, these last few weeks. But what else is there to do as a failing artist? I go over to the clump of trees separating the field from the road. I look along the *Fence* onto over the Wood's wall. And yet still, I don't see the *Fence* as a border line. I used to play in these trees with Tommy when the Gang weren't doing games on the field. And it'd seem like dodgy territory to be away from our familiar parts. But we liked it. We even built a Tarzan once, here in this part. Somebody saw it from the road and cut it down, a day after we made it.

I go through the trees to see if its carcass is still there. And it is. A sad bit of cut rope hanging from the branch. Tommy and I spent so long trying to make this great swing, and we played on it endlessly after it was complete for one night. It was probably one of the Gang members who cut it down. One of many blue-nylon withers hanging from branches in the Woods.

If somebody walking down the road below saw a woman carrying a rope up into the trees, and tying it to a tall branch, what would they think? Suddenly I get all miserable again. Thinking about suicide. To go get some new rope. Easiest way to end it. It'd be so much easier. Maybe it'd be fitting to die by rope in the Woods, the arena of my childhood.

In my dreams of late, regardless of whether Henry's in them, I feel like I can be true emotionally. I experience emotions purely in dreams, of sadness, loss, fear. Whereas in reality I only battle them half-way. And so, I fear sleep, and I shy from it, because it's the only place I'm forced to be real. But sometimes sleep is a relief, and a way to blot out consciousness and thinking for a few hours.

It's a warm morning already, and I brought my mountain coat out with me, fearing a dawn chill. I'm lying on a bed of ivy. The spiderwebs between the leaves don't seem threatening. Only feathery networks under the shade of the trees. Nobody knows where I am. Maybe I can sleep in the Woods, for now, in a non-finalistic way. And my mind starts to invent new dreams, none of them nightmares. I lie down on the ivy and put the coat over me.

Tommy and me are in Homebase, looking for rope. I keep making jokes about suicide and he never laughs. Tommy agrees to pay for the rope, because I have no money and he can see I'm in a wreck. He's embarrassed at the counter because the counter lady stares at me and I reek of alcohol. We head back home on the bus. He tells me he's only doing this because he wants to prove to the Gang we can make a proper Tarzan, one that will never be cut down.

We go back to the trees by the Hospital, which we've never conquered even though we were supposed to. And begin rebuilding our Tarzan on this terrific arching beech branch which goes over this dip. As I'm tying the rope, I hear a thumping noise behind me. I think it's Tommy. But my head doesn't work. I can't look around to see who it is. The thumping gets closer until it's right by my head.

I shoot up into sunlight. I'm lying on a floor of ivy and somebody's standing above me. How long was I out?

The person standing above me is Jim the Janny.

"What are you doing here, Dolina?" he says.

I try to stand up but my brain isn't working. Jim's watching me.

"Nothing, Jim. Just went for a walk."

"Well, you aren't on NHS land this time. But why are you coming back near it?"

I stand up. This is what I wanted, right? To find Jim. I look at my phone: it's 6 a.m. I've been sleeping here for two hours.

"How did you find me here, Jim?"

"That's an insult, you asking me that. How could I not know you're creeping about the *Fence*? I work at the Hospital, Dolina, have done for years as a security man. Tell me why you are here?"

"Because I need to talk to you. About Henry Fowles."

"That's what I expected. Henry."

I'm taller than Jim is. His eyes are far harder than mine. It's his hardness which has retained his character, and Jim is one of the oldest people I know.

"I understand that. But we can't talk about him here." He comes forward and gives me a piece of paper. "Come to me tomorrow night. I'll be home. And we can speak."

"I'll be there, Jim. Thanks very much for –"

"You go home now, Dolina. And stop pretending to be a spy. You're not very good at it."

He walks back toward the *Fence* and disappears behind his door. When I open the paper I read the words:

COME TONIGHT AT 10.

DON'T TELL ANYONE YOU'RE COMING.

And underneath there's an address the far side of the city. I certainly got what I wanted this morning.

CHAPTER TWENTY-NINE

A DIFFERENT JIM

I'd wondered why Jim asked me to come to his place so late at night. It's an hour long bus ride the other side of the city to where he stays. It's such an obscure area, maybe I should've told somebody I where I was going.

But I trust Jim. And when I go to press his flat buzzer, I'm not scared.

"Yeah? Who's there?" a gravelly voice comes.

"It's me, Jim – Dolina."

"Ah, come on up." The stairway's cold and narrow, classic Edinburgh architecture. When I knock at his door and his face appears behind it, I realise why he set the meet so late. He's drunk. Mega drunk. He needed a few hours to get drunk after work before he could speak to me.

"Come in." His eyelids are puffy, face red. He barely has balance as he walks away into the other room. I shut the front door and follow him into his living room. He has his electric fire on even though it's summer. Must be 25 degrees in here. He's lying on his sofa and invites me to take an armchair.

"A drink, Dolina?" There are *two* litre-bottles of whisky on his table – one half empty. I know it might be a bad idea to start drinking spirits, but I also know I need to get somewhere near his level. So I accept. From the kitchen he brings a tumbler choked with ice cubes. I chink glasses with him. It's so odd to see him like this, that image of the gruff-but-with-a-funny-side janitor is replaced with a simple old man, vulnerable in his drunkenness.

The whisky pangs my gullet just as he says:

"So how can I help with Henry?"

"Well … I've been thinking about him a lot recently. I wonder where to start."

"I think about him a lot too, since he went. Though I always have done."

"I'm sorry about the other day for coming out the trapdoor with Tommy. I just –"

"I was only being mean to scare you away. The last person I ever saw come through that trapdoor was Henry Fowles. But yes, you shouldn't be playing the *Game* anymore."

Jim has his TV on, except the volume's off. It's some sports match of two men fighting wrestling and kicking each other. He watches the screen as he speaks to me, constantly necking his whisky.

"There are many things I want to ask you, Jim."

"Shoot."

"First is about an incident when Henry got attacked physically. Somebody gave him a bloody nose. It was when Scotland were playing in the World Cup '98. I heard a rumour that Alec Walker hit him?"

"Yeah, Henry came to me right after that."

"He did!"

"I remember it, yes." he's concentrating on the wrestling game. One of the players has the other grappled on the floor and it looks like he's strangling him. For a moment, I wonder whether it's actually a movie, because both men have blood all over their faces, but it's a genuine sport. Jim claps when the strangling-man's won the game after the other man taps out.

"So Henry came to you right after Alec hit him? What did he say to you?"

"He came to the *Fence* and called for me. Nose was gushing with blood. I took him into my office and waited with him until it stopped bleeding. I knew who did it to him before he even told me. I always thought Alec Walker was a bad man. We should never have gone near the Walkers."

"What do you mean, 'we'?"

Jim turns his eyes to me suddenly, and I retract.

"What is it you want from all this, Dolina? It doesn't matter. Henry's dead."

"Henry is *not* dead! Don't say that!"

"He probably is. People like Alec Walker, and his daughter June? People like us are subhuman to them."

"But why would you say Henry's dead!" My eyes begin to prickle.

"Because he was a stupid kid!" Jim bellows at me. "And he messed with scum like the Walkers!"

"Henry was my friend and I need to know what happened to him. Don't say he's dead if you don't know that."

Jim's shoulders drop and he looks away with shame.

"Do you really know what happened to Henry, Jim?"

"No, I don't. I'm sorry. I wish I did."

"Okay, well please just tell me what you know."

"Right. But first, come through to the kitchen. The game's over anyway. Bring your glass."

When we get to the kitchen the window's open and the temperature drop is a relief. He goes and sits by the window ledge and lights a cigarette. The window offers a view of north Edinburgh, where we can see out to the lights of the Forth bridges. Before those we see the final districts of Edinburgh, carved by streetlamp routes, glowing webs arched across the landscape.

Jim offers me a cigarette and I take one even though I hate smoking. I sit by him at the ledge. When closer to him, I see just how old he is. Those mighty black eyebrows he had are now dotted with white. When he speaks, he's very quiet. But I sense he's about to go on a monologue.

"Henry owed money to June Walker. And I tried to help Henry pay the money back to June. I really wish I hadn't let Henry ever get involved in it. Henry was never able to pay back the money, and I'm afraid that's why he disappeared.

"Alec Walker knew his daughter was owed money, and she wasn't getting it back. So he became involved personally. That's why he hit Henry that day in '98 – because he was late for a payment. And, I mean, if a man is able to smack a boy like that, over money, what else could he do to him?"

He smokes his cigarette feverishly.

"It all started with Linda. She went to score from the wrong type of people. Dealers who were in the mob. She scored from them with fake money. If it was a man that did that they'd just batter him – but because Linda was a woman, they gave her a chance to pay herself off.

"I remember when she came back to the house that night. Me and Henry were there. She was out her mind, hysterical. She said if she didn't pay the mob in two days, they'd come after her. And this mob was bad, the worst in Edinburgh. Anyone that knew of that family was scared of them. But Linda had no money. That night, the three of us were terrified. I offered the money that I had from my savings, but, Jesus – I was a janitor – I barely had any savings.

"Henry used to sell bags of weed to the other kids, and he gave her all he'd made from that. But we still hadn't met the mob's demand even half way. So, Henry said he could find a way to take care of it. He was the calmest of all of us, that night, and we stayed up until 5 a.m., petrified Linda was going to get nailed. But we both trusted in Henry. Let him make his move as if he was the adult and us the youngsters.

"By the afternoon of that same day, Henry showed up at the house with an envelope of money and a massive smile. Linda started crying. We had all the money to pay the mob back. And Linda did, that same night. And we never ever went back to that part of town to score, even though we were junkies.

"Neither of us asked where Henry got the money, we were that desperate. And I didn't even feel bad at the time, that he'd saved us. I knew Henry hated us because we were users. But he loved his Mum and he liked me too. And we loved him. And now, I feel awful I even let him do that. I could have helped him."

Jim pours more whisky, tumbler filled up to the top and passes the bottle to me. He flicks his cigarette nub out the window. Its ember whizzes away, dwarfed by the lights of the landscape.

"But what did you let him do?" I say. "How did Henry get that much money?"

"I already told you. He got it from June Walker. Henry knew she was rich, her father was rich, and he desperately needed cash. Henry told us about it the next day after Linda was safe from the mob. June gave him a loan, because she was his 'friend', and he would pay it back to her by selling more weed.

"When Henry came into my office days later, with his bloody nose, he told me what the real deal was. June charged Henry with 50% interest on what he'd loaned her. And he had four weeks to pay it all back. There were four payments he had to make – one for every week. If he didn't make a payment, June tacked on more interest. So when Henry missed that first payment, Alec Walker punched him in the nose."

"Jesus Christ …" I say, "I thought June was dodgy, but not that bad."

"Yeah. I think she thought it would be some kind of a game, to see if a freak like Henry could get the money back in time. She was manipulative and cruel, but at the start she was only toying with him. After Alec hit him, her game became serious."

"But why would Alec hit him in the first place if there were witnesses around?"

"I don't know. Don't know what Henry had on them. Perhaps Alec was just a psycho. An egotistical bastard."

"So you say Henry never got the money back to them?"

"Well, Henry missed the first payment, so June stacked more interest on his sum. Henry *did* get two payments back to them. I know that for sure."

"I have a vague memory of Henry handing money to Alec. When I was little. Henry handed an envelope through a hole in the wall. He surprised us. But he was making fun. I didn't understand it when I was a kid."

"That was classic Henry: he didn't take things seriously when he really should have. And that was his last payment, because he couldn't make the next one. And that's why Henry left home soon afterward. He feared what the Walkers would do to him if he missed another one. He disappeared for one week, then came back, then a week later he was gone for good."

"Wait, hold up a second. Henry left home for a week? What do you mean?"

"Just that. Henry bailed, and we had no idea where he was. All he did was leave us a note, saying: 'Don't worry. I'll be back soon'. Linda was frantic for seven days … Then Henry just came back home as if nothing had happened. He said he'd been on a trip and that everything was fine now. Then the next time he vanished, there was no note. Nothing. And I think Linda was destroyed after that."

Jim stands up and shuts the window. He yawns. When he speaks, he's still coherent, but his diction is slowed down to almost nothing. I've been here for an hour already listening to him.

"Come back through to the sitting room, Dolina."

He collapses on his couch again, and I'm fearing I'm going to lose him to sleep. He pours another whisky and slugs it like it's a mug of cocoa, closing his eyes. He seems to have forgotten about my company.

"Where is Linda, Jim?"

"I don't know, Dolina. Don't bother Linda."

He takes his phone out and puts some music on, quietly. Puts it on the table. It's Bob Dylan – 'Meet me in the Morning'.

"I always stick Dylan on when I'm heading to sleep. And I think I might turn in, Dolina. But thanks for coming. You're welcome to stay if you like."

"Thanks, but can you just tell me where Linda is? I need to talk to her."

"I loved Linda … And she just fell out of love with me. It's just sad how much I still miss her."

"Please will you help me find her?"

"Don't bother her. She's not well in the head."

"Can I talk to you a bit more?"

"Tomorrow. I'm sleepy."

"You're working tomorrow?"

"No I've got the day off. Enough for tonight, Dolina. Let me sleep."

Jim's not being mean. He's just wasted. A minute later he's dead asleep. Then I'm alone in this bare, claustrophobic flat with Jim the Janny. I take another sip of my whisky, but I nearly throw up after I gag on the taste. I put it down. I've still learnt something crucial tonight. Jim's given me terrific information. But I know he might be the only way I'll find Linda. I need more.

I get crude with my detective skills. I wait until Jim's heavy into sleep. I notice that his phone's still playing Dylan, and it's unlocked. I creep over to the table and take it up. Then look through his contacts. He has five numbers in the entire list. All of these have titles like 'Work' and 'BT Sports', except for the one actual name in it. Linda.

There's a picture of a girl wearing a tiara next to her name. I look into Jim's messages to Linda. And there are endless messages he's sent to her, in long and passionate blocks. There is no rapport from her whatever. And the messages go back months and years. The most recent message from him is from a few days ago.

Jim shakes on the couch beside me and I almost drop his phone. What am I *doing*?

Quickly, I copy Linda's number onto my phone. Then put his phone back and stand up to leave. I put my coat on.

Jim's lying on his back on the sofa, obliterated. I feel a wrenching sadness for him, because I know he's a good man despite his issues. I go over to him at the sofa and lift him across onto his stomach. He's drank so much whisky he might throw up if he's on his back and choke on the vomit. His body is so light it's easy to lift him over.

"I'm just heading back home, Jim. Thanks for having me."

He murmurs incoherently and waves. At the door, I say:

"Night, Jim."

"Night night, Henry," he says.

CHAPTER THIRTY

A PHONECALL

I've already missed the regular buses by the time I leave Jim's. I've never been to this part of the city, and there are no taxis floating about – hardly any traffic. So I begin to walk back home. I'm angry, frustrated. By the time I've made it to familiar city centre areas after 40 minutes, I have enough money to get a night bus, and there are plenty of taxis. But I'm stubborn and self-destructive. So I just walk all the way home. About five miles, and it doesn't even take me that long.

And when I wake up in the morning, it's only a few hours since I got home. And it's as if sleep hasn't had any register on my mental state.

Linda Fowles' phone number is lurking on me. I have it, and I could call her: but it's only 8 a.m.

I hear my Mum get up and get ready for work, and I'm shivering in my room. I don't go to the bathroom because I don't want her to see me. Mum eventually leaves for work. I go downstairs and do the housework. I'm trying to wait until noon to call Linda. But I don't last that long. I need to see if the number I found on Jim's phone will actually lead me to her. I call Henry's mother. The phone brings.

"Hello?"

"Hi – is that, uh, Linda?"

"Yeah."

"Linda Fowles?"

"Yes."

"Hi Linda, you won't recognise my voice, but it's Dolina, from back home. Remember me? I used to live down the road from you.

"…"

"Dolina. I knew your son and I used to play with him. But I was only little. Do you remember me, Linda?"

"Yes, I remember you. Little Dolina. What's up? How are you?"

"Wow! I'm really glad to have found you, Linda!"

"Me too. What would you like, poppet?"

"Can I come see you? I need to talk to you about some things."

"Of course you can. But I'm busy today. Tomorrow instead?"

"Yes! Where can I meet you?"

"Shall I just text you my address?"

"Please, yes."

"Okay. I will. But I have to head out now. So see you tomorrow?"

She hangs up very quickly after I say yes. Then very quickly later I get a text message of her address, alongside the words: 'Come on over any time after 6 x'. The address is farther away from me than Jim's flat was – a polar leap across Edinburgh.

I'm loving all this investigating. To hear Linda Fowles' voice after two decades, the confirmation that she's still alive.

And I noticed she was just as easy and cool as Henry always was. She accepted me, and wasn't surprised I contacted her, and didn't ask why I was calling.

She's given me my next step.

CHAPTER THIRTY-ONE

LINDA FOWLES

She lives in a much quieter area than Jim. Right on the very edge of the city. I'd been expecting a flat, but she has a little house in one of those lonely housing estates you find on the countryside outskirts. I haven't seen a single person as I've walked through the estate.

I ring Linda's doorbell. I meet a thin, wide eyed woman, very old – but she still looks good, with bushy red hair.

"Dolina!" she hugs me in the doorway. "Little Dolina. How are you? Come inside."

She offers me tea and I accept. She leads me out into her back garden to a table. It's an overcast, humid day. In the bleary white distance I watch cars scan down the motorways.

"Haven't seen you in a very long time, Dolina," Linda says to me, "you look terrific."

"You do too. I love your hair."

She chuckles. She lights a cigarette. There's a flooded ashtray on the table.

"So what made you think of me?" She says. "I won't ask you how you found me – but what's up?"

"Well, I'm just glad to see you. And wanted to see how you were. And you seem *great* nowadays."

"Meaning that I used to be a train wreck, and now I've pulled myself out of it."

I blush, badly. That was a stupid thing for me to say.

"Sorry, Linda. I didn't mean it that way."

"No, poppet, I agree. I can deal with this life. I've got a husband, and a job, and as you say, I don't look too bad. And I've been clean for a good while."

"What's your husband's name?"

"Ah – Edgars – he's from Latvia. He's a little bit nuts, and hard to deal with. But, it's worth it. Here, I'll show you," she brings out her phone and shows me a picture of this spectacular looking older-man. Massive jaw, giant build. "And he looks like that, at his age."

We giggle.

"But he's a good man. I share this house with him, and I like it here, in the quiet, away from the city." She lights another cigarette. "You're here to ask me about Henry, aren't you?"

"I. Yes. I just needed to talk to you about him."

"Well, good. The police never wanted to speak to me seriously about him. Only the hacks did. They attacked me every day after Henry vanished. Never left me alone, just wanted a line from a junkie to print. That's why I moved away. The next decade was pretty bleak. After a *long* trial with addiction I finally got where I am now. So what would you like to know?"

"I want to find out what happened to him, more than anything. And – sorry if it makes you touchy – but I went and spoke to Jim the other night."

"Oh, ho-ho, Jim? How's he doing?"

"He's … He's Jim. A bit sad, but still tough."

"Yeah, he'll always be that."

"And he told me something very important. That Henry owed June money."

"Yes, of course. Idiot bloody kid. I'm embarrassed I ever bore him, sometimes."

I go quiet. Linda keeps puffing her cigarettes, looking into the distance.

"He was like that when he was a baby too. Always putting himself into danger. I was always panicking about him. Always had to feel I had to watch him, make sure he was alright.

A clumsy boy. Except he was still a baby when he was a man too."

I gulp two mouthfuls of tea. This is chilling. I didn't expect this from her. I've never seen her angry before. My inclination is to ask her: 'But didn't Henry borrow from June so you could pay back the drug mob?', but her anger scares me off.

"Could you tell me about the time when Henry went out west for a week, Linda?"

"Yeah, he left me and Jim a note, disappeared for a week. He should have just stayed where he was, and not come back. Idiot."

"What happened when he came back?"

"He had bag full of money. Cash. And he had a *limp*. He tried to hide it. But he couldn't walk straight at all."

"Why did he have a limp?"

"Can't you guess? He got it when he was trying to get more money for June."

"He was in a fight?"

"Probably. Henry always attracted fights, and never won any. He was just like that. He never learned that there were awful people on the planet, and the best thing was to just stay clear of them. Instead, he let himself be a target."

"Well, yes. But why do you talk about Henry in the past-tense?"

Linda glares at me. And, though I'm scared of her, I hold her gaze. And I see a weakness there. She looks a lot like Henry herself. She has that same sparky way of talking like Henry did, with the lopsided intonations, all relayed at once. But she's like him only half-way; she has darkness, whereas her son never did. Henry wasn't capable of getting dark. And she never answers my question.

"So, what happened after he came back with his money?"

"Well, we had a massive argument. I was worried about him, because of the Walkers. They were dangerous, and I told Henry to get away from them. He just kept grinning. And showing me the money in his bag. But he had something else in there. He kept describing it as his 'secret weapon' And it would protect him if Alec Walker tried anything else.

"I think he went a little crazy after his trip. I was scared for him, but he wouldn't listen. So I told him to get out of my house. And that hurt him. So, that last week before he finally vanished, I barely saw him."

"Okay. But the 'secret weapon' in his bag. What was it?"

"A video. A videotape."

"I don't understand."

"Neither did I."

"But what was on the videotape?"

"I don't know. I never saw it. That was why I thought Henry was going crazy. He wasn't making any sense."

Linda's finished her cup of tea and she asks if I'd like another. I decline. I've barely touched my own one. I watch the motorway when she's inside the house. I wonder who the people are in the cars, wonder how they make their living, whether they're happy with their lives and know what to do with them.

I'm marvelled by how long I've been obsessed with Henry's case, ever since I found his things. It seems like such a long time ago now. And I *had* planned on telling Linda about his cap and watch. But now I'm not so sure that's a good idea.

She comes back from the house with a new mug, lights another cigarette. She's as easy with me as if I were her own niece come over for a visit.

"I just want to ask about the videotape again, Linda. Are you meaning like a VHS tape?"

"Yes, honey, VHS, it was still in the 90s."

"What did he do with it?"

"He told me he was going to hide it. But then I told him to get out of the house. So he must have hidden it in the Woods."

"The Woods? Why?"

"That's where he stayed after I chucked him out. He took a tent and camped out there for days … I was glad he was gone, but more because I couldn't get any dope and was in withdrawal, and I was at my worst at that point. When I finally did get high again, I knew I'd harmed him. And I got Jim to go and find him and bring him back home.

"That was the night before the big World Cup game – the final. I apologised to Henry, and told him he could stay at the house again, of course. And we made friends again. Jim, me and him were all together that night.

"And that was the last time I ever saw him –" her voice chokes. And her eyes water. She takes a long breath in and stops herself from crying. "And he told me he had some stuff to do the next day, but he'd be home in the evening, to watch the big final game with me and Jim. But he never showed up."

"You must miss Henry very much, Linda. I certainly do."

"Do you think you'll find my son?"

"Yes, I think I will. I know I'm getting closer."

"I hope you do. Even if he's dead, I'd just like to know. Maybe I'm a bad mother, and too weak to find out for myself. But you aren't weak, Dolina. I believe you when you say you'll find him."

The evening gets colder and we go quiet. Then Linda invites me inside to her living room. We try to make conversation on more trivial matters, but the generational gulf is a barrier and we can't find things to say.

Eventually she says her husband will be home soon. And I get the hint that she'd rather that I leave before he gets here, so I make my move to go. But she asks me to call her any time. "Bless you, Dolina," is the last thing she says before I go.

CHAPTER THIRTY-TWO

BACK TO THE WOODS

It was only last week since Tommy and I agreed not to go back into the Woods anytime soon. But I've found out so much more since. There's bound to be more in the Woods to discover. Most of all, I just miss being there. I've called Tommy many times this evening and sent him numerous messages. No response.

After I spoke to Linda last night, I've been thinking again and again about the VHS tape Henry had. And there's a tiny memory I have of Henry back in 1998. I saw him in the Woods when he was over the other side of the river. And it looked like he was *digging* something under a group of trees. Except I couldn't see him clearly enough to see exactly what he was doing. And I didn't go near to him because I thought it was weird.

Linda said that he hid his 'secret weapon' in the Woods. Maybe my memory was of that? I remember the digging location: in the rear part of the Woods near *June's Waterfall* is. Except, further on than the *Waterfall*, where you need to go off-path.

It's a rosy, magical evening outside. The Woods are tingling out of my window, thick with young summer bloom. Beckoning to me to come join them.

Tommy warned that we shouldn't go back to playing the *Game* for a while. But I just want to go for a walk in the Woods. There's no harm in that, right? The next LEVEL – LEVEL 7 – is the *Electricity Box*. That's far away in another part, distant from the *June's Waterfall* area. So I won't need to go near the *Game*.

I head out the house. For a week I've been avoiding the incense of the leaves and plants. Now as I go down the hilly road, the incense returns to me with renewed blast. Arrays of emerald, lime, aquamarine leaves coat the branches above me. I go down past Mr Walker's house. Cut down until I reach the wall where you climb over under the horse chestnut tree.

I *jump into* my Woods. I make a new path through the ferns and nettles as I go down to the river. Sweat's dripping off my face, and I like it. Love the power of life before me.

I reach the river, and go along, past the *Waterfall* and the mill ruins. The growth is so heavy underfoot it's hard to walk along, and it's the same the far side of the river, where I'm basing my '98 digging memory on. But I can't be sure from this vantage point. I remember sitting this side of the river, and he was over on the bankside in the trees. Except the trees are different now. I'll have to cross the river if I want to find anything, and it's very wide at this point.

Hmm. Maybe I should head back home and get my wellies. Should have thought of that before. I stand up and turn around. And I freeze, because I see someone.

There's a man standing behind me in the Woods. He's very tall, way past six foot. He has a dark hoody on, and a maroon football scarf tied around his face.

"Hello?" I say.

He's 20 metres from me on the path I made through the plants. Hovering there, staring at me silently.

"Who's that?" I call. His face is hidden by the scarf. I can only see his eyes. I don't know this man. "Mind if I ask who it is?"

I wait for several seconds, and he doesn't respond. He's blocking the way back. I can't go back to the horse-chestnut wall any other route.

"Okay, I'm a little bit scared," I try again, "and I don't know who you are. Could you at least take your scarf off – if this is just a joke?"

I'm hoping it's just one of Filippo's friends, playing with me. But the man stays still, hands by his sides.

I turn around and begin to walk away. Get out of the Woods, Dolina. I'm alone here with this stranger. Just get to the far wall at the end of the river and climb out of the Woods – hurry up, Dolina.

I hear scurrying and see a flash in my peripheral vision and turn around. The man's sprinting at me. I run.

I crash into the river and the water goes up my jeans and into my face. "Help!" I cry. His body bounds after me. I scream again. The river lugs my shoes down. The man jumps into the water. I launch myself out the river onto the far bank and nip up into the undergrowth, and just run.

I whizz through the plants, aiming for the wall. But I don't know where I am and can't see where it is. There's only jungle. I hear him stomp behind me and it flushes me forward. I pick a direction and race.

As I go, a tree branch nicks me in the eye. I veer over, unbalanced. Feels like my eye's pouring blood. Half blind, I gallop over and find this patch of trees covered by bushes. I crouch behind them, controlling my panting.

"Where's the wall, Dolina?" I whisper to myself. When I pull my hand away from my eye, there's no blood. But it's stinging, dripping. I look around me. All I can see are trees. I don't recognise anything. I can't stay here. I need to go further. Time wrenches by. I don't trust the silence.

I sit up, and peer beyond the bushes.

The man is standing three yards away from me with his back turned.

"Argh!" I shriek. I can't help it.

He spins around to me. I run out the trees and see him jump after me. He catches my foot. I'm thrown down onto the floor. He's on the floor too. I'm shouting: "What's this all about! What's this all about!" I pull my foot away and he pulls my shoe off.

I manage to get away from him and stand up. There's a thick branch on the floor by me. I pick it up as he rises from the floor. I see his skull open under me. I whack him on the head with the branch. He splats back onto the floor.

I run away through the trees with one shoe. Until I find a meadow area suffocated by nettles. Nettles everywhere, running up to my shoulders. Should I just run through them? But then he'll see my path. I spot a long line of trees heading alongside the meadow. The nearest tree to me has boughs stretching out above the nettle field.

I make another path the other way, back through the weeds and further into the trees. Then I go back down the path, and I climb the near tree. I clamber up its limbs until I get to a good height.

The man's prowling through the growth after me – but he hasn't seen me yet in the distance. I step along one of the boughs that's hanging over the nettles. Get as far as I can. And jump into the field.

I thump in. The nettles swarm around me. The nettle leaves punish my face, my hands. They pierce through my sock-foot. I lie there, in this bed of acidic plants in exhilarating pain. But I am hidden. And I wait.

I hear the man's footfalls come nearer. Then I hear him for the first time, growling:

"Where are you, you little bitch? You little bitch – where are you!"

He's yammering away in a frenzy. If he finds me, I'm dead. And he keeps going in that same gibberish for minutes, repeating the same curses.

But then I hear physical thrish-thrash sounds heading away from me. He's been fooled by my trick path – I hope. I wait.

Very slowly, I kneel up and lift my head above the line of the nettles. There he is: he's gone the opposite way from me, far off back into the trees. His tall frame's scouring about the earth

"Okay, Dolina. He can't hear me from here."

I look around. North of where I am, I see where the trees get darker, and less dense. I'm judging this might be near to where the wall is. I'll have to go through the nettles to get there. What else is there to do? I crouch back down and begin to crawl along.

I watch the white pimples rise on my hands. My cheeks are stung with every heave, every bristly stem of the nettles rubs my fingers. When I get out the nettle field and stand up, I'm frying.

But the pain is nothing compared to danger. Where is the man? I can't see or hear him. What I *can* see is ivy. Carpets of the ivy, where the plants fall away. I go across them. The ivy leaves are velveteen under my sock foot. I enter the hazy, dim area, where the trees slip away. Then I hear new noises rushing noises in the distance. Cars! That's the main road. I follow the sounds, and they get louder.

I go on and notice rubbish appearing at my feet. The soil grows damper. Then the river comes back, in sight and sound. I go over to the water. Above the river is the bridge, which looms over me. That's why it's so dark. The bridge is surrounded by the wall of the Woods. The bridge is what ends the Woods: the final geographic point of the perimeter.

I head up the land, up to the wall. There's a weird collection of trash as I rise; beer cans, condoms, bicycle carcasses, a trainer, fluorescent street-cones, a bag of tinsel Christmas decorations … I get to the wall, climb up and over. I hop onto the main street, onto the pavement, beside the thundering cars. I'm so glad to see them – cars, with people in them – just driving on a normal weeknight.

I check myself. I still have my phone and wallet. When I look down at my sock foot, it's bleeding. Blood's soaked through the cotton. My eye is still gushing as well.

I go to the edge of the bridge and look down into the Woods. Trying to spot the man. He's gone. There is only the returned image of the secretive Woods, from this height. Just the river and the banks of ivy. I don't know where he is. I don't know what just happened to me.

A man and a boy are coming towards me down the pavement, walking their dog. They're both staring at me. I know them vaguely. They live down the street, and I often greet the man when I see him around. The dog often nuzzles up to me too, but this time he trots past. As they get close, the man leans his head out, frowning. He's about to ask if I'm okay.

I duck and go past them, limping ridiculously with the one shoe on. They're not real neighbours, anyway. They're not part of my actual neighbourhood: certainly not part of the old guard.

If any of the old guard had seen me like this back in the 1990s, the news would be all over the neighbourhood within hours.

When I get home, I take my shoe and socks off. The cuts on my foot aren't bad. I wash and dry them and put plasters on. I put the socks in the washing machine. In the mirror, my face is laced with nettle stings.

I'm not really sure what to do. Should I tell someone what just happened? Mum is already heading to sleep for work tomorrow. Tommy hasn't replied. It's dark outside, now. Mum needs to get up early in the morning. I should probably just head to sleep.

When I was little, I remember when I stung myself with nettles, I would go to her for help. She showed me how to use dock plants as a remedy, how to mash the leaves up and dab them on the sting.

I wish I could go to her now. But I'm too old for that. So I just undress and get into my bed, naked, turn the lights off, knowing that I won't be able to sleep. And lie there, as the nettle stings pulse on my skin.

CHAPTER THIRTY-THREE

NEW SHOES

I make the mistake of going downstairs the next morning when Mum is in the kitchen. She instantly notices the red marks on my face and freaks out. But I lie about them and tell her that I fell into a bunch of nettles by accident. Which is a white-lie, so I don't feel that bad.

"But how did you do that – fall?" She says.

"I just slipped on some grass, Mum."

"Well, there's some Calendula cream upstairs to put on the marks."

As I'm drinking coffee at the table, I feel her watching me. She knows I'm lying about something.

"What is it you're up to in the Woods, these days Dolina? Why you going in there so often? You injured your leg too, there, the other week. There's something you're not telling me."

"I tripped over on the grass and landed in some nettles, Mum. It was really painful. But I think I'll survive."

She's slightly convinced by this, and she leaves me be. But I'm glad she doesn't see me limping on my cut foot. I'm sitting at the table and she can't see it under the cloth.

Mum is right. I'm not telling her about what I'm doing in the Woods. I haven't told her anything about *Filippo's Game*. I'm more scared about what she could find out than the police, or the Walkers. This morning, when she asks me about it, is the first time I've felt deviant about this whole investigation. And I still don't understand it all myself. But then, why am I not speaking to my Mum about it?

My Mum's a great woman. I admire her. She works as a therapist for a health firm that helps people suffering from depression. She's the boss of the whole firm … A challenging, multivariate woman; a character I've had much strife with – but she's great. There are photographs of her from the 1970s when she was my age. She was a foxy lady back then. And she's aged well too.

I hope she isn't concerned about me. She leaves for work and leaves me alone in the big house. I start thinking. I haven't really processed what happened yesterday yet. A man came out to me in the Woods. He was a stranger. He attacked me. Luckily only got my shoe and I got away before he could do worse.

That was what happened literally. But, why? Why did he chase me? He followed me into the Woods to do what? To rape me? Was he going to mug me? I don't remember seeing anyone when I walked down to the Woods from my house. Did he follow me from the street?

I'm ashamed that I hit him in the head. I've never hit anyone before. Did I hurt him badly? He was trying to attack me, but the guilt of hitting him with a tree branch is what bothers me most. Maybe I'm still in shock. And need to talk to somebody about it. I could try and call Tommy again – but he'll be at work.

It gets to noon, and the house and the Woods overwhelm me. The quiet in the house plays on me until I cannot bare it. And that pair of shoes I had until last night was the only pair of 'casual' shoes I have. I have some good leather shoes and a pair of wellies – that's it for the shoe collection. I need something to do, to get me out of the house, and need new casual shoes. So I put my wellies on and go into town to shop.

I get a pair after 20 minutes. But I don't want to go back home just yet. I find this little coffee shop after getting the shoes, and hang out there, reading newspapers. The papers are just as depressing as always. I order another coffee.

I'm looking to the wall-decorations as I wait. Where there are pictures of an Edinburgh artist; landscapes of the city in chock-block gouache paint. I'm jealous, because the artist's good. I go and check the name of the artist: don't recognise her name, but I wish my paintings were displayed somewhere.

Not sure if I could do better landscapes that she's doing. But then, what *have* I been doing artistically this last little while? Nothing. I claim to be an artist, yet I haven't been at my easel in so long.

I stay in the café until they have to close down late afternoon. I get the bus down the main road to my area of the city. The land arches upward and at the pivot of the hill I see out upon my neighbourhood in the distance. In the close temperature and under the white sky, the Woods and the Hospital suddenly look different to me.

The trees of the Woods are a sickly dark green. The Hospital's cube shies from the horizon, when usually it looms proudly. The housing estates, domineer the skyline in sharp rooflines. Poor lives, hundreds of people strewn there in these areas, these housing estates nearly 70 years old. The Woods are hidden behind them, left in a past world.

I get home, in a huff. Beans on toast. Classic meal. I shouldn't be a diva after reading the news today, all the suffering people in the world. Mum will be home later in the evening. I tidy up and then go upstairs to have a shower. Just as I've turned the shower on, I hear the doorbell ring. I turn the shower off.

I've already half undressed down to my underwear. So I put my dressing gown on and head downstairs. When I open the door I'm just thinking it's a delivery man, so I peek out, covering my body with the door to hide my nakedness.

Two men are standing in my doorway. One wears a bright yellow jacket and the other is remarkably handsome. Alec Walker and my cousin Filippo.

"Dolina!" Alec cries.

"Dolina," Filippo says, "what's up?"

"Hi, chaps, what's happening?" They both have twinkling smiles. "I've just kinda got out the shower, so I'm not really dressed."

"Oh, ha ha, no worries. We'll let you get changed," Filippo announces. "We just came by to see how you were. I came back to see my folks, and I knew you were home. Is your Mum here, too?"

"Umm, no. She gets back a while later. You can come in for coffee, if you like?" I don't know why I'm saying this and I'm thinking this is the wrong idea. But I just keep speaking. "But could you wait ten seconds as I go upstairs to get changed? Then we can have coffee in the kitchen?"

"That's no problem at all, Dolina. Us gentlemen will wait here."

I run upstairs to my room. Why are Alec and Filippo at my house? It's nearly a year since they've visited our house – why now? They only come around on holidays? Why the hell is Filippo up from London, on a weekday? I'm shivering and more terrified than I was last night.

"But, Filippo's my cousin." I say to myself, "Nothing's going to happen." I get dressed and go back to the front door. "Sorry, gents, I was just a bit naked. Come inside. Have some coffee."

They steamroll in. I lead them into the kitchen and put all the lights on.

"So what you up to these days, Dolina?" Alec Walker says. He takes his glasses off for a second, rubs his eyelids, puts the glasses back on. Filippo has taken his coat off but Alec keeps his yellow jacket on.

"I'm trying to become a real adult, Alec, after completing my art degree. And don't know how to do it." They both chuckle as I fill the kettle.

"We all know you're a great painter, Dolina," Filippo says.

"Maybe I used to be, Filippo."

"Are you hungry as well, gentlemen?"

"No, no, thanks. Just a coffee is perfect." Alec says.

They're on my territory, and I know something's off about their visit. But the best I can do is be hospitable. I go into the fridge.

"Oh, come, we've got lots of things. Cheeses, olives: there's some salad I made last night. Have a little bit to eat, friends."

As I get plates and cutlery out I ask Filippo about how his London job is going. He rubs his golden, perfect hair as he talks. He constantly feels the line on the middle of his moviestar chin, too, without realising it.

He's also bad at acting. His voice is overly loud, straining to seem normal. It's obvious there's another reason why they're here. I keep looking at the clock. Mum usually gets home in half an hour.

"So Mum usually gets back soon," I say, "I made some pasta and sauce earlier as well. We could all have dinner and catch up properly, if you like?"

"No, thanks though. We just wanted to check on you," Alec says, and stands up. "Is it alright it I head to the bathroom?"

"Sure, Alec. It's just upstairs. First on the right."

Alec shifts out the room and Filippo and I are left together. I look into his face. The room's warm. I venture into a conversation.

"So is it really doable in London, Filippo? I always had a romantic idea of it when I was a kid, living there. But what's it really like when there?"

"Where are Henry's things, Dolina?" He responds.

"… Huh?"

"Where is Henry's *FIFA '98* cap? And his watch?"

"What's up, Filippo? Why are you –"

"Don't call me that. Filippo. I'm not *Filippo*, not any more. You have a minute until Alec comes downstairs."

"To do what?"

"Tell me where Henry's things are."

"They're not here."

"You don't want to push us, Dolina."

"That's not my intention. What are you and Alec going to do to me? What's with you?"

"Just give us the cap and watch."

"Henry's things are not in this house." I watch him. This man who shares my heritage. His blue eyes, his lips in a constant red pout. But he doesn't intimidate me enough. I'm more aggressive.

"Dolina – even if you just give them to *me*, before anything else happens."

We hear Alec Walker come down the steps in the hall. He appears in the door, studying us. He and Filippo exchange a look and then he sits down at the table. We wait for some time, in silence, none of us drinking our coffee.

"I'm glad your back home in this nice part of the city, Dolina. We all are. It's hard to know what to do after finishing a degree. If you'd done some kind of business education I would've offered you a job, like I did with John.

"We all care about you … But we're a little concerned for you too. You've been out of education for six months. That's a long time. And I'm seeing you walking around out area a lot, acting strangely. Is everything okay?"

"Everything is fine, Alec."

"How far have you got in *Filippo's Game*, Dolina?" Alec Walker says.

"*Filippo's Game*?" I sip my coffee. "I got to the treehouse, LEVEL 3, why? Why you asking me this?"

"We think you've been playing more of the *Game*."

"Well, I played the first three LEVELS, and then I quit. Couldn't get any further."

"Explain."

"I just found Filippo's treehouse in the Woods. Never got that far before, when I was a kid – but so what? It's just a game. And when I did get there, you came out on me with a torch, Alec."

"So you didn't go on with the *Game*?"

"No, I didn't. I was creeped out that night in the woods. But I let it be. And I didn't tell anyone about that, when I could have."

"I think you did tell other people what happened that night, Dolina," Alec says. "And I think you should take your cousin's advice, and give us back Henry's cap and watch. Please."

"Give them *back* to you? They belong to Henry – not you."

"We're just asking you for a favour, Dolina," Filippo says. He's nodding at me: imploring me to accept.

"No, gentlemen. I'm not giving you Henry's things. I'll give them to him myself, when I find him. Besides, they're not in this house. And I'm beginning to feel uneasy with your attitude."

Alec sits back in his seat and drinks more coffee. Filippo does the same.

"So you never got farther than LEVEL 3, Dolina?" Alec says.

"I just couldn't work out what to do for the next LEVEL. Maybe I'm not as smart as the members of Filippo's Gang."

"Then why are there red marks all over your face, your *hands* as well?"

"I have no answer to this question. How is it your business what I look like? I'm not playing your stupid kid's game anymore. Now, I'd like it if you both left. This is my place, and I shouldn't be intimidated you. You're my neighbour, and cousin!"

Alec nods at Filippo. Filippo takes his wallet out. He slips out a little square of paper from it, and hands it to me. Although it's not a piece of paper. It's a photograph.

A polaroid photograph: of *me* sitting at the top of a tree. After completing LEVEL 5 of *Filippo's Game*. I took this photo the other week. Filippo and Alec found it. They know what I've been doing. They've been monitoring me all along as I've played their *Game*. I'm silenced.

"We're just asking you to stop, little cousin," Filippo says, "stop playing the *Game*. It is very old and dangerous. Nobody's played it in 20 years – it's not safe."

They're both standing up.

"It's …" I begin to say. "But, why does it have to be so serious? I don't understand: why's it so big a deal?"

"If it's no big deal, why wouldn't you just tell us you're playing it? Why lie about it" Alec says. "Don't go back to the Woods again, Dolina. If you keep going in, we will know. Thank you for the coffee. We'll let ourselves out the front door."

"Yeah, thank you, Dolina," Filippo says. "Say hello to your Mum from me, too."

Alec heads out the room, down to the front door, opens it. Filippo's still standing in the kitchen above me. He's searching for my expression. This man is the son of my Mother's brother. And he's come here this evening to my house, specifically to threaten me. I think the expression that I return to him says all this. It seemed like he was about to say something to me. But he only buckles under my gaze, drops his eyes, and turns away.

I hear him close the front door.

Until this evening, I'd been hopeful about Henry Fowles. The mystery was liquifying and I was learning big clues at a fast rate. And I'd began to form an idea of what happened. Even after the attack last night by the scarf man, my hope for Henry didn't change. Now, my thinking has altered for the worse. It's rough, and I'm scared for him.

I can't ignore the timing of their visit: the night after I was chased in the Woods. Did they send a man out to attack me last night, to scare me away from the *Game*? Are they capable of doing something like that? I enjoyed the aggression I dealt them, until they showed me the polaroid photo. When that happened, I was scared, I'll admit.

But I'm also exhilarated by it all. And I can think of these things as an advantage. This was a tactical blunder by Alec and Filippo. I now know for certain that they have something to hide regarding Henry's disappearance. And, more than being frightened, I'm now *addicted* to this mystery. And the best bit is that I have Henry's cap and watch hidden. They want them from me and that means that they're scared of me too.

Okay, so they know I'm playing the *Game*. But I know the Woods. I'm an expert of my little woodland. I'm not a bad contender.

I know that there's definitely more about Henry to be found inside the Woods. And I'm not afraid to go back in there to find it. I just need to investigate in a different way. Figure out how to go into the Woods undetected.

I start thinking, plotting at the table. I can channel my creativity into this.

PART III

CHAPTER THIRTY-FOUR

JULY 6TH 1998

WHAT'S HE DOING OVER THERE?

Me and Mum got back from Crail yesterday. I missed Tommy the whole week and I want to see him again. I went to Tommy's earlier to ask if he was coming out. His Dad said he was already in the Woods. So I went inside and checked the places where we normally play, with no luck.

Sometimes we go down to where *June's Waterfall* is – so maybe he's there. I climb over the horse chestnut wall and head to the river. I see the ruins of the mill and I feel tingly. That's part of F*ilippo's Game*. But I just can't see what can be done there – they're only lumps of stone. I always try and imagine what game could be there, but I can't even imagine swimming across the river.

Anyway, I go along the path, looking for Tommy. The path runs down to the riverbank, where the river turns in a crescent moon shape, and you can see across to this group of trees the other side of the river. Just as I get there I see somebody moving across the water.

I'm about to yell Tommy's name. But it's not him. It's someone much bigger. I crouch down behind some nettles, and watch. Whoever it is is digging at something on the floor. At least that's what it looks like. His arms are moving angrily and he's kneeling under this big tree with yellow flowers. The yellow flowers look like yellow grapevines. The person stands up.

It's Henry. He's drinking a bottle of something, his football cap turned up to the sky. Looks like spirits this time, except he's *downing* the bottle, gulp, gulp.

"What's Henry doing over there?" I whisper to myself.

I don't know why I thought it was Tommy at first, because we never cross the river. How did Henry get there? He finishes drinking, and then he gets back to the digging. I can't see anything clear from here, and I don't want to go closer because I'm scared.

What I do see are bags with him. Lots of bags. He lifts one of these bags up and places it into the place where he's digging. Then he stands up and begins kicking at the ground. He drinks while he kicks. Except, only with one foot, and he leans against the yellow tree. He stops that, and he puts his bottle in his pocket, gets his bags, and moves down to the river.

He has a *limp*. One of his legs is really bad, he can barely put any weight on it.

He's just splashed into the water. I dart out of the nettles and run away down the path. I've never been scared of Henry before. Something doesn't seem right. I run down to the horse chestnut tree. He's probably coming back my way. But I check to see. He's not there, so I go forward a little.

Then spot him, down in the trees beside the path. Along with the bags he's wearing full camper gear, a hiking bag and boots, like I saw him at the bus stop last week. He's carrying a whole bunch of other stuff in his arms too. He staggers off the path and goes into the trees. I follow him. He limps at a snailspeed under the weight and keeps stopping and starting to rest his bad leg.

"I should go and help him ..." but I can see how furious his expression is. If he had his usual smile I'd already be with him.

He goes a far distance on the path, then he drops flat on his face. His bags spill everywhere. Has he fainted? But I see his back, panting air. Five minutes later he sits up and drinks more from the bottle. Then he begins clearing things off the floor with his feet, throwing sticks away, ripping plants out, tossing them too.

He gets one of the bags back and brings out this mesh of plastic. He shakes it open into a square. It's a tent. He lays the plastic across the floor he just made. Then he starts getting the pole bits out of the tent bag.

"Why's Henry making a tent in the Woods?"

Henry shoots up and spins around. I duck. He's scanning over where I am. Did he hear me talk to myself? He watches, but then relaxes, takes his bottle out and drinks a long gulp. He gets back to making his tent again. I should go home. Henry's obviously being strange again, but on a new level this time. I want to help him – but what can I do? So I go back out the wall and head back home.

I never found Tommy, oh well.

CHAPTER THIRTY-FIVE

JUNE 7TH 1998

A QUESTION

Tommy and me are playing catapult with bottles on the wall. We're by the Hospital where the road's quiet. We went up to the shop earlier and bought loads of juice, drank all of them, and I knew Tommy had a catapult. So we put stones into the bottles so they wouldn't fall off in the wind. Then we take shots at them the other side of the road to hit them off.

Tommy's won all the games so far, of course. Sometimes I get a bit insane that he always wins. If he gloated about it, I could smack him, but he never even celebrates, which makes me want to smack him even more.

But we're on a match now, and the score is 3 – 2 to me. We play it like penalty shootouts in football: best out of 5 is the winner. I *could* win a game against him for once.

Tommy's on his third shot. He's taking his aim. I'm watching his hands and eyes. He springs the rubber out and the stone whizzes and it *just* touches the bottle on the wall. The bottle sways, but it stays rooted.

Perfect. My stomach feels heavy, I want to beat him so bad. He gives me the catapult and sits behind me to watch. That's another annoying thing he does. He watches me to see how I use the catapult when he's obviously better at it than I am. And it always puts me off and I bet he does it on purpose.

But I ignore him this time. I look at the bottles on the wall. Choose which one I'm going to hit. There's a small one on the far left, which none of us have hit yet. Runt of the pack. It's the hardest one to get. Go for it, Dolina. I pull the rubber strap back, nuzzle the rock in my fingers, *see* it hitting the bottle in my mind. And it does! The bottle pongs off the wall. 4 – 2 to me.

Unlike Tommy I always cheer like crazy. I jump up and clap and sing to myself. It's embarrassing, but so what? It's good to celebrate when I can. Tommy's just smiling at me on the pavement. I still haven't won the game. He still has two shots, technically. But if he misses the next one, I've won.

Just as I go to give him the catapult, I notice somebody walking towards us down the road. She's wearing a white sweater and her dark hair drips over her breasts. The Hospital bulges in her background. June Walker.

Suddenly I get embarrassed. Tommy hasn't even noticed her yet. He takes the catapult and immediately hits one of the bottles on the wall: 4 – 3.

June reaches us. She waves at us. That's weird – she doesn't say hi a lot.

"Hi guys," she says, "what you up to?"

"Just playing catapult." I say.

"Ah, that's nice. Who's winning?"

"Tommy usually wins."

"Ha ha."

"You want to play too?"

She looks away and pretends to chuckle.

"No, thanks," she looks at me with her thick black eyes, "I just wondered: have either of you seen Henry recently?"

"Hmm, no," Tommy says.

She's only looking at me.

"No …" I say, in a high pitched voice.

"You sure? I'm trying to find him."

I saw Henry making a tent in the Woods last night. But I'm not going to tell June that. Why's she looking at me like this? Why's she even talking to us?

"No – don't know where Henry is."

"Okay," she walks on from us. "Enjoy your day, guys."

She goes down the street and I can't stop watching her. With June, it's like she doesn't care about anything, but she knows everything at the same time. She always walks slow, but with confidence.

So does she know I saw Henry in the Woods yesterday. Is that why she was looking at me like that? Why's she looking for Henry anyway?

"It's your shot," Tommy says. He's holding the catapult out to me.

I can win the match now. But I've lost my courage. June's spoiled it. I hold the catapult out. If I hit one more bottle, I win the game. If I don't, Tommy has another shot to take the game further. Maybe I'm not good at anything in life?

I don't even try to hit the bottle when I shoot. I know I'm not going to hit it. The stone sails into the Woods.

Tommy hits another bottle on his next try to make it 4 – 4. Then I miss the next shot. Then he wins in the knock-out bit, 4 – 5. Tommy's won. Again.

I care, but not really. Because I'm confused and distracted about June.

She wasn't the only one who's asked me if I've seen Henry any time recently. Filippo did as well earlier on, when he saw me near the Woods. And Jim the Janny came down from the Hospital and asked me when I was playing by myself.

Spooky. I didn't tell any of them the truth. I *did* see Henry yesterday. But I felt like I had to protect him. So I just lied.

CHAPTER THIRTY-SIX

MAY 2018

RAIN

The summer weather has been good thus far, the days sunny and hot. But to be honest, as a Scot, I prefer colder weather, and when the rain comes this morning, I relish it. I set out of the house before dawn. I climb over the fence in the back garden, then nip up the streets into the housing estate. I'm going the long way around to the main road. A different route back to the Woods.

The scent of the rain rises from the pavements and the rooftops darken by the water. My wellies tip-tap the floor. I only have my keys and a garden trowel in my bag. The fresh water rolls down my cheeks and neck, onto my breasts. The cut on my foot's sore, but I don't register the pain.

I walk until I get to the main road. The colours of dawn are just beckoning on the horizon. I see the trees of my Woods in the distance, then go along them at the roadside, until I get to the bridge. Looking into the gloom, I see the navy blue river rolling. I climb into the Woods over the wall.

The canopy rushes with rain, and as I go through the branches, I'm soaked by the time I find my path from two days back. I see the path through the weeds where I traipsed, and follow it back again. Back to the nettle field. Ha! – the nettles are sodden, now, and I don't need to make another path through them.

I find the scene of the chase and then the bit under the bushes where I wrestled with the stranger. And: "Wow, there's my shoe!" It's lying there in the weeds, collecting rain. The stranger didn't think to hide it? Well, I've got another pair of shoes back now. I put it in my bag and go on.

I come to the river, disks flying across its surface in the rain. And try to judge where I saw Henry digging in 1998. From this side of the river, I see the current turn in a bow shape the other bankside. I think that's where I saw Henry when I was a kid. I look over to the left to a clump of trees. I remember one of those tall Laburnum trees – the one that have the yellow flowers. He was digging under a Laburnum. But when I get to the clump now, I don't see any such tree or yellow flowers.

It was bare ground here in '98. Now it's all overgrown. I look around the area. Can't think what to do. Maybe it wasn't this spot at all and the tree is further down the river. I look down the bankside but can't see any.

Then I notice that a once-lofty pine tree has fallen, a little further down the river. I go to it. It hangs across the forest floor, a 50-foot carcass. And, during it's fall, it's taken down other trees. I flatten down the weeds and study the pine's victims. There is one thick-boughed tree I can't discern the type of, which obviously isn't a *Laburnum*. I do find another one, with smaller branches. It's decimated by years of weather and ivy growth.

I go to the bottom of the trunk. It hangs a yard off the ground, poised from its original stump. Underneath it the ground is thronged with nettles and weeds. I should have brought my Mum's gardening gloves too. But I take my top off, use it to protect my hands from more blooming stings. And rip the growth out under the trunk.

Then I dig with the trowel. Roots, stones, parts of brick, worms; I wasn't wise in my equipment selection. But I hack and churn at the ground, sitting on the floor in the rain, my pants sodden through my jeans, hair smeared across my face. Until I reach a different texture. I see a familiar fluorescent logo in the growing light. *Reebok*, '90s style. That's Henry's bag.

I dig around it and lift the thing up. It's so crumpled and worn by dampness that the zipping comes away in my hands as I open it.

Inside, are plastic bags, tied around a square object with string. I undo the string. Unravel the bags. Under three layers of bags is a Tupperware box. I open it. Now there's a cloth tied around a cuboid object.

"Pass the parcel, pass the parcel … But here we go; there it is."

Classic vintage VHS cassette tape. Black and unmarked. I was right, but I was lucky I had that memory from 1998 too. It's cold to the touch. Of course it is – it's been in the ground for two decades. Does it still work? That's the key question. It's still raining hard, so I put the tape in my bag.

Should I put the soil back into the hole? The ripped weeds are all scattered about the area. It's obvious somebody's been searching here. I can't hide my tracks. But, even if Alec and Filippo come out to find what I've been up to, and find a hole undug – what're they going to do? Tell everybody that I've found Henry's VHS tape? His secret weapon?

I need to get free from the Woods whilst it's still early. There's an old VHS player back home in the attic, and an old school TV as well – that's the next step.

CHAPTER THIRTY-SEVEN

THE ATTIC

I successfully sneak back into the garden and the back door without waking Mum up. I have to wait four hours until Mum goes to work. If she sees me going into the attic, she'll want to know what's up. When she finally heads out the house, I instantly head upstairs. I carry one of the kitchen chairs up with me.

Of all the climbing I've done in the last few weeks, this is the most difficult task yet. I'm a short woman, and I can't even reach the door which you have to push up and over the hole in the ceiling. I use a wooden spoon to do that: and then I jump up to the ledge, clutching with my hands. I manage to pull myself up.

I'm met with a sleepy smell of dust and history. I turn the light on – the bare bulb winces my eyes. Strewn all around the floor are bin bags with all kinds of things in them. There's one bag filled with Halloween costumes my Mum used to make me; black capes, witches' hats, hockey masks, plastic knives.

I find my old stash of *Pokémon* cards, too. I begin to look through them – all the old characters coming back to me. It's a terrific collection. I used to be so proud of it when I was a girl. They're antiques, now – could probably sell them on the internet. The bastard teachers at our school banned *Pokémon* cards when the craze was at its height.

I go on and step on something in one of the bags. Suddenly this jingly music fills the attic. A little toy-box melody; it's so sad and pretty, and I pause, listening to it. I open the bag and it's filled with my toys I had as a baby. The music comes from this plastic phone with rainbow buttons where each button plays a different tune.

Can't believe it still works. I'm thrown into nostalgia. I feel old. Feel the loss of childhood. There are all my other old toys too. It's strange how memory works like that – how they would've been precious to me when I was a kid, and I haven't thought about them in so long, but their magic returns to me through a little melody. I can see why my Mum didn't have the heart to chuck these things away.

"But, calm down, Dolina," I put the toy back, "You're 25 now. Childhood's gone. Get back to the mission."

By the end of the attic lie the TV and the VHS player. Complete with wiry antennae, a moon-grey screen and jagged plastic. It's amazing how bulky technology used to be. I pick the TV up first – god, it's heavy – and lug it over to the trapdoor, then the VHS player.

With some effort I get the apparatus down from the attic and take it all down to the kitchen. Henry's secret weapon videotape is lying on the table.

I put the TV and player up on the kitchen desk near the mains. I blow the dust away, wipe the screen. When I turn the TV on I'd forgotten it makes this gnarly hissing sound when it's not connected to a channel, flashing grey and white dots. But it still works. I connect the VHS wires into the audio/visual sockets and it still works as well.

Breathing deeply, I put Henry's tape into the player. It works too! I sit down to watch. The visuals are in black and white. I quickly gather that it's showing CCTV footage. At first, all I can see are two walls of a building's corner, and a cement floor. There is a date at the top of the screen, which is: 06 / 07 / 98.

I keep watching for minutes, and nothing happens – the view is exactly the same. I fast forward the tape, and after it wizzes by with nothing, two dark shapes suddenly flash into view. I rewind, and watch.

The dark shapes are two people. One of them is a boy who leans against the wall. He's wearing a hoody. When takes it off and I see Henry's face in ghostly shades.

My palms turn cold when I see who the other person is. Alec Walker. He's standing over Henry by the wall, close to him.

They are just talking. By their body language, Henry seems relaxed, not giving eye contact, whilst Alec is very serious and direct. This goes on for minutes. Then Henry does this dance move with his arms – he spreads them out and circles them around, now looking directly into Alec's face.

Alec *springs* at him and I clap my hands to my mouth. Alec's holding Henry by the neck against the wall with both hands, his face right in Henry's like he's kissing him. He's holding his body *up* and I can see Henry's shoes swaying off the floor.

Blood's thumping in my temples as I watch Henry being suffocated. Henry lifts his hand up and pushes Alec's face away. Alec releases him and Henry falls onto the floor choking. Alec says something else to him, then walks out of the frame down one of the corner walls.

Henry sits back up against the wall and puts his head in his hands.

I can see why this is his secret weapon. But *where* are they? Where is this filmed? The date is the same day that Henry came back to Edinburgh, the 6th of July. From the light on the screen it looks like day-time. Henry somehow caught CCTV footage of Alec attacking him, and I'm guessing that he provoked Alec with the dance move, so Alec would do that. But how did he get the tape?

I saw him on the 6th in the evening – after he'd had the fall-out with Linda and went to live in the Woods. So when he went to his Mother's later that day, he showed her he had the tape as a weapon against Alec.

Back on the screen, Henry stands up, and slowly disappears the other corner of the wall. I watch the tape until it ends and nothing else happens. My hands are still icily cold. Mr Walker attacked Henry *again*, after the nose bleed? Why? I assume because of the money? Was Henry late for another payment? But Linda said that Henry had lots of cash money with him that day. And presumably he'd gotten the money specifically to pay the Walkers.

Henry robbed the money from out west? I'm still surprised that Henry did that. How would *Henry* rob anybody – the small goofy kid? But then I still don't know exactly what happened on his trip, so will need to find out. And also, how he provoked Alec again to attack him. This happened on the 6th July and Henry went missing on the 12th. So what happened in between those six days?

I'd been elated to find the videotape and to get it working again. Now, I'm even more terrified of my oldest neighbour who lives across the street. I need to talk to somebody about this, now. I'm too afraid to process it all on my own.

It's near lunchtime – and Tommy might be on his break from work in Glasgow, so I give him a call.

CHAPTER THIRTY-EIGHT

TOMMY THE SAGE

"Dolina, what's up?" He says. I'm glad to hear his voice.

"Tommy, my friend. Have you got a spare amount of time to talk?"

"I do, Dolina. You sound ... energetic?"

"I am."

"I'm guessing you have something to tell me?"

"Yes, but it might take a while so I don't want to spoil your lunch break."

"No, I like to hear you. Tell me what's up."

I gush the story out, everything since I last saw him. About my meeting with Jim and Linda, and that Henry owed money to the Walkers. Then I go on to the VHS tape. And I tell him how I found it, what I saw. And recant how Alec and Filippo came to my house last night. I'd expected him to react at this bit. But he doesn't.

I really should tell Tommy about the incident with the stranger who attacked me. But I don't think it's right at the moment. I'm trying to leave that block out. I'm hoping that Tommy's calculations won't be based on that one incident. Plus, I'm ashamed that I went against our vow to not go back into the Woods again soon.

"Are you still there, Tommy?"

"I am. Well this is all very helpful for the case. But it's still scary, and it's not looking good for Henry."

"Which part?"

"Well, with the tape. With Alec Walker."

"Go on?"

"Why would Henry bury the tape in the Woods?"

"Because he wanted to hide it from them in the meantime."

"But Henry set the camera recording up – don't you see that? If he'd gotten what he wanted, why would he postpone it by hiding it in the Woods?"

"I don't understand, Tommy. How Henry did all that. I don't even know where the recording takes place. Where are they?"

"It's outside the Hospital, Dolina. From what you described in the video, they're behind the *Fence*. The two corners of Jim's janitor office are what you saw on the CCTV. I thought you knew that too."

"Wow. Of course! You're right!"

Jim's little office building lies behind the Fence. We always saw it from the football field and I remember seeing a camera on the corner of the roof as well. I feel stupid for not realising where the CCTV footage was, when I'm familiar with that area so well.

A memory whacks me. That day I saw Henry tease Alec with the money payment through the hole in the Woods' wall. The day I finished school for summer holidays. After that, Filippo and Alec went up to the *Fence* by the Hospital. Jim must have let them in.

"That's right." I say. "Alec and Filippo were going behind the *Fence* around that time to meet with Henry and Jim. I remember seeing them go in there."

"Yeah? Well, now it's proven on tape. And, so, that day on the 6th, Henry planned the 'secret weapon' videotape with Jim. Jim knew that the CCTV camera was outside his little office on the corner. Jim was the janitor of the entire Hospital and could monitor the camera footage. And Henry knew that he could annoy Alec to the point that Alec would attack him. Jim wanted to help Henry. It's most likely that Henry came up with the whole idea. But it's definite that Henry got that VHS tape from Jim."

"Tommy, you're like a sage, you're so good at this stuff."

"Ha, thanks. But, something's bothering me. Why didn't Jim tell you about that – any of this, when you spoke to him?"

This is suspicious, I agree.

"Yeah, that is a bit odd. Maybe he just wanted to help Henry, and was getting desperate? He *did* tell me that Henry was in danger from the Walkers. And he seemed to hate Alec as well."

"But he didn't tell you anything about when Henry came back in that final week?"

"Hmm. No, he didn't. But I believe Jim cared about Henry. And he was really drunk when I spoke to him – maybe he just missed stuff out because of that."

"I agree, but Jim's version of that last week should be the next step: you should try and speak to him today."

"Yes. But, crap – I forgot to even take his number. Stupid. I can't exactly crawl through the *Fence* trapdoor again …"

"But you have his address, right? You still got it?"

I go get the bit of paper Jim gave me and read the address out to Tommy.

"Hang on two seconds, Dolina." I hear him tapping on his keyboard. Four minutes later there's a ding on my phone. "Okay, so I found out his landline number. Couldn't see anything for mobile. I sent you a message."

"You're the best, Tommy – how'd you even do that?"

"It's easy to find people with an address and name."

"Thank you. So that's Jim's landline. He'll be at work today so I'll need to wait until tonight to call. You think he gets drunk every night? What if it'd be better to talk to him sober?"

"It might be vice-versa – better when drunk. But anyway, Jim seems the best person for the next option. I think another version of Henry's last week is important – from somebody on Henry's side."

"Thanks for all this, Tommy."

"Any time."

"But, just one more thing. About Filippo and Alec coming to my house: what do you think is up with that?"

"Well. Yes that shows they've got a strong issue with this. And I don't think you should go back to the *Game*, maybe *never*, Dolina. Okay?"

"Hmm. I thought you meant just postpone going back?"

"I think we should rely on informational clues for now. Don't head back into the Woods."

"It's our Woods Tommy. I'm not being intimidated into not going there."

"I think if we have reasonable logic and collect it all. And if we find something that suggests Henry got hurt by the Walkers, we should just take it to the police."

"Okay. But we already do have evidence. I've got a tape of Alec attacking Henry."

"Of course, good point. But leave it until tonight. And call Jim and see what he says."

"Fantastic."

We say bye. Now I've got the whole day to think about the phone call with Jim. I don't last until night or even late afternoon; I try several times but he's not at home. Just have to wait.

CHAPTER THIRTY-NINE

THE GRUFF JIM

The issue of *evidence* came up earlier. If we have evidence that something dark happened to Henry, the police will welcome it. I decide to call Jim on speaker phone on my next try, and record the call on my laptop. This feels a bit unpleasant, because I still trust Jim, and I'm not going to let on that I'm recording him. It's just that if I could document what he says, it could be a key moment.

At 7 o'clock Jim picks his phone up.

"Hello?"

"Hi, Jim? It's Dolina here."

"Oh, Dolina. How are you?"

"Umm, I'm good, thanks. I just wondered if you had some spare time to t –"

"I just got home from the Hospital, Dolina, and haven't had dinner yet – okay if you called me back in an hour?"

"Okay, perfect. See y–"

He hangs up. By the time it gets to 8 o'clock I'm a bit afraid of him. I call, and press record.

"Dolina," he picks up, "How are you?"

"I'm good – yourself?"

"Not bad. What'd you want to talk about?"

"Well, it's about Henry again. Is it okay to ask a few questions about him? Or would you rather we spoke another time?"

"No, ask away."

"Okay. Well, do you have any memories of Henry during his last week at home? You said he went away for a week out West, and then he came back?"

"Yeah. He'd stolen a bunch of money. It was from *Glasgow* – not 'out West'. Where else would he get money like that?"

"How'd you know it was Glasgow? And that it was a theft?"

"Henry told me."

"But, who did he steal from?"

"He wouldn't tell me who."

It's obvious that Jim is *not* drunk. He's the gruff, curt talker I remember from youth. And he sounds angry.

"Well, I heard, that … When he came home from Glasgow, he had a limp, and that he fell out with L–"

"So you spoke to Linda, then?" Jim breaks in. "I asked you not to do that."

"I did speak to Linda, yes. She's Henry's mother, of course I needed to speak to her."

I hear his nostrils puffing.

"Well, what did she say to you then?"

"That Henry and her had a big fall out when he came home and she kicked him out the house."

"Yeah. Henry was delirious. He was acting like crazy. He robbed some people in Glasgow and they roughed his leg up. But he managed to get away."

"But why did Henry come back home at all?"

"I don't know. Because he was homeless."

"Well, I remember people looking for him. June was looking for him. I remember *you* asking me if I'd seen Henry. Nobody knew where he was."

"This was in *1998*, Dolina – I don't remember that. I was high on skag all the time. How can I be of help to you?"

He's breathing fast and hard into the phone.

"But Linda said that she asked you to go get Henry back from the Woods … It was the night before the World Cup final, right?"

"I found out he was in the Woods eventually yes. But honestly, my memory from then is nothing reliable."

"But Linda definitely –"

"Dolina!" He shouts my name, and the volume pangs my body. There are seconds of silence, then Jim sighs. "I'm sorry. But please, don't say her name. I can't bare it. But I know you're trying to help Henry. Just hear me out:

"When Henry came back home, he was drinking and smoking like mayhem. He was jabbering incessantly, twitching, jumping about. He wasn't making any sense, and he'd repeat the same sentences over and over.

"That's what freaked his Mother. She was wrong to kick him out. She was furious with him that he'd left for seven days and then when he came home he was smiley and mad. She couldn't handle Henry, and flipped out. She cried when he left with his bags. But I couldn't handle him either. I kept trying to ask him what he was up to. What was he *doing*? I tried to get him to sober up and explain thing – but what kind of sponsor was I?

"Henry constantly repeated the same two things. That his 'deadline' was on the Sunday. And that he needed to complete *Filippo's Game*."

"The 'deadline'? You mean he had to complete *Filippo's Game* by then?"

"No, it was the deadline he had to finally pay back the Walkers."

I look at the recording on my laptop screen, watching how the decibels flicker on the volume receiver. This is good evidence.

"Well, Jim, that means Henry went missing on the same day as the payback deadline."

Jim does not say anything.

"Okay. And what about the *Game*? What was he saying about it?"

"He kept going '*Electricity Box*! *Electricity Box*!' He had to get the *Game* done quick! 'I need to complete it, Jim. I have to get there.' He was just manic. I couldn't help him."

"*Electricity Box* is one of the LEVELS of the *Game*."

"I know it is."

"So did he ever get there and do LEVEL 7?"

"I don't know. The memories are so small. I can't help you much with that period. I don't even remember the World Cup game. I don't even remember the moment I realised Henry was missing. Then it all turned dark. Those were ugly times, Dolina."

"Yes I remember all that too."

We're both quiet for a period.

"Thanks for talking to me, Jim."

"Um-hm."

"There's just one more thing I wanted to ask … It's about a VHS tape. Henry was using it as a 'secret weapon' against the Walkers?"

Jim doesn't respond.

"It's a tape of recorded CCTV footage. Know anything about that?"

He's gone silent to the point that I can't hear him breathing.

"Did I say something wrong?" I say.

"Dolina, am I on speaker phone? It sounds like I am."

"Yes, you are."

"Why am I on speaker phone?"

"I'm. Just taking notes because I'm interested in what you're saying."

"Could you turn it off."

"Yes, I will," but I keep the recording on.

"What is this, Dolina? Why are you really talking to me about this?"

"You know why, because I need to find Henry."

"Do you think I'm a *culprit*?"

"A culprit? For what? No, I don't!"

"Then why are you asking me about a videotape?"

"It was just one of my questions. Linda told me –"

"Do not say her name. Jesus, if I'd never met that woman, I wouldn't have been into any of this bother. No, I don't know anything about a videotape. The hell with this. Dolina, I don't want you to call me again. How did you even get my number?"

"I just looked it up, Jim – you gave me your address."

"I don't like this. Don't call me again, or come to my flat. And don't come *anywhere near* the Hospital. I won't let you off again if you cross onto my turf."

"Jim!"

He hangs up.

The decibel levels lean stagnant on the laptop screen. I stop the recording.

What just happened? Did I just lose him as a lead? Why? I thought he was on our side. What made him react like that?

CHAPTER FORTY

JULY 8TH 1998

FILIPPO AND HENRY

I'm at the Bonfire Site where Filippo's Gang have their parties. Tommy's supposed to meet me here, and I'm waiting for him. We've got some matches and newspaper and we collected some sticks. Mum doesn't like us lighting fires, but it'll only be a small one.

It's a great spot for bonfires. There's a circle of branches surrounding a middle bit for the fire, and at the back is a massive old tree that fell down years back. The fire is in the centre and the smoke rises through the hole above in the trees. So it's like a room inside the Woods.

I hear noises behind me and I stand up, thinking it's Tommy. But it's Filippo and Henry, coming through the trees towards me. They haven't seen me yet. I panic, because Filippo knows I'm not allowed to make fires. And he might tell on me. So I grab the matchbox and the newspaper and run toward the fallen tree. I scramble up it and jump the other side.

Did they hear me? The tree trunk is so big they definitely won't be able to see me. I'm hidden in the shade. A minute goes by and their voices come nearer. When I realise that they don't know I'm here, I'm excited to listen in. Henry is talking in a weird, fast way.

"But you know I can do it, Mr Inzaghi. I'm sure I could do it all, so why not?"

"I'm sure you could as well, Henry. But June doesn't want you to."

"June is not the leader, my boy, you are, you're the king. Do you not want me to? June's just miffed about the deadline. The stupid, over the top deadline. I've already said I can make it. Make the deadline, make the deadline by Sunday!"

"Then why don't you do it already, I know you have the money – so just get it back to her."

"Look at where I am? I only have enough money to pay June. Then, I have nothing. So just let me play the *Game*."

"How would that even help anything, Henry?"

"Wouldn't you like me in your Gang, boyo?"

Henry begins singing. He's sings a song from 'The Sound of Music'. I can smell the alcohol and marijuana from him from here. It's obvious he's out his mind. And it's even more strange, the way Filippo's talking to him. Filippo never tries to help Henry understand something. It's like he's genuinely concerned for Henry.

"Henry, hush up for a second, and listen to me. And stop drinking that wine."

"I will postpone my singing, and hear you, my liege, but I will *not* stop drinking my fine wine!"

"Okay, but, I'm a bit worried for you. What happened in Glasgow? Who did that to your leg?"

"I'll never see them again. My leg's fine – it's already healed up."

"Alec and June know what happened in Glasgow."

"So? I got away with it."

"They're scared you might snitch them out, Henry."

"But I'll pay them back on Sunday, no bother. No more cold war needed."

"But it's not a cold war, Henry. I mean, look at you. You're all mucked up on the booze, getting beaten up!"

"I always have gotten beat up! So many times. All my life. Don't you think that's why I drink so much? Because I'm the one that always gets beaten up." Henry's voice snaps shut.

I hear him scratching a lighter into flame and then the smell of marijuana sails over to me.

"It's always, attack, attack with people." Henry's quiet, now. "Why do you think I got into all this mess in the first place? So I could help my Mother out. Now my Mother tosses me out her house, hurls me out the nest to splat on the floor. How'd you think that feels, Filippo?

"Christ – I'm just asking you – *you* specifically, John, to protect me a little bit. If you let me join your Gang, nobody will be able to touch me anymore. I just need a little bit more money before I can pay June the whole thing. But I can do that by dealing the next few days."

"Have you got new stuff to sell right now?"

"Not now, but I will by tonight. Promise. Just believe in me, Johnny boy."

I hear Filippo sigh, but it's a happy sigh.

"Okay, I trust you. But you promise to have it all there for June by Sunday? You can even give it to me before, if you like, and I'll get it over to June."

"Okay, but what about that other thing, friend? Will you let me join your illustrious Gang? You can banish me later, if you like – but just for a few months. I've been dying to play *Electricity Box* for so long."

"Sure, Henry. The *Box* is my favourite one. Meet me tomorrow at the hole in the wall."

"*The hills are alive, with the sound of music*!"

I can hear Henry running around. He breaks into other random Musical songs in his celebration. Filippo laughs.

"But, Henry, about the booze. Maybe clear it up for tomorrow? LEVEL 7 can get a bit intense."

"It sounds spectacular, my dear."

"Seriously, *Electricity Box* shouldn't be played drunk."

"Okay, Inzaghi. What time?"

"Noon."

"Henry, listen. When it comes to June, and Alec. They're my friends, but. They don't like you, Henry."

"I'm perfectly aware of this. Not everyone has to like me."

"I'll tell them your plan. I'll put a word in for you."

I hear them clapping each other's backs in a hug. That's weird too. Filippo is never this friendly to Henry.

"So, you want some wine to celebrate, Filippo?"

"Jesus, Henry. Why don't you just throw it away?"

"I'll stick to the one bottle for the rest of the day, king."

Their voices fade away. They're leaving the Bonfire Site.

As they spoke, I noticed this bit of stone in the shade of the trees, lying close to me. It looks like a chimney – like an orange chimney cone lying in the leaves, but I've no idea why it's here. There are no houses near here, and it looks too modern to be part of the old school or mill.

But anyway, I wait until Filippo and Henry have completely gone. Then I climb over the fallen tree and go back to the fireplace to wait for Tommy.

I enjoyed listening to Filippo and Henry, but I wish I understood what they were talking about. What did he mean by *Electricity Box*? I didn't get it. And why were they talking about June? I thought June totally hated Henry and she never goes near him.

Who knows? I'm still waiting for Tommy after so long. Has he forgotten again to come play? I could go back to his house. But I'd rather just start the fire myself. So I lay it all out, scrunch the newspaper into balls, then put the sticks on. I light it. The woodsmoke waters my eyes and fills my nose, and I like it.

CHAPTER FORTY-ONE

MAY 2018

ELECTRICITY BOX

I barely sleep the night following the call with Jim. I doze in an out of disturbing dreams. I keep thinking about what the call means. It's 2 a.m. now, and I have nothing to do but brood about it in my room. I could wait until tomorrow afternoon to call Tommy about it. But I ultimately just want to be alone.

Alone, not just with the case, but with the whole thing of *Filippo's Game* and the Woods. I've already decided to head out at dawn and complete *Electricity Box*, LEVEL 7. So it's good I'm already up early.

Filippo's Game ... It seems like such a long time since we completed *Fox Dens*. Whilst I agreed with Tommy that returning to the *Game* will be dangerous and we shouldn't do it, I knew that I'd probably break the promise.

I just might be the last person to ever play the *Game*. The final contender. I *must* complete it for Henry's sake, but for my sake too. It's something I need to conquer within my relationship with the Woods. Before I found Filippo's treehouse last month, I thought I was an omniscient guardian of the Woods. But, whilst I am a guardian, I'm not omniscient just yet.

I do not desire to be in Filippo's Gang. Of course, it's in my competitive nature to want to win. But it's more than that. The *Game* means something different now than it did in the 1990s. Winning the *Game* will be a way to divide myself between Filippo's generation and mine, whilst conquering the transition into adulthood and blessing childhood with victory.

It's raining more heavily than yesterday. I wait until faint light comes in the east and then sneak out the house. I take the route out my back garden onto the main road, as to avoid Alec Walker's possible viewing. But the route to the *Electricity*

Box is by the bottom of the long road which runs down our street, so I need to cut back homeward anyway.

I get to the point in the wall where there used to be that hole, and you could peek through and see the *Box*. The council built the wall up years ago – but you can still see where the boulders are lighter than the older parts. I climb up the wall at that part, and indeed, there's the little cuboid of electricity hanging under the trees, not far from the road. I jump into the Woods.

I head through the leaky leaves and the ripe scent of soil. The *Box* is just as foreboding as I remember it in childhood. I know I won't be able to climb the three-meter steel fence, with spikes on the top of each pole. The yellow signs with the black stick-man being struck with a thunder-bolt would make anyone uneasy.

Am I really supposed to go inside this area? There is one enormous padlock on its gate. Do I have to find another key to unlock it? I start to search the area for signs. It's too dim to see much. The sun hasn't yet taken the sky, and it's hot too despite the rain. I scour the place for half an hour. But there's nothing except the *Box* and its impenetrable fence.

I sit by the side in the trees, where the branches give me respite from the rain. I gaze up at the canopy, to see which types of trees are flowering or changing … Then I notice something unnatural on one of the branches. I stand up and go closer to it. It's a coil of rope, wrapped around the branch, and the branch hangs over into the *Electricity Box*.

I'll need to climb up the tree. It's a birch, a very tall one. So tall its first branches are a meter above my head height. I monkey crawl up the trunk until I get to the first branches and keep going until I reach the branch overhanging the *Box*. It's another good distance off the floor from here, but the bough is long and thick and will hold my weight – so I edge across it.

I journey over the metal spikes below, then find that the rope is directly above the *Box*. I uncoil the rope, and it droops down to the rooftop, plus it has knots tied into it so one can climb down, which I do. I lower into this lethal square. My wellies clang onto the *Box's* roof. Ignoring the spikes and the DANGER signs, I notice a little container on top of the roof.

It looks like a recycling box, except it's much smaller and is sealed. Moss grows on its top. When I open it, the inside is completely dry, and there are two pieces of card. One says:

HEAD TO THE BONFIRE SITE: FIND THE CHIMNEY

GO THROUGH THE TARZAN CIRCUIT TO GET THERE

The other card is a map, of the Woods – it has the same outline of the Woods as the map Robin gave me. Except it's drawn differently. There are no pictures of the locations except the *Electricity Box* and the Bonfire Site. There are little pink circles in a zig-zag line leading over from here to the Bonfire Site. Intriguing. I return to the other card and I notice smaller text under the main directions:

Look to the right of where you are. This is your first Tarzan.
Hook it to the oak bough nearest to you. Swing, and you'll
see the next tree.

I still don't quite get what to do. But I look over to the right, down by the side of the *Box*. In the wet shadows I find another container like the one on the roof but bigger. I find a stack of bricks piled up against the wall of the *Box*, so I can climb down to it. As I climb down, a stick-man's being electrocuted right in my face, and my hands tremble. But I'm outside the *Box's* walls so I hope it'll be fine.

In this new box is another coiled rope, coiled around a long plank of wood, with a loop tied in the rope at the far end. It's a ready made Tarzan swing, dry and in good condition.

"Ahh, I think I see it now!" and I climb back up the bricks onto the roof. I look at the map and the first pink circle is poised to the left, close to the *Box*. There's an oak tree in the same place as I look and I find a bough which overhangs the *Box* too. "So you have to make a Tarzan on this bough!"

This bough is taller than the birch's above me, and I can't throw the rope up to it from here. But I could, if I climb back up the birch rope. So I do, taking the coiled Tarzan with me.

I used to make swings with Tommy all the time when we were little. You judge the length of the rope, the distance between the branch and where you are, and you throw the loop up first up over the branch. Then when it comes back down, you put the wooden saddle through the loop the other side. Then hoist the rope up to the top to tighten the hold.

The distance between the oak and birch branches are so perfect that I do this on the first try. And I'm assuming that Filippo cut the rope to an exact angle as to make the rope swingable to the 'next tree'.

Day has arrived within the Woods and myself, now, in a swirly light embalming the trees. I take the map with me and swing out on the Tarzan. It dips down and charges into a gulf of air where land dips away. The rope goes in a huge arch so that I flume up into a treeless stretch.

"Woah."

The arch surprised me so much I didn't take anything in, and I reach the top and let myself be sailed back to the original birch bough, panting. This is fun. I jump out again.

This time when I reach the arch's pivot, I notice something draped against one of the other trees – something *pink*. But I just can't get close enough to see it before my body's taken back by the swing. I jump out this time with all my weight and gusto, and when I get closer to the tree I grab out to the nearest branch and catch it, suspended in the air. I pull myself off the rope and climb onto this new tree.

The Tarzan drops away from me back to the *Box*. I sit on this bough, take some breath in, then go examine what this pink thing is on the branch above me. I find two bits of large pink cellophane sheets, wrapped around another coiled rope and saddle. I take the rope out from under the cellophane and drop the rope down. Then I look at the map.

And so I'm at the next pink circle. The zig-zag circles follow from here and go north-east towards the Bonfire Site. Filippo made a Tarzan course across the Woods? All built throughout the trees? And if you go through them, you get to the Bonfire Site.

I go down to the rope I've just uncoiled. And there's a convenient branch under me to propel myself from. As I swing across the air I see another glimmer of cellophane tied to a branch and catch onto it, climb up. Uncoil the new rope and saddle. Before I swing the next Tarzan, I again study the map. I'm definitely at the next pink circle of the zig-zag line.

I'm high up, and I can see wondrous areas of the Woods from these parts, like a living map itself throbbing under me. I can just see the river from here, and so I continue with the LEVEL.

The Tarzans are so perfectly made. Even after two decades, where the trees have naturally been modified by age, the circuit works so well, and it's easy to swing across to the next tree: there's always a sturdy branch to launch yourself off from and another to latch on to.

I swing until I come to the river. From this tree I can't see any more cellophane. I try several flights, but can't see anything, nor can judge where the new pink circle is.

I swing out and up and hop onto the boughs on the next tree, a fantastic horse chestnut which I always adored as a child. I've never even thought about climbing it, it was always too gigantic and the grandest tree which overhangs the river. I'm proud to be up here. But what about the next pink circle? I look at the map, and look at the Woods to the east.

From here I can just see *Filippo's Tarzan* – which of course is LEVEL 1, which starts the entire game. The Bonfire Site is only a short walk from there. And I'd thought the Tarzan course would lead that way. But it goes around another way in a detour. I see that the new circle is located ahead of where I am, but all I can see is air. Perhaps if I climb I might see more? I notice that this circle is red and not pink. Maybe because it's the final one?

I rise and rise above the river. It's amazing to think how many times I've walked the path below me, and never knew there was a secret Tarzan network above me. I get into the upper branches of the tree, and look out, following the map's hints. "Yes – there it is!" I see cellophane wrapped on the tree the other side of the river. There is no Tarzan under me, but I can climb across to it because the horse chestnut branches arch over to it. Beautiful. I shimmy across and reach the next bit and uncoil the rope.

It's not until I'm swinging out that I realise how high up in the air I actually am. There are thick clumps of holly bushes far, far below me. I've gone up an extra fifteen feet without realising it. But the next Tarzan is easy. And, though this up high, I get to the next bough without bother. Plus, I can see a different angle of where the Bonfire Site is.

I climb down to the bough below me. I straighten the saddle, and I see another tree directly ahead. That must be where to go. Once more unto the breach, dear friends. I head out.

The rope lurches down immediately and I feel a thud in my palms through the nylon. Then the rope snaps off the branch above me.

I fall. I'm falling, still holding onto the saddle as if it's going to save me. The shapes of trees whizz through my vision. Don't land on your head, Dolina. The holly leaves cut my limbs. I flap my arms out. Don't land on your wrists, Dolina.

WHAT'S UP?

Mum didn't notice the woodsmoke smell on me the other day after our bonfire. I know she doesn't like me doing that, but I don't see why. She has bonfires often in the garden when her girlfriends come around to party at weekends. So why can't I do it in the Woods?

That was a great fire I made the other day too, and I can tell Tommy was jealous I did it so well. He turned up late and it was all roaring. I love lighting fires. And I want to make another one today. I still have matches from last time, and I nicked some new newspapers from home. I go into the Woods with them, and head to the Bonfire Site.

It's in the morning and Mum usually doesn't get up until lunch time because she's tired from work. So if I can light the fire fast and get it done, then change clothes when I get home, she won't know a thing.

I jump across the river fast. I go past the giant hogweed plants with the scary stalks. Mum said they're poisonous to the touch – the stalks are bristly and their leaves flap over your head. But it's the only way to the Bonfire Site. I spot the shoe prints of Filippo's Gang in the mud and follow them. I'm nearly there, when I suddenly hear a noise.

I freeze. It's a sad sound. Somebody's crying. It's coming from the Site. I come out of the hogweed stalks and come to the circle where the fire is. Henry's sitting there beside the cold fireplace. He's sobbing, loud. I can't see his face. His green hood's over his head, head in his hands. Bags and wine bottles are lying all about him.

"Henry?"

He shoots up from the floor and spins around to me blinking. His face is puffy and it looks like he's been crying for hours.

"Little Dolina. What's up?"

"Are you okay?"

"I'm terrific. What's up?"

"Are you sad about something?"

"No … Just drunk and stupid. I'm good."

He's embarrassed that I caught him crying. But I don't want him to be. I'm sad to see him upset. He drinks his wine. Then turns around and rubs his eyes so I can't see him. Then with his back turned, he says:

"So how was your trip out to Crail, my friend?"

"It was fun, yeah."

He coughs and holds his throat. Drinks more.

"You sure you're not sad about something?"

He turns around with his huge grin. His face is red but the smile still makes me want to smile too.

"No, little one, I'm good," he looks down at what I'm carrying. And I only just realise I've got the matches and newspaper in my hands. Henry's smile widens: "Uh oh, Dolina! You came here to light a fire, didn't you?"

I go purple in the face and laugh nervously.

"Yes."

"Ha ha! You minx! Got a pyromaniac here, have we! Was that you that lit a fire the other day as well? I saw smoke coming from here and I knew there was no party on or anything, so wondered who it was."

"Yeah, that was me, I'm sorry."

"It's all right, Dolina. I just don't want you to hurt yourself. I'm good at fires too. We can make one together and I can show you how to be safe. You got any sticks for your fire? You want me to help?"

We go about collecting sticks from the ground and the trees. Henry's fast and he picks much better sticks than I do. And he sits next to me by the fireplace and shows me his way of making the newspaper bunches. He tells me how to light the bunches in a square-pattern which gives the flames the power to light the whole fire. I really like Henry, showing me all this. And gives me his lighter to do it that way – and we watch the fire spark. His face has cleared up and his eyes aren't shiny anymore.

He still drinks from the bottle, like he's attacking it with his mouth. Every thirty seconds he drinks. And he keeps checking his watch too.

"So that's a great start, Dolina," he says, and stands up. "So just keep adding your sticks in. I'm sure you know what to do to keep it going. For now, I've got to go."

"You're going home?"

"Yeah. But I'll see you soon?"

"Be safe with the fire, though, Dolina."

He moves off into the hogweed. The poisonous leaves and the stocks whack against his face and hands, and he doesn't care.

CHAPTER FORTY-THREE

MAY 2018

THE CHIMNEY

I wake up with a giant heave of air.

It's white and wet wherever I look and feel. The blood's in the back of my head and I'm lying with my feet in the air, on a bed of something sharp and spiky. I try to stand up and the sharpness goes up to my waist.

I'm lying in a bed of holly bushes. I stand up and see the river over the top of the bushes dizzily. I trudge out of the holly and get to the river.

Okay, so I'm in the Woods. But I don't remember how I got here. What just happened? It's day time and the birdsong clangour is maddening. When I check my phone it's around 5 a.m. I look up in the trees above the holly bushes … There's a bit of rope dangling from a branch, cut off at the top. Then I remember. Jesus. I fell.

Did I get knocked out? Wow, this is bad. I sit down by the river. My body seems fine; nothing's physically hurt. How long was I out for? Did I hit my head? I've never been knocked out before. Mum won't be up for work yet and has no idea I'm here.

I take the *Electricity Box* map out my pocket and work out where I got to. That was the Tarzan that snapped above me. I find its circle: and I realise why the circle is coloured in red when all the others are pink. This is no accident.

"Wow … It was designed that way. The last Tarzan was designed to snap."

I must've fallen about 30 feet. Thank God the holly bushes were there. The *Tarzans* were so fun to do that I didn't recognise the warning clue on the map. The red circle meant the Tarzan was a dummy. I missed yet another warning in *Filippo's*

Game. But this time I'm not angry with the *Game*, or myself for not playing it well. I'm just disillusioned with all this.

Disillusioned for the first real time. Why am I falling out of trees and getting knocked out? I look at the other card I got back at the *Box*: 'Head to the Bonfire Site: Find the chimney'. Chimney – that sounds familiar. I'm closer to the Bonfire Site where I am now than when I was up in the trees. The hell with the *Game*, why don't I just walk there?

I head down the river and through the hogweed plants and come out into the circular bit. The old patch where the Gang used to light fires is swamped by greenery now. It all seems smaller than I remember it. You wouldn't imagine a horde of teenagers partying here nowadays. I pass their old glass bottles underfoot, and even come to the boulders which were set around the fireplace, all overtaken by moss and ivy now.

Chimney … Chimney. I have a shred of memory about something like that. Only it wouldn't have been within the Site's open circle, else I would've remembered it better. That massive fallen tree which acted as the back of the Site is still there. I go over.

The weeds have overtaken the tree too, as if it's just a continuation of soil. I jump up onto it and study behind it. Just a dark bed of dry leaves. I step down, misjudging how deep the leaves are, and sink in up to my kneecaps. I search around with my feet, feeling around. Until I tap something hard. When I pull the leaves away, I find it. The orange chimney.

I don't know how I remembered it was here, and have no clue how it ever got here. I go to lift it up, expecting it'll be heavy. But it's nothing weight wise, and it's not a complete cone-shape. Half of it is missing underneath, so it just looks like a full, heavy thing placed this way.

Underneath it is a long wine bottle, corked at the top. It's been protected well from the weather by the chimney. When I look inside there are small sheets of paper, folded in half. It's their names. The Gang's. Filippo is there, June. I unfold all of them. Henry Fowles is in there too.

I put the papers into the bottle, the chimney back over it. I'm not going to be adding my name to the bottle. I can't pretend to have passed LEVEL 7. I almost don't want to be part of the *Game* anymore.

I head home. I just go the quick way. Alec Walker can see me walk past his house if he likes. I don't care. I lie in my bed and text my boss at work:

Hi Claire: I got knocked out last night and at the hospital the doctors told me I shouldn't work for the next few days. Looks like I can't come in this weekend. Sorry about that. I will give you a call ahead of next weekend.

Which is basically true in a way. I can't go back to that damn place again anyway, so this is a convenient excuse. What are you supposed to do after you get knocked out? I really should just rest for a while. And, of course, Tommy Hepburn was right. I shouldn't have gone back to *Filippo's Game*. I was doing it too fast, rushing the process when I knew it was dangerous, that it shouldn't be underestimated. It's a *twisted* game.

I try to sleep, but I can't. I'm too sad, sad for Henry Fowles. I lie for hours without noticing time, until I hear Mum get up for work. I head down to the kitchen and put the kettle on. She comes down after me.

"You're up early, Dolina," she says, "everything okay?"

"Yeah, I'm good. Cup of tea?"

"Please."

I sit at the table. I feel ill, wiped. Haven't slept well for weeks I realise.

"Mum, this might sound a bit random. But do you ever think about Henry Fowles?"

"I often think about him, yes. Why'd you ask that?"

"No reason … I was just passing his old house the other day. It's like something out of a horror film now, with the big abandoned house. You think that's why nobody ever bought it again after Linda left? Because of Henry?"

"It could be, yes. It was just shocking how Linda was forced out her home that way. I wonder where she is too sometimes."

Mum sits down at the table with me.

"Do you think Henry's still alive?" I ask her.

"It's too hard to answer. All we can do is guess. Henry didn't have an ugly heart. I remember him when he was little, he was a bit of a toerag, in a cheeky way. But he didn't misbehave that badly. I'm sure the other kids were just as bad."

"How was he a toerag?"

"Hmm … Well he went through a stage of stealing bikes one time. That wasn't good."

"He did?"

"Yeah, there was one summer when he kept riding around the street with a new bike every week. He'd head up to the housing estate and nick them, then dump them in the Woods. I knew what he was up to, so the next time I saw him with a new bike I confronted him. Asked him where he got it. He became all bashful and I got the truth out of him. I made him take the bike back up to the estate. He was ashamed, and he never did it again.

"But he was only nine or ten. You can forgive a kid that age. I don't think he was capable of doing anything worse than that."

"I never knew that. There are a lot of old bike carcasses in the Woods."

"Things like that made the neighbourhood distrust Henry. His mother's condition did as well. People didn't want their kids going up to Linda's house. I knew that Alec didn't like

Henry, even when he was little, and didn't want him hanging around with June. But, to me, Henry was just a nice lad. He was funny and quirky."

"I agree. Do you think we were too mean to him? The other kids? He was so different to all of us, it was easy to be mean to him."

"I think the *world* was mean to him. He was born unlucky. He had a shoddy home life from a young age. I remember another time, actually. When he was even younger – maybe eight – when he was playing with John outside in the street. Just on the road outside this house. I was in the kitchen making food and suddenly I heard a boy crying, so I went outside to check. It was Henry.

"There was a police car hovering on the road. Two policemen. They rolled their windows down and were talking to Henry. 'Where's your Mum?' they kept asking him. The policemen just pulled up and questioned him like he was a thug they were after. A little boy. I would've started crying as well.

"So I quickly realised that the police were alerted because Linda wasn't at home, and Henry was on his own in the house. Which is basically child neglect. But instead of the police taking Henry away, I said I would take him. I took him into the house. I made him dinner and he stayed over. But he was crying for ages, and I sat with him at the table."

"That was very kind of you."

"It was just instinct. I couldn't let a boy be taken off by two policemen who were insensitive enough to approach him like that."

"Well, what happened after? Did Henry just go home the next day?"

"Yes, pretty much. He thanked me a lot at the door. And he went back to his Mum. I never reproached Linda about it. It was awful to neglect him, but I don't know what happened behind the incident either. Did one of the neighbours call the police on her maybe? Or was it child services or something? I couldn't judge her for it. I was just glad I could help Henry out that one night."

"I never ever knew that either, Mum. You were a real hero that day."

"It was a natural maternal impulse."

"You can learn new chapters of another person's history so quickly, just by talking. It's amazing."

"You *can* … But anyway. I should get ready for work."

She heads up stairs. Gets ready. I was almost about to tell her all my secrets of the past weeks and all that I've learned. I wanted to – but I know she'd worry. And it'd spoil her day before she went to work. And it's too long a story for this early in the morning. But she'll probably figure out why I've excessively been going to the Woods, eventually. Maybe mentioning Henry Fowles was a way to start.

When she leaves, I discover how helpful it was to talk to her. Of all the people I've talked to about Henry this far, she was the most empathetic about him. Mirroring my empathy for him, it helped to hear somebody else talk that way. Linda and Jim did, in their own way, but they were far more critical of Henry.

Now that I've embraced my sadness for Henry, I start to return, nicely, to a field of anger. Angry is what I should be and not sad. I was a bit miffed when I failed *Electricity Box* earlier. And it scares me that the *Game* was dangerous enough for me to get knocked out.

But is it really that important? I still found out what I needed. Henry played LEVEL 7 and completed it. The next question is: did he get to LEVEL 8? The final LEVEL of the *Game*?

Also, I have a new attitude towards the *Game* itself. Gone is that petty rivalry and the memories of the laughing kids when I was little. Finding Henry's name scribbled on a piece of paper has made it different. I'm not part of Filippo's kin group, even though he's my cousin. His Gang doesn't even exist anymore. I'm playing the *Game* for Henry, not for Filippo.

I remember that I still have the map from the Tarzan route in my pocket. It's another terrific drawing, my cousin made. Yes, but I see his artwork in a refreshed way now. Filippo was good at drawing, good at this course he built – but does he have a love for the Woods the way I do?

I walk out the kitchen into the garden, taking the map with me, alongside a box of matches from by the cooker. I take the map to the old bonfire cage where Mum has her parties. And set fire to Filippo's Tarzan map. I watch the flames raise the red circle where I fell out the tree.

Matchstick sulphur and burning paper in the summer heat. The best smells. I was despondent the last few hours, but I'm not going to stop with this mission just yet. LEVEL 8 is what's needed next. Before, I'd thought I needed to induct myself into the Woods, through *Filippo's Game*. Now I know I need to *reclaim* the Woods and banish the pretenders.

CHAPTER FORTY-FOUR

JULY 12TH 1998

WORLD CUP FINAL

It's early and I've just picked up some sweets and crisps for Tommy and me from *Spar*. He was too lazy to come to the shops with me. We need some snacks because the World Cup Final is on tonight. I'm going to his to watch it. I just get out of the shop when somebody shouts from behind me.

"Dolina!"

Filippo smiles and he's wearing this white t-shirt which makes his chest bulge.

"Hi, Filippo, how's it going?"

"I'm good. What you up to today?"

"I was just going home to watch the game with Tommy."

"Ah, perfect – I'm watching it too! Should be a good one."

He's holding a CD in his hand.

"Who you think will win?" he says.

"Brazil? Because they have Ronaldo in their team?"

"Maybe, little cousin. But you can't doubt Zinedine Zidane."

It's weird how quickly Filippo saw me after I left *Spar*. He doesn't usually come up to the shops here.

"But anyway, I don't suppose you've seen Henry today?" he says.

"No, don't think so."

"Could you give him this for me if you do?"

He gives me the CD. It has a blue front cover. There's a picture of a baby floating naked underwater. It's a baby boy and I can see his penis. I've never seen a penis before. He's reaching for an American $ note in front of his face.

"This is for Henry?" I say.

"Yeah, well it's already his. He gave me it a while ago and he was asking for it back. Just give it to him, please, if you find him."

"Is he not at home?"

"He isn't sadly. Please, Dolina – if you see Henry give him that? Or if you don't see him try find him? Will you do it?"

"Yes Filippo."

"Okay, enjoy the game. See you around."

He walks away from me without saying anything else. His long hair swishes down his back. He doesn't walk back the short way home with me. Instead he goes back towards *Spar* and down to the main road.

I don't understand. Why's he giving me a CD to give to Henry? Why couldn't he give him the CD himself? I don't mind, it's just I don't get it. The CD is by Nirvana, called 'Nevermind'. Never heard this CD before.

I go down our street under the trees. The bags are heavy with snacks and juice. Why didn't stupid Tommy just come up the road with me? Now I've got to pass on the CD to Henry as well as bring the stuff over to his. Henry. I saw him crying yesterday. But he seemed to cheer up before he left me. When I get to my house, I leave the bag of snacks inside my garden. I have a bit of time before the game starts to find Henry.

I go into the Woods and my first thought is to go to where I saw him build his tent. But when I get to his tent patch, there's nothing there except trampled weeds and no other sign of him. Should I go to the Bonfire Site where I saw him last?

It can't be long until the game starts now, and I don't want to miss it. Maybe I should just give Henry the CD tomorrow? Won't he be watching the game too rather than listening to Nirvana?

Bring! Bring! Bring!

This berserk noise suddenly gives me a fright. I jump at a sound of bells and alarms. It sounds like it's right next to me, but I don't see anything. It's like church bells and alarm clocks joined together, all rattling against my head, but I just don't see anything near me except trees and plants. And it's terrifying. Is it just me? Am I going crazy?

Then the noise stops. The wood pigeons and the blackbirds return. I've no idea what just happened. I'm scared. Maybe I *am* crazy – what on earth was that noise? I should leave.

I get out of the Woods, and I run up the hilly road. I'm sure Henry's CD doesn't matter so much just now. When I get to my garden, I see Tommy: he's just about to ring the doorbell.

"Tommy!"

"Dolina! I thought you were coming over to the house?"

"I *was*, I am!"

His expression changes. He's looking at me strangely.

"Are you all right, Dolina?"

"Yes, just annoyed you got me to bring down all the shopping."

"Dolina, your face is bleeding …"

"Huh?" I wipe my face and my palm has a smudge of blood on it. "Where's it coming from?"

Tommy comes closer to me. He dabs at my forehead with a tissue.

"Well, it's just a little cut. It's not bleeding anymore." he says. "Sorry I didn't come up to the shop with you."

"It's okay. The snack bag is there. Let's go watch the game."

"Did you go into the Woods?"

"Yeah."

"Why?"

"I was looking for Henry?"

"Oh, I saw Henry earlier. He went into the Woods. He was with June."

"June? *June* was hanging out with Henry?"

"Yeah – I thought it was odd too. What's that, by the way?" He points to the CD. "You listening to Nirvana?"

"No. It's nothing. I just … Doesn't matter." I go into the front door and put the CD onto the shoe rack. "Let's go watch the game, Tommy."

We go out the garden onto the road.

"Did you hear the news, Dolina?"

"What news?"

"Ronaldo swallowed his tongue."

"What do you mean? The Brazil player?"

"Yeah – Ronaldo had a seizure."

"How can you swallow your own tongue? Is he still *alive*?"

"Yeah, he's not in trouble or anything."

We go into Tommy's garden, into his house, to his living room. His Dad is on the couch. He gets drunk a lot but I still like him.

"Hey Dolina! How's it going?" he says. "Would you like a Coke or Pepsi?"

"Pepsi please."

I sit next to Tommy on the sofa. On the TV is the warm up coverage to the match. And a news bulletin thing comes in just as Tommy's Dad hands me the Pepsi can, which announces:

RONALDO BACK IN STARTING LINE UP

"Oh!" Tommy's Dad goes.

"He's back in the team?" Tommy goes.

There's a reporter talking into the camera. He's saying that nobody knows yet what happened with Ronaldo. He had a seizure earlier tonight, but it's not serious, and he is included in the team tonight to face France in an hour's time.

Tommy and his Dad start clapping and cheering. They both like Ronaldo and they're glad to see him play. But I'm nervous. Ronaldo had a fit? That's quite bad isn't it? If I had a fit I wouldn't want to play a football game after it. Eventually the game starts, and we're all looking at him – Ronaldo's face – to see how he is.

It must be scary to have the whole world watching you like that.

CHAPTER FORTY-FIVE

JULY 14TH 1998

DOORBELL

I'm in the garden helping Mum with her tomato plants. She's teaching me how to tend the tomatoes. She grows tomatoes from compost bags in her greenhouse. They have this zappy smell only tomatoes have – except they smell better than supermarket ones. The little bulbs are still green at this point in the year, I see. In a few months, she says, they'll be red and ripe. She lets me spray the vines with the water-spray.

We hear the doorbell back at the front of the house.

"Okay – just going to check the door, Dolina, keep watering those vines."

I do so. Mum's gone for so long, that I wonder who's at the door. I take my gloves off and go back into the house. Mum's not in the front door, but the front door is open. She's standing in the garden next to Linda. I pause in the corridor. They both look serious. Linda's face is puffy and her hands are shaking as they talk.

Mum spots me watching them.

"Dolina – come outside for a second."

Linda's red hair is unwashed and crazy. Her whole body is shaking and she's looking down at me paranoid.

"Have you seen Henry any time recently, girl?" she says to me.

I don't know how to answer. I really want to but don't know what to say.

"Henry. I saw him the other day. Umm. Maybe it was longer than that. I saw him on Saturday, why?"

"What time on Saturday?"

"Tell Linda when you saw him, Dolina," Mum says.

I don't want to let Mum know I was making fires and that Henry was helping me. But it's serious Linda wants to know where her son is.

"It was just in the day time. He was in the Woods. He seemed okay."

"But you haven't seen him since?"

"No, no. Is he all right?"

"No. He's missing. My son's missing." Linda starts sobbing. Mum hugs her.

It's morning and the sun's shining down on us. Linda looks distraught. I don't know what's happening.

"Linda," my Mum says to her. "Don't worry about Henry. I'm sure he's fine. We can help you out. Have you called the police yet?"

"No. He was supposed to come home on Sunday. But it's two days now. I hope he's just gone away on a trip, but it feels different this time."

"Okay, Linda. Come inside, and we'll call the police, just as a precaution. Henry might be anywhere. But we'll just let the police know, okay?"

Linda comes into the kitchen with us. I can see how scared she is and it makes me scared. Her body vibrates with fear, and I wish I could help her. But Mum seems to be doing a good job. She's boils the kettle and brings Linda a cup of tea.

Is Henry in *real* trouble this time? I want to tell Linda that I saw him hiding in the Woods with a tent. But I don't have the nerve.

Mum types in 999 to the phone.

"Hello, there," she says, "police please …"

CHAPTER FORTY-SIX

AUGUST 7TH 1998

POLICEMEN

I have to go back to school in a week. The summer's been miserable. It's barely felt like a summer. So many strangers are walking about the street that you can't go outside.

Journalists keep coming up to our front door to ask questions. They always wear suits and they already have their tape machines buzzing with their wide eyes. Mum was polite at first when they came; now she just shuts the door on them. They talk to me the same way as her, they just say: "Good afternoon, ma'am, you know anything about Henry Fowles?" the instant they see you.

Kids from the other neighbourhoods come down too, and they're even worse. They all come here to see what's happening as the police investigate the streets. I don't know *what* they're trying to see here. They all want Henry Henry Henry. But he's not here.

The kids chant in the street: "We want Henry, We want Henry!" They seem to think that we're hiding him from them. Somebody even threw a brick into our kitchen window yesterday. Me and Mum were in the kitchen eating dinner and after the brick hit the floor we heard a boy shout, "Posh Bastards!" Did that have something to do with Henry? I've never thought of my Mum as 'posh' … Just because she has a big house? Does that deserve having your window bashed in?

Mum and I are having dinner the *next* evening and our window is still broken. She put a wooden pane over it before the window man comes to fix it tomorrow. Then the doorbell rings again. Mum rarely gets angry, but you *know* when she's properly mad. She stomps down the front door, and I expect she'll start shouting at another reporter.

But her voice is calm. I hear other footsteps come into the house, and the door shut.

Two policemen walk into the kitchen. They're mega tall and navy blue.

"Dolina," Mum comes through them and I see she's intimidated by them too, "these are two police officers. They're here to ask us about Henry. They're not like the reporters. They just want to help, okay?"

"Sorry if we interrupted your dinner, ladies," one of the policemen says.

We all sit down at the table. The police ask Mum about Henry. When did she last see him? Does she know his mother Linda? What does she know about him?

I'm still confused by what they're saying. I'm confused about Henry and have been for a month. But I don't think he's in trouble: he's just not in our neighbourhood anymore. Mum isn't really talking back to the cops. She just frowns, like she's trying to answer maths puzzles. They finish talking to her. Then they ask if it's okay to speak to her daughter. Mum says yes.

"And what about you, Dolina?" The policeman nearest to me says. "Can we ask you about Henry? Do you remember the last time you saw him?"

"I do. He was in the Woods."

"The woods? Which woods?"

"*The Woods*. Next to our house. I saw him the day before the World Cup final."

"Uh hu, and what was he doing?"

"He was … He was making a fire, with me, and he was showing me how to make a fire."

I watch to see how Mum will react. But she only looks down at her feet. The policeman's smiling at me.

"You mean, like a bonfire?" he says.

"Yes."

"And did you see him on the day of the World Cup final?"

"No."

"Okay, thanks Dolina." The policeman stands up. The other one does too. "Thank you, ladies, for your time."

"But, wait," I say, and everybody looks at me, "I think Henry was playing *Filippo's Game*. With John and June. *Filippo's Game* – it's a game my cousin made in the Woods. Henry wanted to join John's gang. But something wrong happened to him."

Mum's embarrassed. The police just look away.

"Don't you know *Filippo's Game*, Mum?" I say to her but she doesn't look up. "I think he was in trouble with John and June. He was crying the last time I saw him too."

"We thank both of you for your time," one of the policemen says. "Have a nice day."

They leave the house. Mum puts out plates back into the oven to warm them up again. I feel stupid and left out. Because nobody listened to me. I was sure I had something to offer them. But nobody could hear it. Mum's still embarrassed of me. She puts our plates down again and begins eating. And says nothing for the whole meal.

CHAPTER FORTY-SEVEN

MAY 2018

NEVERMIND

'Nevermind' came back to me in a dream before I remembered the 1998 memory when Filippo gave me the CD.

In the dream I'm walking in the hills and fields beyond Edinburgh. As I get farther from home, the image of the Hospital cube and the swathe of the Woods fade out. There's a frantic pace in my walk. I don't know why I'm afraid or where I'm going. The sky darkens to a brown-grey, and a mighty wind gains courage. Grass swishes me in the face as I crawl up and up until I reach new terrain.

Whereupon the wind stops and I'm climbing something much larger and barren. I don't want to climb, yet I trod on through a type of duty. Grass turns to rock and the steepness sharpens. Until I'm climbing at such a slow speed with wet hands and flickering limbs.

It's then that I hear music booming in the distance, up and over the mountain. I like it and I want to be closer to it. Spitfire drumming, crazed guitar, a doomed man's voice. I reach the top, on a straight slab of rock, vertical drops on all sides. The music thunders down in the valley, far below.

I wonder why I've come up to this place. I know I've been here before, so why do I keep returning? Everything else is other worldly. There is only the sky and the rock face here. And it's not so much the climbing up that scares me. It's the journey back down.

It would be so much easier to just jump, rather than climb down. I have to head towards the music. But I'm too afraid to approach the edge, and I'm stranded here with no hope of rescue.

Across on the horizon a city simmers, insects writhing on their backs, black legs sprawling at the sky. I begin to descend the mountain face. Somebody appears above me, climbing down the same route as me. They're fast and have better climbing skills. I can't tell if it's a man or a woman. I call out, "Who's up there?"

The person gets a fright, looks down. At the same time the person loses grip on the stones above, and falls. The body hurtles towards me and there's no scream. I hug the wall because I can't let the body hit me. I can't try to catch him or her because I'll be carried down too. There's nothing I can do.

I wake up.

And the first thing I do is head to my CD collection. I have the memory and the dream. I need to find the 'Nevermind' CD. I'm in my underwear and a t-shirt, panged out of sleep. It's very early, still dark. Mum's still asleep. The collection's in the sitting room next to the stereo. I go through the alphabet and find N. And there it is – Nirvana, 'Nevermind'.

I open it up … What am I supposed to be looking for? This is Henry's CD, right? I'd forgotten altogether this was his possession since 1998. I look through the booklet for clues. There are only pictures of the band being grungey. Am I supposed to listen to the album? A message hidden in the lyrics? No, that's unrealistic. What about the physical case? There's the black plastic bit which you press the disk into. I remove that. Out slips a piece of paper. It was hidden behind the back cover's track list. On it is written a message. I recognise Filippo's handwriting from all the signs I've read in his *Game*:

DON'T GO TO LEVEL 8 TONIGHT HENRY.

JUNE WILL HURT YOU.

FORGET MY GAME.

LEAVE TOWN. DON'T COME BACK.

CHAPTER FORTY-EIGHT

LEVEL 8

Where is the last LEVEL? I supposedly know all areas of the Woods, yet I can't figure out where it is. I'm in my garden, thinking in the dark. Filippo's note to Henry is more significant than anything else I've seen yet. I've got to find out whether Henry reached LEVEL 8. I remember Tommy saying, on the day of the World Cup Final, that he saw Henry go into the Woods with June.

It's Saturday, and people will be busy around the streets today, walking their dogs. I need to be covert. I have to be in the Woods, even if it's dark, before the public wake up. But I just cannot guess where LEVEL 8 might be … After an hour in the garden, going over the same logistical thoughts, I go inside and get the Map Robin gave me.

My cousin tried to warn Henry not to play the *Game*, and get out of town? Is Filippo a bad guy, or not? – I can't decide. He knew June was going to 'hurt' him if he didn't vanish, so sent him a message, which never arrived. Does this mean he's been a friend of Henry's all this time, and I should trust him more? I hope it does. Finding Filippo's note has given me hope that he represents something apart from the Walkers. This is why I go back to his Map – one of the retro originals from the '90s which he drew.

I study it in my room. As Robin mentioned, there is no depiction of LEVEL 8: you have to find it yourself. There was also no clue at the end of LEVEL 7 as to where to go next. I go over all the LEVELS. I feel that I've covered the land so well, and yet it's taken me this long to discover the LEVELS, so maybe I'm being naïve.

Filippo's drawn the river's circuit expertly and I'm pretty sure I know the river line just as well. I've been all along it, from the *Fence* by the *Fox Dens*, down to the bridge at the far end leading onto the motorway. I don't think there are any more water-based LEVELS. Maybe it's a trick LEVEL – and there is no 8th part? Maybe I've missed a clue somewhere within the *Game*?

Filippo's depicted the paths of the Woods in brown pen, in thin diagonal strokes as you would see on a land map. I visualise where I'm going as I trace them with my finger. north east to *School Ruins*, south west to *Electricity Box*. I do all the path lines, until I get to *June's Waterfall*, ending with the long path which edges around the river.

But what's this? There's another path at the very northern part of the Woods. It's drawn in a thin, short line, and it extends beyond the trees, near the urban areas. I never knew this path existed. Unlike any of the others, I don't have any memory of a path in this part. I know there are trees there, yet I never considered the northern section a part of the Woods, for some reason … Why? This might be where to go.

I head out the house into the festering morning.

I haven't showered in days. I smell so bad. My boss didn't message me back yesterday when I told her I was sick. Am I fired? Good, if so.

I walk down the hilly road to the horse chestnut tree. The orange streetlamps shine in the dark. My breath transcends my body as I walk; I have no mouth, no tongue. I don't feel ill, or healthy, don't feel anything physical. I only just realise when I get to the wall that I'm only in my t-shirt. Forgot to even dress properly. But I go on.

There is only the Woods, now. Its aura dwarves everything else. There is nowhere else I'd rather be. I'm supposed to be here.

It's stopped raining, and the ground is drying in the heat. I go past *June's Waterfall*. It's like a chain, how I walk. I don't venture with my own legs – I'm simply pulled towards the trees. Until I find the little square patch where Henry built his tent 20 years ago. This is where he lived. Tree saplings spark up to the sky in the patch, now, vying for sunlight.

I suss where I am, using the direction from the *Waterfall* to head north. The land rises up and the trees grow thicker. I go slow to be careful. I'm bemused why I never came to these parts. Because it's overgrown with nettles and thorns? Yet it doesn't seem like the *Fox Dens'* jungle parts. There's something different about this area, a sense of finality, of urbanity approaching.

Suddenly I hit something hard as I go through a pair of trees. As I step forward something catches my kneecap. But in front of me there are only trees and grass.

"What the hell?"

I reach forward with my hand and touch a hard surface. Then realise I can see *myself.* It's a reflection! It's a *mirror*, taller than I am! A long sheet of glass, old and musty with rain, but still reflective.

I move the mirror out the way and go behind it. Once there, I see a host of more tall mirrors propped up against the tree boughs behind me, placed in a circular order. It's a disguise to make it look like the Woods keeps going on into the distance if you see it from far away. You only see more trees if you're far away from them.

Now I see the northern path under me. I've got here. I follow it.

I remember the reason why I never considered this part of the Woods the actual Woods. The trees break off after 30 meters, leading onto this long unkempt field. It's fenced off from the public. I think it's owned by the Hospital, but it's just been a derelict stretch of grass for as long as I can remember. This fence marks the end of the Woods.

Where I am now, the trees are still thick, and the path's like those of the others in the Woods, a nimble mark of history. I'd been fooled by the mirror disguise when I was a child, which was why I never thought anything was here.

I come to a clump of lush ivy, smothering new stone ruins.

"So that's why there's a path here. The mill or the school must have had a building here."

The trees arch across this little enclave, making it darker and hushed, and when I go closer, I spot a wooden hut in the gloom.

It's like a large garden shed. Windowless, with moss on its walls. But it's well made and properly painted, with clean timber and tarmac on the roof. It seems forgotten rather than derelict. Then I see the sign, painted in skyblue letters by the door, reading: '*JUNE'S HUT*'.

So *June's Hut* is LEVEL 8. This is definitely it, but why June and not Filippo?

There's a padlock on the door. Where's the key? I search around for what to do.

It doesn't take me long to work it out this time. On a pine tree behind the shed there's a blue arrow pointing upward. When I climb, it's easy, enjoyable. And when I get to the top, I find a key in a jar. From here, I can see out across the entire span of the Woods. It tingles in the dark. I feel like I'm carrying the Woods and they are carrying me, that we're nearing a climax of history together. I go back down the trunk.

Okay, so I've got the key. But this is all too easy for LEVEL 8. I don't trust it. You only have to climb up a tree to unlock *June's Hut*? I'd been expecting something epic, something even more elaborate than *Electricity Box* or *School Ruins* … And when I put the key into the padlock it turns easily, and I go inside.

I turn my phone's light on. I find a table in the centre of the room with chairs around it. The walls are decorated with colourful things. Then I discover a light switch on the wall and turn it on.

"Wow, the *Hut* even has electricity?"

A lampshade hangs down over the table with homely warm light. On the table I see a single sheet of paper. When I go closer I find it's made with thick card, bordered in gold lines, like a certificate:

WELCOME TO FILIPPO'S GANG

PUT YOUR CERTIFICATE INTO THE CHEST IN THE BASEMENT

There's a fancy pen lying by the paper. So you sign your name on the paper and put it into this chest. I see a trapdoor at the end of the room, which must lead to the basement …

I look around the walls, and the rest of the room. Whilst the table seemed ceremonious, the rest of the place just seems *young*. There are desks and stools placed around the walls, strewn with mouldy beer cans and ashen marijuana pipes. There are porno magazines, uncompleted card games, a CD player with all sorts of music by it, Radiohead, Oasis, Britney blooming Spears … I even find an old *Tamagotchi* toy. I remember they were huge when I was little. I try to turn it on but it's dead.

On the wall above me there's one of those World Cup fixture pop-outs you get in the newspaper, where you fill out the scores as the games go on. The paper's yellowed with age. All the 1998 World Cup scores are inked on it, except the Final score which is missed out. Even I know that. It was 3 – 0 to France.

"This is creepy."

Is this really the final LEVEL of the *Game*? It just looks like a party zone. Where the Gang used to hang out. There seems nothing finalistic about this. There must be something else. It feels like the *Hut* was abandoned one night amidst one party and nobody's ever come back.

The rest of the wall is even stranger. In one part there's a poster of Kurt Cobain, followed by a poster of the film 'Groundhog Day'. Other parts are lined with nude Page 3 models out of *The Sun*, with the silicone breasts and all that. There are photos of Filippo and Robin hugging and smiling at the camera, surrounded by trees – are they in the Woods? Medals and trophies as well, with Filippo's name on them.

Football trophies. One of them is a golden football on top of a podium, with 'Golden Boot' under it. Why aren't these things in Filippo's house at home? Why would he leave them in this forgotten place?

Above the door where I came in there's this single shelf filled with alarm clocks. The old fashioned clocks with the two nobs at the top that make the ringing sound. And bells, too, assorted bells as you'd find above antique shop doorways, except they're just stacked on the shelf anonymously.

When I get to the far wall beside the trapdoor, I see a little blackboard above me. I can see the chalked inscriptions on it. At the top is written, 'HENRY FOWLES'. And underneath his name is a series of boxes next to each of the LEVELS. From LEVEL 1 *Filippo's Tarzan* to LEVEL 2 *River Jump*, and so on until *June's Hut*. All of the boxes for Henry are ticked in with chalk, except for *June's Hut*.

"So this is where the Gang made tabs on the contenders for the *Game*? It just doesn't seem right, though – how the *Game* was so clever – and this is the ending?"

I go over to the trapdoor at the end of the room. It's unlocked.

I remember that the light inside the top floor of the hut is still on, and the door is open. So I go back and turn the yellow light off, shut the door, then use my phone's light to go through the trapdoor, down to the basement.

There's a ladder which leads down into the room. The air goes cool as I descend. I shine my light around the basement. There are no objects, only walls and an open floor. When I get to the bottom of the ladder I can only hear myself breathe. I shine my phone's light forward – nothing. Stupid me. I could have brought an actual torch.

I look by the ladder side and I see a light switch. When I turn it on, an acidic white blue light blasts the room. It's not a *room*. It's a rectangular cement floor, surrounded by brick walls. At the far end is a chest. I expected the chest to be a little thing like a safe. Instead it's the size of a horizontal freezer, made out of wood, painted in blue and yellow with flower patterns around the edges.

But in the glare of light, I notice something sitting in front of the chest. It's crumpled and green. My pulse is jumping under my tonsils. I go closer to the green thing. It's very cold in this basement – is there even any air in here?

The green crumpled thing is Henry Fowles' hooded top. It's his green hoody he always wore in the 1990s. There's a hole torn through the right breast area. The fabric is lined with dark stains around the hole, blotchy black stains covering the green. I don't touch Henry's hoody. I just study it, sprawled on the floor.

"Okay, Dolina," I bring my phone out and stand up. "Now's the time to call the police."

I take my phone out and when I see the screen I notice there's no reception.

I hear a *bang* of the trapdoor shutting above me.

And when I turn around, the lightbulb goes out.

I'm thrown into dark.

"Who's there!" I shout.

I'm on the floor, crouching. Somebody's in the basement with me.

"Who is there? Who are you?"

I have my phone and I could shine my light – but then they'll see where I am. What do I do next?

"Look, just turn the light back on. I'm not doing anything wrong. Who are you?"

I hear a *sigh* … It's sassy, overdone.

"Can't you guess who it is, Dolina?"

It's a woman's voice. She lights a match, *scratch*, and she's standing over in the corner of the room.

It's June Walker.

She has her back to me. Before her I see one of those old antique lanterns, with the glass case and the wick inside. It sits in a hole within the bricks. She lights the wick and the room glows rosy.

She goes over to the other side of the wall in the corner. There's another lantern in a hole there too. By the next illumination I see her face and body. Her dark hair's short these days. Her breasts are larger than ever. The scent of the candles comes across to me. We're standing only metres apart. She's in front of the ladder.

"What are you doing here, June?"

June brings out a knife from inside her pocket. She points it at me.

"What are you doing June" Why do you have a knife!"

"Stop shouting."

It's a vegetable knife. My Mum has the same one, stainless steel blade with a nifty handle.

"We need to light the candles for LEVEL 8. The induction ceremony," June says. "We can't only have electric light."

"June, just let me go. I don't care anymore about the police or anything. Please just let me go home. I'll move away. I —"

"Dolina. Take this paper and pen. You forgot to sign it up stairs."

She reaches into her pocket with her free hand and comes towards me. The knife's dangling in her other hand. I snatch the paper and pen. It's the certificate thing.

"But before you sign it," she says, "Open the chest."

"June, please just let me away. How can you even threaten me like this and get away with it?"

"Open the chest, Dolina."

She steps towards me with the knife and I stand up.

"What's Henry's hoody doing here? What did you do to him?"

"Henry deserved a lot of things. Time put him where he was supposed to be. Open the chest, Dolina."

"What's in there?"

"Open the chest."

"Okay, but put the knife away."

"No, just open the chest. Jesus, your family members are all the same – stubborn. Your cousin is just like you. Let's get this over with."

I go over to the chest, past Henry's bloody hoody. June follows behind me with the knife. I try to think how I can run past June and get out the basement. But she *has* me; I'm too scared of her.

I get to the chest and put my hands on the door to lift it up. It's even bigger than a freezer – like something out of a church. And I kneel down because I know June Walker's going to stab me … And I know what I'm going to find inside the chest.

I lift it up.

"Congratulations," June says, "you completed *Filippo's Game*."

Inside are sheets of paper. Certificates, like the one June's just given me. They're all lined out across the chest's bottom neatly.

"Aren't you proud?" June says to me.

She has an expression of nothing. I sit, breathing at her.

"Write your name on the certificate," she says. "You did well, and you're the first one to do it all by yourself. That's a big feat."

"I don't understand what's happening ..."

"You should be celebrating. You've completed your cousin's coveted *Game*."

"Where is Henry?"

"I don't care where he is. Sign your name on the certificate."

"Where is Henry?"

"Your name, please."

"I didn't even complete it all – the *Game*."

"You were the best contender that's even been, Dolina. You had a little help from Tommy, but you were the best I can think of."

"What do you mean? I didn't even complete LEVEL 7? The Tarzan game."

"You were the fastest contestant ever. We timed you. You *did* complete LEVEL 7: you just fell off at the red dot Tarzan. We made the red dot one to see if players would realise it was a dummy, or if they would fall into the holly bushes. There were no Tarzans after that one anyway."

"You're an insane person, June. You and my cousin. You're sadistic people."

"You completed the *Game* in the fasted time we ever monitored. Bravo. Sign your name on the sheet."

I write my name on the line. I put the certificate down with the others.

June puts her knife away.

"I remember past players looking around for LEVEL 8 for months. And you found the *Hut* just like that. Really good." June walks to the chest and she shuts it.

She walks over and goes up the ladder.

"Blow the candles up when you come out, please."

CHAPTER FORTY-NINE

RELEASE

I follow June up the trapdoor and out of the *Hut* and she locks the door after me, after I give her the key.

"We do admire you, Dolina," June says to me. "Honestly, we were impressed with your desire. You were the final contender. I assume that's what you wanted?"

"Who is 'we', June?"

She doesn't answer.

"What's the time even?" I say.

"It's 4, maybe 5 a.m. ... Beautiful, aren't they, the Woods."

We're standing in the glamour of the new morning Woods. Of course they are beautiful.

June's looking into the trees. I can't see her knife anywhere. I can run away from June. I can attack June. I could call the police. But I don't. There's something different she's going to tell me.

"But I know you're somebody who actually *loves* the Woods, don't you?" she says. "Me and Filippo only saw this place as territory. But you see this place as love. Right?"

"I do."

"Dolina. Stay away from my Dad and me, and don't go near your cousin again. Don't ever talk to him about this. He seems like a big man, but he's not – he's weak. If you leave us be, we will leave you be. Can you accept that?"

"I can."

She brings something else out her pocket and hands it to me. It's a bit of card. A postcard.

"We needed to scare Henry away from here. So we injured him. Injury was the only thing he understood. And he needed to leave. He just didn't realise it at the time. It worked for all of us. Him too. And I hope you understand that's how it needed to be to be.

"We intercepted this postcard in July, 1998. It was necessary for all parties. Linda couldn't see it. Henry couldn't be found at that point. It would've been damaging for us. But it doesn't matter anymore if you see it. I hope you have the sense to just keep things the way they are. I hope you realise what me and my Father are. We're not like you, or Henry, or your cousin. Stay isolated from us.

"Of all people, you're the person who's tried the hardest to find Henry. And I admit, I commend your spirit. You can stop trying now. There's his postcard. Henry never completed *Filippo's Game*. But you did, Dolina. That's all the conclusion you need. Put the mirrors back when you're done, if you would."

June's already going away. Walking off into the trees with the haughty gait. I hope this is the last time I ever see her.

PART IV

CHAPTER FIFTY

MAY 2018

Henry Fowles is still alive.

CHAPTER FIFTY-ONE

THE POSTCARD

15/7/98

Dear Mother,

I'm very sorry I couldn't come back to watch the final with you and Jim on Sunday. I really wanted to. But I got into some trouble, again.

I want you to know I'm alive and I'm all right. But I can't come back to Edinburgh any time soon. Maybe I won't ever come back. I can't explain it all here on a postcard. If you want to find me, just come to the address at the top.

If you're too mad with me, and don't want to see me again, then that's fine too.

Love

Lucas

CHAPTER FIFTY-TWO

THE JOURNEY

So what can I learn from the postcard? It's addressed from a place called Plockton, in Ross-shire. Has an obscure postcode. No idea where that is, but Ross-shire sounds Scottish. On the front of the postcard is a picture of a little village by a loch, which clearly suggests Scotland. Pretty white houses and multicolour boats. I look up Plockton on the net, and indeed, it's a tiny village of 300 people, up in the far north west coast of Scotland. The proper highlands.

I'm in a kind of mental throng. Whilst I'm exhilarated that Henry might still be alive, I have to see him physically before I can believe it. That postcard was written 20 years ago. There's a horrible current in me that he might have passed away for some other cause, after that. The Walkers didn't kill him, but he drank so much. He could have died from liver disease? Or a heart attack?

But the exhilaration is too strong and overrides my fears. I have a free day. I'm going to go up to find him. It's still only six in the morning. I figure out a journey up north. I can get a train up to Inverness, which is on the east coast, and then there are two shaky bus rides out west. It will take a long while to get to Plockton. And the train fare is astronomical. But I just have to do it.

The final thing is 'Lucas'. He signed his name with 'Lucas'? Why? Because he was trying to be safe with an alias? So when I get to Plockton, I won't be asking for Henry Fowles, just Lucas.

I shower and pack my bag. The bus for Inverness is in 90 minutes. Mother suspects something, obviously. I tell her I'm going through to Glasgow to see some old friends. She knows I'm lying, but she can see how bright I am today, so she only smiles and says cool, she'll see me when I get back.

The train takes me out into the hills. I'd forgotten about the majesty of the countryside. Vending pictures through the window, rolling in green, blue, yellow, the fields trembling in the sun, the hillsides handsome. The clouds send aquiline shadows over the land as they move. And the clouds are fast today. The wind's nippy. Sunshine for ten minutes, met with angry showers for half an hour. Classic Scottish weather. I'm liking this.

When I get off the train, I wait an hour for the first bus out west. It's late afternoon. Then the bus takes me into the highlands. Mum used to take me up north on holidays, and I'd forgotten the *different kind* of beauty within the mountains. The fathomless lumps of rock and heather. The one-way roads, millipede paths under these towering shapes. Ruins of cottages standing anonymous in the lowlands. Once the host of families, children, who then left for America, Canada, Australia, 150 years ago.

I wait two hours for the next bus at some stop in the road, miles from any civilisation. And, of course, it starts to rain. When I finally get on the bus I feel bad for making the seat so wet. But by early evening I come to Plockton. Looks exactly like the postcard photo. A sweet village overlooking a loch.

I'm pretty tired after the journey and could do with resting somewhere. I walk into the village street. Elderly people walking about with their dogs. Quaint little tea shops. Is Henry really here? What do I do – go up to an elderly married couple and ask if I've seen this weird kid who went missing in 1998?

The first time I hear noise of any kind is when I approach the Plockton Inn. Looks warm and inviting through the orange windows. May as well relax for a while and have some drinks.

When I go in, it's what I'd expected. Old men in caps, drinking, the occasional older woman with them. But I'm by far the youngest person here. There's a little moment of silence when I go in, when they turn and look at me. Then they go back to drinking. I ask for a whisky and an ale at the counter and sit at one of the stools. A smiley lady bartender serves me. She's short and quiet. She's the manager.

The whisky and ale are nice at first. The lady's name is Eileen. We start chatting away. I tell her I'm an artist, and I paint. I'd like to do some paintings of the mountains and the loch too. She tells me her husband paints as well and she even invites me round to their house the next day to meet him. She asks me if I came up here just to paint, and where I'm staying?

I'm such a shoddy liar. I tell her I'd planned to stay in the hotel. And yes, I'm here on a painting project. She must know the owner of the single hotel in a village of 300 people, know that I wouldn't come to a place as random as this for so simple a reason.

The alcohol's knocked me down a bit. The men's laughter behind me is too jarring. I order one more ale from Eileen, to try numb them out. After a third into the ale, I just go for it. I lean towards Eileen.

"Okay, Eileen. I'm not just here to paint. And I'm not staying in the Hotel."

She just giggles. And I blush.

"I'm looking for somebody. Lucas. Do you know Lucas?"

"Umm, yes, he'll be here in a few hours, honey. This is his favourite place."

"Lucas? Really? He comes here?"

"Everybody loves Lucas, yes … What, are you an old friend?"

"I am, yes, definitely. Do you know where he stays?"

"Sure, he stays up on his farm. But honestly, you can just wait for him here – he'll be down in a few hours."

"Lucas has a *farm*?"

She giggles again.

"Yes, somehow he manages. I can get my husband to give you a lift up? It's quite a way."

"I can walk, thank you though. So which way is it?"

"I'll get Keith to give you a lift up the road, honey. The farm's quite a trek from here."

I accept her offer.

She goes to the telephone behind the bar. Five minutes later Keith appears in the door. He's bald and peaceful, and doesn't seem suspicious at all of who I am.

"Keith, take Dolina here up to Lucas' farm?" Eileen says.

He just nods, and I follow him out the room.

"And I'm sure Lucas will bring you back here later on, Dolina," she calls after us.

Keith is a naturally silent man, I find, as he drives. It's like he's half asleep, old and serene.

I can see why Eileen offered the lift to Henry's farm. It takes ten minutes to get there on curvy highland roads. Keith parks by a trail which heads up to a house and barn in the distance.

"Okay this is it," he says, "you just head up there and you'll find him. You want me to give you a lift back into the village later on?"

"No thank you, Keith. You were wonderful. Eileen is as well. Thanks so much."

He drives off back to the village.

I'm left with a trail leading into a field. There's a small light in one of the house's windows up ahead. I go up to it.

I didn't even bring my wellies up to the highlands, when I really need hiking boots. I'm just in the boggy fields in my flimsy trainers I bought the other week. The mud oozes up into my socks.

The house is very small. There's a gate and a long fence by its side. The barn by the end of the field looks closed up for the night. I can't see any animals, or crops. What kind of farm is it? I go closer to the gate, and suddenly this whirling shape of black and white shoots towards me.

It's a dog – a border collie dog.

"Hi dog," I say. He puts his paws up on the top of the gate. He's not barking at me, just curious to see who it is.

"Who is it, Bell?" I hear a man's voice. I look ahead. There's a man, standing outside the doorway of the house, hunched over a plant pot. He has his back turned to me, and he's just talking to his dog. "Who's there, Bell?"

Bell the dog squeaks at me.

The man's hair is totally white now – thick and bushy, like his mother's. He's wearing old jeans and a brown jacket. He's grunting at the plant pot. I think he's trying to put sticks into the pot, so the stalks of the plant will wind up it. But he's not doing a good job, getting frustrated with himself, swearing under his breath.

"Henry?" I say.

He spins around. That's Henry Fowles. He squints at me. Then his face brightens, and he stands up.

"Well, now. It's little Dolina!" he says.

I go through the gate and run up to him. And he catches me as I jump into him.

"I knew I'd see you again one day, little Dolina!"

I try not to sob. But I can't help it. He's hugging me just as tight as I am him.

I see the mountains and the loch below the fields as I drop my head behind his back.

CHAPTER FIFTY-THREE

JUNE 14TH 2018

THE WOODS

I could tell you about what Henry and I talked about. We went back down to the Plockton Inn after I found him at the farm, and talked for a long, long while. That was weeks ago. He was much changed, as a man. But Henry still had his boyish wit and humour. It was just fun to hang out with him, get drunk with him.

I could tell you about what exactly happened on June the 12th 1998 and how he got injured. How he escaped from the Walkers. But somehow I don't feel I need to. Because when Henry told me about it, he didn't regret any of it. He was glad that it happened.

He was even more glad to see me. And he repeated the phrase that he'd always imagined he would see me again in life. He knew it would happen.

There was one spooky revelation he gave me, but it also made sense. Henry left his football cap and his watch in Filippo's treehouse before he went missing. He did it deliberately, because he anticipated somebody would try to find him. He knew nobody would be playing the *Game* after he did, so nobody would be going back to the LEVELS anytime soon. But eventually, somebody would. And he wasn't surprised that that eventual person was me.

He didn't show much anger towards the Walkers, and he said he still considered Filippo a friend.

I showed him the post card that June and Alec intercepted in the summer of 1998. The one he tried to send to his mother. Even then, he didn't get angry, whereas I was furious.

The Walkers were cruel enough to prevent a boy's letter getting through to his mother, telling her that he was still *alive*? Solely to protect themselves?

Henry got a bit emotional when he knew Linda never got the postcard. He'd thought, for all this time, that she just didn't want to see him again.

I gave him her phone number. But instead he asked me to go back to Linda when I got home to Edinburgh. He wanted me to give her the '98 postcard. And he wrote down another letter in an envelope and gave it to me to give her as well. Out of respect for their privacy, I never opened the new letter on the train back to Edinburgh.

I went to Linda's house and gave her the letters. And told her that her son was still alive. And I'll let you imagine for yourself how she reacted. And I know that the mother and son are reunited now. Linda invited Henry to come back to her, and he did. They made peace. And I am proud to have enabled their reunion.

And so, what's for me, now? After all that's happened this summer … The giant mystery which has consumed it. I'm still in the comedown, the hangover, from the mystery. It's taken such a chunk away from my life, so much that I want to experience it all over again. Which is odd, because I never will.

It's June the 14th today. The day that the *World Cup 2018* starts. I could go into town and watch the opening game. Russia versus Saudi Arabia. It's not that I don't like football – I just don't understand it. Everyone can surely love the atmosphere of the World Cup, though. I do. I'd like to watch the game, but going to the pub on my own would be a bit sad. I don't have any friends in Edinburgh these days. All my old pals are in Glasgow.

What do I realistically have going for me in life? I graduated last year and it's not gotten me anywhere. I still have the one depressing job. Still live my Mum, at 25 years old, and I'll be 26 next month. I apply for 'adult' jobs, and never hear back from them.

For a long time, I've thought of myself as a good artist. Other people seemed to love my paintings. And actually, I've returned to painting a lot more recently.

But I still have my doubts about my art. Maybe if I was the archetypal *savant* when it came to painting, I'd be satisfied in life? If I was famous; if my paintings were in Venice, London, Paris, New York – would I be happy? Is fame what makes an artist? If my paintings just made me money, and I could be some spectacular diva *artiste*, dying young after three marriages, would that give me satisfaction?

What's most likely is that that's all a sham. That concepts of success aren't what they're labelled to be. These were things that I wanted earlier in life. I'm still young, but those ideas seem childish now. What's most probable is that I'm not going to be a great painter. And I'm just one of many people who are okay at art.

I still have the house and the day free today. I can do anything with my free time.

I open my bedroom window wide and look into the Woods.

It was immensely windy last night, and still is today. The wind bats the trees of the Woods around with anonymous violence. Apparently, these are the strongest winds in the Scottish summer time for seventeen years. It's in the news. I watch the leaves shunning themselves from the wind. And yet they don't buckle or retire easily, they don't allow the wind to take them without a battle.

I head out of the house and go into the Woods. The floors of ivy, the ancient paths, the river, are sprinkled with ripe branches, seeds, leaves. All taken down by the wind. They clatter down on my head as I cross the river, and I hold my hands over myself as I go, eyes blinking, in case something properly heavy lands on me. But I'm in awe of this flurrying brilliance.

In this way, the wind is not something destructive. The wind and the Woods are merely conversing in chaotic dialogue, in an alternate kind of creation.

When I was little I would listen to the sound of the wind in the Woods through my window. The rushing leaves and the creaking of the boughs. And it seemed like the safest sound, to know that I was sheltered in my bed.

Now that I'm an adult, in the midst of this chaos, inside the place itself, I hear the noise the same way, and I feel the same safety, the same love for the Woods. It surprised me, when June spoke to me, after we'd left the *Hut* – that she recognised my love for this place.

Somehow, I know that these Woods will never be torn down. They will not be demolished for new houses or for another supermarket or anything urban. First of all because the land is too erratic. The steep valleys, the gigantic trees, the scattered masonry ruins. It is too miscellaneous a place, too unusual to infect with urbanity. I don't think any architect or building group will come here and feel they can invade.

But it's more than the practicality of it. It is a special arena, filled with magic and history. And you'd have to be a proper fiend to try to dismantle all of that.

And I believe *I* am the one true owner of the Woods. And always will be.

I don't know what my future will bring. Don't know whether I'll ever be successful, whatever that could be.

What I do know for certain about myself, is that I solved the mystery of Henry Fowles. I loved him and cared about him. And I'm overwhelmed with joy that he is still alive on this planet. Now I can say that I *still* love and care about him. It was a feat, to find out what happened to him, when nobody else could.

And that's a personal triumph nobody else can meet – and a feat regardless of revenge, competitiveness, or being the sole champion. I'm just glad I found an old friend.

The wind charges up in the trees above me. I go further into the Woods.

THE END

ACKNOWLEDGEMENTS

Thank you to my family who raised me in a house next to a magical woodland. This place is, if one hadn't already guessed, what the book is based on.

Many thanks to Alasdair Gillon's encouragement after I wrote this novel. (He was the first person to read the original manuscript.) Ally is a writer himself and you should check out his stuff.

Printed in Great Britain
by Amazon